THE
FOUR
LANE

J. DENNIS MAHONEY

authorHOUSE®

AuthorHouse™
1663 Liberty Drive
Bloomington, IN 47403
www.authorhouse.com
Phone: 833-262-8899

Published by AuthorHouse 12/04/2020

ISBN: 978-1-6655-0977-0 (sc)
ISBN: 978-1-6655-0980-0 (e)

Library of Congress Control Number: 2020924059

Print information available on the last page.

For "Edith"

Acknowledgements

The author would like to express his appreciation to Audrey Jean, Irene Ann, Cynthia Irene and most of all to my wife, Janice. Without all of their assistance and encouragement, this book would never have been completed. J.D.M.

Chapter 1

Dublin, Georgia – Wednesday (July 4, 1979)

Beverly

This time she was really scared ....

Beverly tried to get that terrible picture out of her mind, but it wasn't working.

He was like some horrible stranger. The look of hate in his eyes was piercing and that *look* actually hurt her much more than the sharp sting of his vicious slap.

Her mother had left them two years ago, and ever since then her father had grown more and more mean and distant. His boozing had gotten worse and the accusations had become a daily part of Beverly's life.

She loved her father very much and tried to understand his sadness. She was even willing to put up with the verbal abuse. Beverly had hoped that he would ultimately conquer his depression and enable them to pick up the pieces of their broken lives.

She prayed for this to happen daily, for her own sake, as well as for Mike, her brother.

This night it was different. She heard the front door slam and saw her father stumbling down the hall, toward the kitchen. He was obviously drunk and totally disoriented. An alarm went off in the back of her head when he called her Claire.

He was screaming at the top of his lungs, "Claire,

you little bitch, I know he was here while I was at work yesterday. Don't you think I know what's been going on?"

"Daddy, it was just my friend Eric and all we were doing was looking through the "Help Wanted" ads. Now that high school is over, I want to find a job so I can help out around here and save some money to begin college in the fall."

And then she cried, "Why did you call me Claire? I'm Beverly not Claire! Mommy's gone, don't you remember?"

That was when he hit her.................

In all her eighteen years, her father had not so much as threatened to hit her or Mike, but now his big hand slashed across her face and he screamed, "I'll teach you to screw around on me."

She could feel her cheek throbbing as she lost her balance and fell back against the kitchen counter.

She recovered just in time to see him readying another blow. Jumping out of the way, she grabbed her purse from the kitchen counter and ran toward the back door, not fully aware of what she was going to do.

For some reason she snatched her brother's leather jacket from the back of one of the kitchen chairs.

Beverly extended the hand holding the jacket and pushed as hard as she could against the screen door that led from the kitchen to the backyard.

She didn't notice that the latch was still in the eyehook, but it made no difference..... her adrenalin was flowing so fast that the hook ripped from the casing and the door flew open with a crash.

Rather than opening the back gate, she ran straight through the hedges that separated their yard from the alley. Because she was wearing Bermuda shorts, her bare legs were exposed to their sharpness.

As she ran down the alley, she could still hear the horrific sound of her father's voice screaming, "Claire…. Claire, you whore, don't you ever come back! Do you hear me?"

In a state of near hysteria, Beverly had neither felt the pain as her legs scraped against the sharp hedges, nor did she notice the droplets of blood that fell quietly onto her clean, white tennis shoes.

The only thing that mattered was to escape this nightmare as quickly as possible and she ran, at full speed, until her lungs hurt.

When she could run no longer she continued her escape by intermittently walking and jogging.

As she fled, time had ceased to be a conscious dimension. When she began to regain normal focus, several hours had already passed and darkness had descended around her.

She thought she could hear muffled booms. Then she remembered that it was the Fourth of July and everyone was celebrating. Well, almost everyone.

She was now nearing a highway and a sign told her it was Interstate sixteen.

Other than her own labored breathing and the distant booms, all was quiet. Now that all of Beverly's senses were returning, she could smell the familiar, sweet perfume of the Georgia pines, which lined both sides of the Interstate.

She walked up the freeway on-ramp and stood by the side of the highway. As she paused there, not really knowing what she was going to do next, she found herself staring down at her shoes. The little red specks on them stood out sharply against her bright white tennis shoes.

When four girls in a yellow Buick convertible stopped to give her a ride, she wondered how awful her legs must look. She hoped they wouldn't notice.

"How far are you going?" asked the young, redheaded driver. "I'm going to visit my mom in Atlanta," Beverly lied.

A cute little blonde, who had been riding shotgun, slid over to let Beverly get in. She said, "We're going as far as the Forsyth cut-off on I-75, just above Macon."

"That's great." Beverly said, "You guys are real lifesavers, I'm sure I can catch a ride into Atlanta if you can just drop me off at one of the rest areas."

Beverly had half-walked, half-stumbled almost eight miles from her home to where the girls had picked her up and she was happy for any ride that would take her away from Dublin.

That had been about forty-five minutes ago. The girls chatted back and forth and every now and then Beverly nodded and smiled.

She had no idea what was being said. The driver pulled over to the side of the road and said, "This is as far as we go honey, you better tend to those cuts on your legs." Beverly thanked them for the ride and climbed out onto the gravel shoulder of the road.

Now as she looked alternately, from the red spots on her shoes to the diminishing red dots of the Buick's fading taillights, she began to sob again. She couldn't erase the memory of the look of hatred on her father's face.

Chapter 2

Marietta, Georgia July 4, 1979

The McCords

It wasn't often that the "Farm Fresh" store was closed.

When you're running a "Mom & Pop" operation it's pretty much a twelve hour a day, seven day a week commitment.

Well, not today. This was the "Fourth" and Roger McCord (Owner and Proprietor) had decided to shut down and enjoy the holiday with his family.

Actually, it wasn't quite accurate to say family, since of his five children, only two still lived here. Roger's eldest son Johnny was living with his wife and two sons in Virginia. His oldest daughter, Liz, had migrated to the left coast, and the middle girl, Kate, was also married and living in Pennsylvania.

Here in Georgia, the "family" consisted of Roger, his wife Martha, their youngest son Pete and their youngest daughter Carol, who they fondly referred to as their "mid-life miracle".

Martha had given birth to Carol thirteen years after they thought they were no longer complicit in the procreation of the world. Roger didn't mind, though, because having a twelve-year-old around helped to keep him on his toes and feeling young. In reality Roger really did look deceptively youthful. He had always kept himself in good shape.

His brilliant white teeth (usually clenched on a big cigar), a full head of close-cut, dark-brown hair and the tattoos on his arms, relics of WWII, would enable him to pass for forty if he were ever so inclined to try.

Roger and Martha had seen their share of good times and tough times. These last ten years, since they had left Baltimore, MD and moved back to his home state of Georgia, had been good ones.

All of that was about to change............

As Roger steered his Caddy convertible west on The Four Lane, Carol, Pete and Pete's wife Gloria (who was closely approaching the delivery of their first child), knelt on the back seat facing the rear so as not to miss the Grand Finale of the annual "Marietta Fireworks Gala".

Roger had never liked fighting the mob at the end of the show and had made a ritual of slipping out ten minutes before the extravaganza.

He hung a left, off The Four Lane, and proceeded the six blocks to Maple Drive. As he swung the car left again, two blocks from their house, he turned his head toward the back seat and said, "You kids ready for the big cook-out?" The backs of three heads nodded in unison and Martha laughed.

Carol said, "I want to give King a hot dog with all the dressings, ok dad?" King was their prized Irish-Setter. "Just don't get him sick like the last time," said Roger in an overly authoritative fatherly voice.

As Martha leaned over to quietly remind Roger that it was he who fed King the plate of baked beans at the last cook-out, her attention was captured by the ominous glow of flashing red lights coming from the direction of their big rancher.

"Oh my god that's our house!" she gasped. "Them damn boys must have caught our roof on fire with their roman candles."

Roger slid the Caddy to the curb with a screech of brakes and tires.

"Stay in the car until I find out what the hell is goin' on."

He jumped out of the car and sprinted across the three lawns that separated him from his own yard.

Yellow banners bearing the words "FIRE LINE - DO NOT CROSS" were strung in front of him; he leaped over the banner and turned toward his front door. He could see that one whole wing of his home was ablaze.

He felt a hand grab his arm in a tight grip and heard a gruff voice say, "Where y'all think you're goin' mister?"

Roger turned to confront the police sergeant who was restraining him. "Damn it officer, I'm Roger McCord, that's my home and my dog is in there!"

The sergeant lowered his voice and said, "I'm sorry sir, but the firefighters already found your dog, he's gone. Was anyone in there with the dog?" "No", said Roger, "Thank God, they're all with me. How bad is the house?"

"Don't know exactly", the officer replied, "but you won't be stayin' there tonight!"

Chapter 3

I-75 North of Macon, GA July 4, 1979

Bear

The Harley-Davidsons peeled off from their four-abreast formation, much like a squad of fighter jets rolling over to make a strafing run on a Viet-Cong stronghold. In actual fact, the pilots of these shiny, growling bikes fancied themselves just as awesome and deadly as their winged counterparts.

As they thundered down the off-ramp of I-75 and into the service area of the Citgo station, the riders observed the noiseless, person-less indicators of inactivity. This particular station was chosen over the last two, which had been bypassed, because of the inviting, flashing sign announcing "BEER & WINE SOLD HERE".

Three of the motorcycles carried two passengers each. From any distance it would be difficult to distinguish, with any certainty, the gender of the riders. Their clothing was identical and in lieu of helmets they all wore long hair.

The lone rider, on the lead bike, stood out from the rest. He wore the same leathers and long hair, but he wore it on a six foot-four inch frame that outlined two hundred & fifty pounds of muscle and bone.

He extended the kickstand, dismounted and rocked

the massive Harley gently onto the support as if it were a Schwinn.

The brilliant station lights illuminated the back of his leather jacket, announcing in bold script letters that he was **"Bad News Bear"**.

Chapter 4

Johnny

To say that Johnny was a "redneck" would be slightly off-the-mark. Although he was born and raised in the Mid-Atlantic area of the country, he could not deny a certain amount of the "Deep South" ingrained in him from his Georgia born father.

At his first opportunity he had moved his family south from Maryland, deep into the state of Virginia. This extricated him from the hustle and bustle of the big city, where he had never felt comfortable. Camping, rafting, motorcycling and shooting with anything that expelled bullets or arrows were his favorite pastimes.

Johnny McCord, christened "John Larry McCord", had been driving south for about eight hours.

I-95 & I-85 were all smooth sailing and having just passed Augusta, he figured to be about three hours from Marietta.

Johnny was excited about surprising his Georgia relatives. He couldn't wait to show off his newest toy, a 1972 Porsche 911T. It may have needed some work on the body, but it was still quick. He also hoped to kill two birds with one stone. After showing off the "Targa", he would get his dad, Roger McCord, to take a critical look at his extensive gun collection that now resided in the boot of the Porsche.

11

Roger had been a gun aficionado ever since his time in the war. He introduced Johnny to firearms at a very young age. Johnny had taken to it like a fish to water. He definitely had the gun bug and didn't miss an opportunity to add to his collection.

His dad knew which arms were valuable and which were not. He could help Johnny make the best decisions on what guns he should trade or sell, and which ones he should hang on to in order to improve the value of his collection.

Johnny, like his dad, was also one helluva shot with a rifle or a handgun.

Chapter 5

Wally

Walter "Wally" Higgums was pretty contented with his position as the Night Manager at the Popes Ferry Citgo Gas Station & Mini-Market.

It was somewhat off the beaten track, which afforded Wally all the time he needed to drink "free" Mini-Market coffee and indulge in his favorite hobby, which was restoring his 55' Chevy BelAir.

The last thing Wally was concerned about was being robbed.

Anyone, with half a brain, would know that the pickens would be pretty slim at this remote station. But just in case, and to insure that Wally didn't lose his "redneck" status, he kept a Browning 9 mm on a hook just beneath the cash register.

Only six years removed from his duty in 'Nam, Wally was confident that he could discourage any *dumb shit* that might have lost his way in life.

Wally was in number two auto bay admiring the "Power Pak" under his BelAir's hood when he heard the unmistakable rumble of multiple motorcycles. This wasn't unusual for this part of the country, since lots of folks around here had bikes. He figured they were stopping for a pack of smokes and a bottle of *Jack*.

"Well," he thought "it would be a welcome relief from the extreme quiet of this particular night."

Chapter 6

Beverly exited the women's restroom and walked over to the vending machine area of the rest stop.

Although she was alone, the soft lights and gentle hum of the vending machines helped to offset the quiet of this dark and lonely stretch of road.

She had cleaned the blood from her legs and shoes as best she could, and replaced her makeup. This had helped lift her spirits up a notch from the sadness and depression that had enveloped her.

After getting a diet Coke and a pack of cheese crackers, she sat down at one of the rest stop's three picnic tables and debated with herself about what to do next.

Returning home was out of the question. She still loved her dad and knew she would miss her brother Mike terribly, but she was not going to subject herself to any more abuse, physical or otherwise.

Her mother had never contacted them after running out on them, so that was a dead-end even if Beverly had the inclination to be with her mother, which she did not.

She could call Mike, but there was nothing he could offer her except a return trip to *hell*.

Beverly thought about her cousin in Rome, Georgia. They had always gotten along well. Maybe if she just showed up, her cousin wouldn't be able to turn her away, at least not for a few days.

That would be long enough for Beverly to make some kind of plan. What Beverly needed now was another ride. With any luck at all, this rest stop would be the best place for her to catch one.

Chapter 7

Roger returned to the car and looked into three anxious pairs of eyes. "I'm sorry, but King didn't make it."

He said this in as gentle a voice as he could muster.

They all began to tearfully console each other when Roger interjected, "King had a good life, but this was a helluva way to go. There isn't any more we can do for him now except lay him to rest. We need to get into the garage. We'll get a shovel and bury him in the backyard, by his favorite tree. I'll grab the army cots out of the garage so we can spend the night in the storeroom at the store. It won't be terribly comfortable, but we can make do until we find out how bad the damage is to the house."

Pete said, "C'mon dad, I'll help you with King."

Martha tried her best to smile. She looked up at Roger and said, "Hon we'll take the cots over to the store and try to fix it up nice for us. You men can drive my car over once you take care of poor old King."

Roger and Pete went to the garage and got the cots. They loaded them into the Caddy's trunk along with the four sleeping bags that Pete had in the back of his Jeep.

Martha slid behind the driver's seat and slowly drove the Caddy away from Roger and Pete and what was left of their home. Gloria, who had moved to the front passenger seat, began to cry once more.

Martha reached over, patted her on the knee and

said, "Honey, I know you're upset, especially with the baby due and all, but you've got to try and be strong.

We've always been a strong family and we'll get through this together."

Chapter 8

Bear lumbered over to a forest green Harley. He smirked as he viewed the painting of a cobra on the gas tank. It was a black cobra with red eyes and looked as though it would gladly strike anyone foolish enough to get close.

Straddling the chopper was a biker equal in height to Bear, but weighing in at a slender one hundred sixty-five pounds.

Snake was an apt name for this rider. Both of his arms were tattooed with replicas of the slithering thing that decorated his gas tank. As he gripped both handlebars to dismount from his bike, his posture and attitude put one in mind of a snake slithering over a log.

Bear looked at him and said, "OK wild man let's party."

Snake slid off the bike and turned to the brunette who was sharing his ride. Her open leather jacket revealed a halter-top that was woefully inadequate for the task of restraining the breasts that were seemingly attempting to escape their prison. Snake reached over with both hands, roughly squeezed her breasts and said, "Rache, this is for luck."

Rachel, obviously enjoying this public display, smiled up at Snake and replied, "Hey hon, don't forget my Marlboros. You know I'll pay you for them later."

With an ugly sneer, which is what passed for a smile from Snake, he released his grasp on her breasts, turned to Bear and said, "Let's do it partner!"

Chapter 9

Wally grabbed a shop rag to wipe the grease from his hands and headed for the door that separated the auto bays from the Mini-Market.

As he passed through the open door, he heard the buzzer that heralded the coming of customers through the front door.

He positioned himself behind the cash register just as two bikers approached the front of the counter. One of the bikers, with snakes tattooed on his arms approached him and said, "Hey man, lemme have a pack of Marlboro hundreds in a box."

Wally nodded his head and smiled, thinking to himself, "Right, and a fifth of Jack Daniels."

Wally turned to get the cigarettes from the counter behind the register and he heard a different voice say, almost in a whisper, "If you still want to be breathing tomorrow, keep your hands where I can see them and don't fucking move."

Just the way he said it gave Wally a cold chill. He didn't know what to do. He always figured that if this ever actually happened, he would be facing the cash register within easy reach of his gun. The cigarette play had totally screwed him.

Before he had a chance to make a decision, he felt himself being pushed roughly away from the register. He tried to maintain his balance to keep from smashing headlong into one of the glass enclosed display cases, when he heard the same voice that had asked for cigarettes. "You wasn't thinking about goin' for this were you asshole?"

From the corner of his eye Wally could see the tall, skinny biker menacingly pointing Wally's nine millimeter at him.

There was nothing for him to do now but to just try and survive the situation.

He said, "Hold on, I'm no hero, take whatever you want."

Snake turned to Bear and said, "You know this prick would have blown us away if he'd a had the chance. I think I'll do him."

Wally began to panic. He said, "Wait......wait, I'll open the register for you, Just don't hurt me."

Bear said, "Then open it quick, son-of-a-bitch."

Wally moved back to the cash register as quickly as he could. He fumbled in his shirt pocket for the key to the register. He finally got a grip on it, pulled it out and slid it into the lock on the register and began to turn it.

There was a flash of white light before his eyes and a searing pain on the side of his head. Then everything went blank!

As Snake leaned down over the prostrate body and drew back the gun for another blow, Bear snarled, "Fuck it, he's had it, don't get any more blood on that piece, that's a nice piece and it's mine. Go out and get the others, tell them to bring in all the saddlebags. It's Christmas in July at the Mini-Market."

Chapter 10

Roger and Pete completed the sad task of laying King to rest. They buried him in the far corner of the backyard, under the tree that he'd often used for shade and to bark at the birds.

As they were walking back to the garage to replace the shovel, they saw a fire department official approaching them. The official, who they observed by his nametag and helmet, was a lieutenant of the Marietta Volunteer Fire Department, reached out to grasp Roger's hand.

He said, "Hi, I'm Mike Barnes, sorry for your loss."

He told Roger that the fire was completely out and had been restricted to the area where it had started, that being the wing of the house that included the master bedroom and bath, along with the hall closet.

He advised them that the fire had been started, as Martha had surmised, by some fireworks that had gotten out of hand. He explained that the police had a statement from their neighbor's fourteen-year old son, admitting to setting off the illegal fireworks. He said that the neighbor was extremely sorry and had already asserted that he would take responsibility for all of the damage.

He told Roger that the balance of the house could be entered safely, but that the smell from the smoke and water damage would make it impractical to live there until repairs had been done. Roger thanked the lieutenant for his help and said, "We appreciate your department's fast response and for limiting the damage.

We're good for tonight. We'll be staying at my place of business over on The Four Lane and we'll come back to take a better look at the damage, in the light of day."

He handed Lieutenant Barnes a business card and said, "Here's the phone number for the store. You can reach us there in case you need us."

He turned to his son and said, "Let's go Pete, the girls are bound to be wondering what's taking so long and they'll need some help fixing up the storeroom."

Pete answered, "Ok, dad, nothing else we can do here."

Chapter 11

Beverly mused, "When it rains, it pours." While there was a reasonable amount of traffic on I-75, nobody seemed to need a "pit stop". Not one car had pulled into the rest area since Bev had arrived.

She decided to leave the rest area and begin walking up the highway, thumb out... *The old- fashion way.*

Even though it was early July and very warm, she somehow felt more secure by putting on her brother's jacket.

It made her feel less vulnerable. Each time a car or truck came into view; she would get closer to the road and extend her right thumb.

After trying for about thirty minutes, with no success, she faced forward and began to walk.

She was in deep thought, rehearsing what she was going to tell her cousin, when she first noticed a low rumble that was growing louder and louder each second.

She turned and watched as four motorcycles passed her, slowed down and then pulled onto the shoulder where she was walking. This was not the kind of ride she was looking for she thought, and she continued to walk.

As she began to walk past the bikers, Beverly heard a commanding voice say, almost in a whisper, "Hey babe, I got a spare seat here, hop on." She turned toward the voice and saw a huge biker smiling at her. She quickly said, "Thanks, but I'm afraid of motorcycles."

The biker responded, "Then whatta you wearin' a biker jacket for?"

She said, "It's not mine, I borrowed it." Then he said, in a not so friendly voice, "If you're scared of bikes, I can always tie you on so you won't fall off."

At this point, Bev was getting nervous. She had no idea what to do, but realized that when you hitchhike you are always taking a gamble. She could see that there were girls on the other three motorcycles and decided that there was some safety in numbers.

She really wasn't afraid of bikes; in fact, she rode with her brother on his Suzuki 750 quite often.

She figured that she would just try to be friendly and tell them she was only going two exits up. She laughed and said, ""You don't need to tie me on. I'm sure you know how to ride that thing. I'm just going up to the Griffin exit; I think it's exit 67. If you could take me that far, I can walk home from there.

Bear said, "Ok good-lookin', jump up behind me and hold on tight."

Beverly put her foot on the peg and swung her leg in front of the sissy bar. She noticed that the two vertical spikes had a small bear's head, teeth bared, tied between them.

Bear pulled her arms around him and said, "You're gonna enjoy this babe."

Chapter 12

As Johnny drove past the intersection of I-85 and I-985, he felt a grumble in his stomach and realized that it had been about five hours since he had eaten.

He decided to pull off the highway near Suwanee and look for a place to eat. It was getting kind of late and while he wanted to get to his mom and dad's house as soon as possible, he didn't want to make his mom mess up her kitchen this late at night.

Luckily, he found a Bar & Grill open on this Fourth of July night and pulled into the parking lot.

There weren't a lot of customers, which made sense on a holiday night. He sat at the bar where he could easily watch the wall-mounted TV, hoping to catch the local news for Atlanta if not for Marietta.

The bartender asked what he wanted and Johnny told him just coffee and a burger. As the bartender went back to the kitchen to get the order, Johnny looked up at the TV. He saw a newscaster standing out in front of a Citgo station interviewing a police officer.

They were talking about a robbery that had just occurred this evening and about the station attendant who had apparently taken a pretty bad beating.

The newscaster asked if they had any leads. The police officer replied, "All we know is that the night attendant's name is Walter Higgums and he was hit in the head pretty hard."

The newscaster asked if the attendant had provided any description of his attackers.

The officer stated that Mr. Higgums was pretty disoriented, and he kept repeating something about a "snake".

The interview ended and the weather report came on. Other than a few possible thunderstorms, it was going to get much hotter in the next few days.

Johnny got his coffee and burger and after finishing the burger, he lit up a Camel to go with the refill on his coffee.

His belly full, he paid for the meal, told the bartender to take care and went out to complete the last leg of his trip.

Chapter 13

Roger pulled Martha's car around to the back of the "Farm Fresh". He saw the Caddy parked under the large, covered truck pull-in that they used for deliveries. There was enough space for two cars and he pulled in next to the Cadillac.

Roger used his key to unlock the back door. It led into a large storeroom at the rear of the store.

When he opened the door he could see that the girls had already set up the cots and sleeping bags and they were sitting there talking about King and their house.

Fortunately, they had plenty to eat and drink and Martha had made some coffee from the coffee service out in the main store. She had also opened up a few bags of cookies and put them on some paper plates.

She looked at Roger and Pete and said, "It's not the Ritz-Carlton, but, I bet you both are hungry."

Pete went over to his wife, Gloria. He gave her a hug and said, "How are you and the baby doing?"

Gloria had finally stopped crying and she attempted to smile. She said, "We've been fixing this place up for us and it kinda got my mind off things. I feel a lot better now."

Carol, Pete's youngest sister said, "I helped make the coffee and I picked out the cookies. Sit on the cot and I'll bring you some."

Carol, while almost thirteen, could easily have passed for seventeen. Not only had she developed physically, but her mannerisms and the clothes she wore made her appear older. No doubt her two older sisters, whom she always tried to imitate, had influenced her.

Roger said, "Well let's finish our coffee and cookies and hit the sack.

Tomorrow is going to be a busy day. I'll open the store and then you guys can take care of things here while I go check out the damage to the house and call the insurance company."

Chapter 14

After they had ridden for about ten minutes, Beverly saw the sign for the Griffin exit. Since there was no windscreen on the bike, it was very hard to hear.

She cupped her hands together like a megaphone and shouted, as loudly as she could, to remind Bear that this was her exit.

She knew something was terribly wrong when he cranked back on the throttle, sped up to ninety miles per hour and blew right past exit 67.

Beverly was really scared now. How do you get off of a speeding motorcycle? She figured the only thing she could do was wait until they stopped and then try to get away from them.

Every now and then, she could feel small road debris striking her unprotected hands. She alternated putting each hand into the pockets of the jacket for some temporary relief. When she slid her right hand into her brother's jacket, she felt something hard.

Wrapping her hand around the object, she realized it was Mike's penknife! She wasn't sure what she could do with it or when she might have the chance, but if it became necessary, she was going to put up a fight.

She had just left one abusive situation and she would not allow herself to be abused, in god knows what way, by these jerks. If they tried anything with her she would make them sorry.

As they got on the beltway that looped around Atlanta, she tried one more time to tell Bear to let her off. He just turned his head back to her, shook his head "No" and smiled.

Beverly gripped the penknife tightly and wondered if there was any way that she could attract someone's attention. But, she thought to herself, "Who's going to get involved with a girl in a black leather jacket sitting behind this big piece of shit, with all his asshole buddies around?"

When the motorcycle gang sped off the beltway and once more headed north on I-75, Bev knew she was still heading toward Rome. If only she could get away, before they got to Rome, she could call her cousin and have her come and get her. But, how could she get away if they didn't stop?

Then she saw a sign announcing "Welcome to Marietta, Population 3,500." Under that sign was one that said, "SPEED LIMIT 40mph – Slow Down and Live".

Bear stuck his hand down, with the palm facing backward to let the other bikers know he wanted them to slow down. He certainly didn't want to get locked up for speeding, in this little hick town, especially with this girl and all the goodies from the Citgo station.

Beverly thought, "This might be my only chance. Once he speeds up again, it might be too late."

She stuck her fingernail into the larger blade of the two and slowly worked the knife open. She pulled the knife out and screamed for Bear to let her off the bike.

When he just laughed at her, she stuck the knife, as hard as she could, into the meaty part of his thigh.

Bear pushed the brake pedal and squeezed the brake grip on the handlebar and the bike slid into a darkened parking lot. He didn't seem to be phased by the wound at all.

Beverly threw her leg over the seat, jumped off the bike and started to run as fast as she could. She slipped and fell on the gravel of the parking lot. She looked up and found herself looking into the headlights of the other three bikes.

Chapter 15

Johnny lit up another "cancer stick" and turned on the car radio. After playing with the dial for a few seconds he found a local station, "WFOM 1230AM" from Marietta. He thought to himself, "Almost there, Hoss."

It was a top 40 station, and while Johnny preferred country music, he wanted to hear all he could about Marietta.

Since it was the top of the hour, the news was on and they were discussing the robbery at the Pope's Ferry Citgo station.

According to the latest information from the Georgia Highway Patrol, they were looking for a couple of longhairs in leathers. One of them had snakes tattooed on both of his arms and all that was known about the second assailant was that he was big.

They were considered armed and dangerous. The "armed" caution was due to the fact that they had apparently taken an automatic pistol from the station attendant. They said the attendant was hurt pretty badly and would be hospitalized for an unknown period of time.

Johnny thought, "You can't get away from it. Even here in the boonies there are dickheads looking for a free ride." Just another couple of hours and he would be seeing his folks.

He wondered how Gloria was doing.

He was looking forward to the arrival of another

McCord boy and he knew that Pete and Gloria were excited. He would have to give some big brotherly advice to Pete on bringing up a boy.

He felt fully qualified to do so; since he felt that he hadn't done too bad a job with his own three sons, Randy, John and Michael.

Chapter 16

Ricky and Phil jumped off their motorcycles and grabbed Beverly. She started to scream, but Phil put his hand over her mouth and yelled, "Shut up bitch, if you know what's good for you."

Snake had already gotten to Bear's side and he could see the knife sticking out of his thigh. He said, "What the fuck, she stuck you!"

"No shit Dick Tracy!" roared Bear. He reached over and pulled out the knife. The blood immediately began to flow.

Snake said, "We need to get something to stop the bleeding."

Ricky piped in, "They probably got something in there we can use," and he pointed to the darkened sign on the front of the building that sat on this parking lot.

It read, "McCord's Farm Fresh Store" – If We Don't Have it, You Don't Need it."

Bear said, "Looks like nobody's home, but just in case, you guys go around back. Snake and me will check out the front."

Bear walked over to where Phil was holding Beverly and said, "Let her go."

Phil said, "But she's gonna scream again."

Bear replied, "No she won't." As soon as Phil took his hand from Beverly's mouth, Bear punched her hard on her chin. Beverly crumpled to the ground.

"Now get your asses around the back, like I told you."

Ricky and Phil didn't need to be told again. They

hopped on their bikes and rolled around the building, toward the back.

Bear looked at Rachel and said, "Watch this bitch, we're gonna go in the front."

Chapter 17

The McCords were fast asleep and didn't hear anything until the back door slammed open. The only light was from a small bathroom, in the back. They had left the light on, but closed the door 'til it was only open a crack.

Roger jumped up off the cot, realizing that something was wrong. He looked around and saw the baseball bat that he kept by the door that led into the market.

He saw two figures coming through the door and he made a leap for the bat, hoping to get there before they got to him.

As Phil kicked in the back door, Ricky said in a cocky voice, "Shit man that was the easy way."

Just as they came through the door they saw movement half way across the room.

Phil said, "Somebody's in here." Phil was holding the lug wrench that he had tried to jimmy the door with, before he decided to just kick it in. Ricky reached into his pocket and pulled out a six-inch switchblade and with a flick of his wrist the deadly blade protruded in front of him.

By this time the others had awakened and Martha shouted, "Roger, what's happening?"

All Roger could think about was protecting his family. He made it to the baseball bat and rushed back to get between his loved ones and the intruders. Seeing the glint of the switchblade from the thin strip of light, Roger didn't hesitate.

He swung the baseball bat at the arm that held the knife and he didn't miss. Ricky screamed with pain as he felt the bone in his wrist crumble and saw his knife fall to the floor.

Bear could hear Ricky's scream all the way from the front door. He had been trying to open the lock with a credit card. When he realized something had gone wrong, he reached over and picked up one of the empty milk crates that were sitting beside the front door. He lifted it high over his head and sent it crashing into the plate glass of the door.

There was a loud crash as the glass gave way to the force of Bear's missile. Bear reached into his pocket and pulled out the nine millimeter that they had taken from the gas station attendant. After knocking a few large pieces out with the gun, he climbed through the opening. Snake was right behind him.

Roger heard the glass break and his heart sank. "How many of them are there?" he thought.

Phil's eyes had gotten used to the semi-darkness and he could see Roger moving toward him. He lifted the tire iron and swung it at his opponent's head. His aim was off and the tire iron glanced off Roger's shoulder.

Roger's adrenaline was pumping so fast that he didn't even feel the blow. He swung the bat, one more time, and felt it hit the intruder solidly on the side of his head. The intruder went down like a sack of potatoes.

Roger turned toward the door between them and the market and attempted to close it and lock it from the inside.

By now the biker girls had gotten into the act, Rachel left Beverly and climbed through the broken door after Snake. The other two girls entered the back door and saw Roger running toward the front.

Chapter 18

She felt the gravel pushing into her cheek. Her whole face felt numb. As she turned her head and attempted to sit, Beverly remembered what had happened.

She looked around and was surprised not to see anyone. Pulling herself to her feet she saw the front door of the store being smashed in and heard loud shouting from the conflict inside. Still dizzy from the blow she received, she tried to concentrate on what to do. They might return at any moment so she must hide now!

But where?

Looking to the left side of the store, she saw a large trash bin with the top open. She stumbled to the bin and climbed up and over the side. She lowered herself into the trash, which was made up mostly of broken down cardboard boxes. The smell was pretty awful, but the alternative could be much worse.

Beverly crouched down, as low as possible, and pulled as many boxes over her as she could. Lying there, afraid to breathe, she closed her eyes and tried hard not to hear what was happening inside.

Chapter 19

Pete was afraid, not because he was a coward, but, because he knew that his family was in jeopardy. At the age of twenty-nine, Pete still looked like a teenager. His five foot, ten inch frame carried only one hundred and thirty five pounds. He knew that in a hand to hand fight with these intruders, he would lose.

The son-of-a-bitch that his dad had hit in the head wasn't moving, but the other one seemed to be looking for something on the floor. Pete turned his gaze to the biker on the floor and he saw the tire iron just inches from the outstretched, unmoving arm. He ran over and picked up the tire iron.

Ricky couldn't move his right hand and it hurt like hell. He also couldn't find his switchblade. He turned toward the three women, who were holding each other on the cots and trying to be invisible.

As he moved toward them, someone jumped in front of him. It was a boy, not very big but with a tire iron held high over his head.

Ricky said, "Don't hit me man, I'm already fucked-up."

Pete told him, "Then lie down on the floor and don't move."

The two other biker girls slowly, cautiously moved toward Pete and Ricky.

Pete said to Ricky, "Tell them to get out of the store or I'll split your head like a watermelon."

Ricky shouted, "Shelly, Linda, do what he says. Back the fuck out of here."

Shelly, who had been riding with Phil, saw him on the floor not moving. She screamed, "What about Phil? They killed him."

Ricky screamed again, "He's not dead. He just took a bad hit. Get out of here like I told you, we'll take care of him later."

Bear saw the dim light from the back of the store and realized that it was coming from a back room. Ricky and Phil must have run into some trouble, but he would take care of it.

Still bleeding from his thigh, Bear found that he was hobbling instead of running. He reached the back door, just as he saw it closing on him. He hit the closing door with his shoulder and sent it flying back the other way.

Roger had gotten to the door and started to close it, when it came swinging back and almost hit him.

There, outlined in the doorway, was one of the biggest men he had ever seen, and the man had a gun.

Roger, relying on his old combat experience knew that he must act quickly. He rushed at the man and grabbed the arm that held the gun with both hands. The gun was pushed back toward the front of the store and a loud report rang out as the gun was fired.

Snake heard sounds behind him and turned to see Rachel running toward him. Just as he heard the shot, he could see Rachel. She appeared to be slowed in suspended animation and then frozen in place. Snake saw a small hole appear, just under Rachel's right eye.

She looked surprised as she toppled backward and fell to the floor.

Roger saw the gun fly out of Bear's hand. It slid across the floor and came to rest under the vegetable counter.

But with both hands free, Bear simply overmatched Roger.

Bear spun around behind Roger, grabbed him around the chest and lifted him off the floor. Roger felt that all his ribs were being broken as this giant kept squeezing his chest. He felt himself going into semi-consciousness as he was thrown to the floor.

Snake was standing over Rachel, watching the blood ooze from the wound under her eye. He spun around in rage and saw the pistol lying under the tomatoes and spinach counter. He grabbed the gun and ran to where Bear was standing over Roger. He looked at Roger and sneered, "You killed my girl, you cocksucker, now you're gonna die."

Before Bear could do anything, Snake pointed the gun at Roger and shot twice, into his chest.

Martha screamed, "Roger, Roger oh they shot my husband!" She jumped off the cot and ran over to where Roger had fallen. She knelt down beside him and tried to lift his head, but he didn't move.

Bear grabbed the gun from Snake's hand and shouted, "This is all fucked-up. We gotta get out of here now."

He hobbled back through the doorway, past Martha

and Roger and saw Pete holding the tire iron over Ricky's head.

He immediately pointed the gun at Pete's mother and said, "If you don't want her to join him, and he pointed to Roger's unmoving body, then you better drop that."

Pete couldn't believe all the mayhem he had just seen and heard. But seeing his dad lying there, he knew this man wouldn't hesitate to shoot his mother. He dropped the tire iron and just slumped down next to his sister and his wife.

Bear looked at Ricky and said, "Get up, we gotta figure out what we're gonna do. Snake, go find me something to put on this cut, I'm bleeding like a stuck pig!"

Snake was standing there in a quiet rage. He looked at Rachel's body and then he turned to look at Carol, who was huddled with Martha and Gloria. He said, "I'll find something for your cut, but I ain't leavin' here alone."

Snake moved toward a rack that was marked "Johnson & Johnson". He said to Bear, "Tell Shell and Linda to take Phil and Ricky's bikes and head up to our place at Red Top."

Bear, kept the gun trained on Martha, walked to the back door and gave the girls instructions to meet them at the campsite.

Shelly said, "What about Phil?"

Bear replied, "He can't ride, I'll take that Caddy

parked out back and he'll go with me. Now, get going and don't get stopped by the cops."

Snake came back with an armful of bandages and a tube of antiseptic he had gotten from the rack.

He gave them to Bear and said, "Give me the gun. You fix yourself up while I straighten things out here."

Bear slipped, gingerly, out of his jeans and began to clean and bandage his wound. As he was doing this he remembered Beverly. He said to Ricky, "What happened to the bitch outside? Rachel was supposed to be watching her. Go out front and get her."

Ricky, holding his shattered right wrist with his left hand, walked to the front door, climbed through the broken glass and went to where he had last seen the girl....... She was gone!

Chapter 20

Beverly was terrified. She had heard what she was sure were gunshots. There was a lot of screaming and shouting, but now it was eerily quiet. She thought she heard footsteps in the gravel on the parking lot. All she could do was stay as quiet as a mouse and pray, "Please, God, don't let them find me."

She heard the sound of motorcycles being started up and heard them growl as they left the area. She knew that they hadn't all gone because she could still hear footsteps very close to where she hid.

Ricky knew that Bear was gonna be pissed, but the chick must be long gone by now.

He thought, "I better get back in there and see if I can fix a splint for my wrist and maybe find something for the pain." He knew that Linda had a whole bottle of Oxycontin pills that she had gotten with a fake prescription, but she and Shelly had just pulled out on the bikes for the campsite at Allatoona Lake. Well, he'd just have to make Excedrin do until they caught up with the girls.

He climbed back through the broken door and told Bear that the girl was gone. Bear told him to get Snake to help him wrap up his wrist and then put the family in the freezer box. Snake gave the gun to Ricky. He held it in his good hand, still pointing it at four family members who weren't dead.

Snake found an empty wooden orange crate. He

stomped it with his boot and picked up two pieces of the broken wood to splint Ricky's wrist.

He wrapped gauze around his wrist, applied the wooden splints, and then secured it with adhesive tape.

Ricky gave the gun back to Snake and went to find something for the pain.

Chapter 21

Johnny smiled as he saw the sign for Maple Drive. He knew he was just a few minutes away from the big surprise.

His mom would be a little aggravated that he hadn't called to let them know he was coming, but she hadn't seen him for almost two years and it would quickly become all hugs and kisses.

As he swung left onto their street, he lit up another cigarette. He knew that Gloria was expecting and she hated when anyone smoked around her. Even his dad made sure to go out on the deck to smoke his cigars.

About a block away from the house, Johnny could tell something was wrong. While it was extremely dark, there was a street lamp just in front of the rancher. He could see piles of furniture and what looked like roof tiles all over the front yard.

Johnny slid the Porsche to the curb, turned off the ignition and jumped out leaving the keys in the car. He couldn't believe his eyes. A big chunk of the house was destroyed. He saw the yellow DO-NOT-CROSS tape and realized that whatever had happened was over.

He thought to himself, "Was anyone hurt?" He prayed that they were not.

He ran to the house next door, without even considering the fact that it was after midnight. He banged hard with the knocker that decorated the neighbor's front door.

A light went on in the front foyer and the door cracked open a few inches.

Mom's neighbor, Evelyn (he couldn't think of her last name), stuck her head out the door and said, "Johnny, Johnny what a bad time you picked to visit!"

Chapter 22

Bear walked over to Snake and said, "Gimme the damn gun back, you crazy son-of-a-bitch."

Without hesitation, Snake handed the Browning back to Bear.

Snake said, "Well what's the plan?"

Bear said, "The girls are gone, but that leaves us with an extra bike, unless Ricky can ride with one hand."

"Whatta you mean?" said Snake, "Ricky can ride with me and you can take your bike."

"Not gonna happen", responded Bear, "We're taking some insurance and you need to drive one of the cars to do it."

"He's not gonna ride my bike with one hand, he'll wreck it."

"Either Ricky rides your bike or we leave it here", said Bear.

"Ok", said Snake. "But if I'm driving the car and "dickhead" is riding my bike, I'm taking the young, sexy chick to replace Rachel."

"Suit yourself, but you're taking Phil and the pregnant girl too."

They walked over to where the McCords were huddled. Bear pointed at Pete and said, "You and the old lady get in the freezer box. Snake, you and Ricky can drag that asshole's body in there with them."

Pete took his mother by the arm and said, "Come on mom," and he led her into the freezer.

Snake and Ricky dragged Roger into the freezer with Ricky using only his left hand to pull one of Roger's legs.

Martha's face reflected her total panic and she screamed, "What about my girls?"

Bear said, "Don't worry Lady. Just keep your mouths shut, until we get away, and we'll leave the girls somewhere safe." With that he slammed the door to the freezer.

Carol and Gloria were sitting huddled together on one of the cots. Gloria was crying uncontrollably and Carol looked at the intruders and screamed, "Leave us alone. Just go away and leave us alone."

Snake noticed the switchblade, which had been knocked out of Ricky's hand by the baseball bat. He picked it up, walked over to Carol and grabbed her by the hair. He bent her head back and stared into her face. He said, "Shut up you bitch, you're both going with us, and if you don't keep your mouth shut, I'm gonna cut your little friend here."

Snake noticed a set of keys, a wallet and a lighter, lying on the floor next to one of the cots. He picked them up and saw that one of the keys had the word "Cadillac" etched into it.

He turned to Bear and said, "Hey, I got the keys to the Caddy. Let's load up."

"I checked on Phil. He's history," said Bear, "but we can't leave him here. Ricky, get your sorry ass over here and watch these girls. "You and me gotta put Phil and Rachel in the Caddy's trunk. We'll bury their asses at the campsite."

They carried Phil out through the back door.

Snake opened the trunk and they hoisted the body into the trunk. Then they went back and got Rachel, from where she had fallen. They carried her out and piled her on top of Phil.

Snake returned to where Ricky was watching the girls. He looked at Ricky and said, "I'm gonna tape your right hand to the handlebar grip. That way you should be able to drive my bike. If you drop it, I'm gonna kick your ass."

They brought Carol and Gloria out to the car, taped their hands behind their backs and put several pieces of adhesive tape over their mouths.

After shoving both the girls into the back seat of the Cadillac, Snake told Ricky to mount up. Ricky got on Snake's bike and Snake taped his right hand around the accelerator grip. Bear mounted his own bike and Snake jumped into the Caddy.

Bear said, "Head on up to the lake. We'll be right behind you."

Chapter 23

Evelyn, the McCord's neighbor, told Johnny as much as she knew. She assured him that the family was ok, but that they had lost their dog. Johnny asked her if she knew where they were and she replied that she wasn't sure. Johnny figured that they would probably go to the Farm store and he asked if he could use her phone.

Evelyn said, "Go right ahead. I'll put on a pot of coffee for us."

Johnny dialed the number from memory and when it rang continuously, with no answer, he thought maybe his memory had failed him. He pulled out his wallet and checked the little phone number reminder sheet that he kept there.

The number, as he remembered it, was correct. "Well," he thought to himself, "it is kinda late, I'll call again and let it ring till' they answer." He dialed the number again; slowly to be sure that he dialed it properly.

After about twenty rings, he started to worry. He said, "Miss Evelyn, I think I better drive over to the store, no one's answering the phone."

She poured his coffee from the coffee cup, into a large paper cup and said, "Sure hon, take this with you and be sure to call me so I know y'all are ok." She wrote her phone number on a small memo pad, tore off the sheet and gave it to him.

Johnny thanked her for the coffee, assured her that he would call and hurried out to the street. He jumped into his Porsche and sped off toward his Dad's Store.

Chapter 24

She didn't know just how much time had passed, but it felt like close to an hour. Beverly had only heard a few cars pass by and apparently, none of them had noticed anything to make them stop. She had heard muffled voices, coming from the direction of the store, but that was all.

Now there seemed to be a lot more activity going on. She heard a car trunk slam and the sound of motorcycles starting up.

As the sound of the motorcycles faded, she decided that she would wait a few moments before leaving the safety of her hiding place. After the passing of what she guessed was about five minutes, she hadn't heard any sounds.

She climbed to the top of all of the boxes and let herself over the side of the trash bin and onto the gravel of the parking lot.

Her heart was beating very quickly as she tried to decide what to do next. Her first inclination was flight. The sooner she put some distance between this place and herself the better.

She slowly walked toward the highway, which forced her to pass by the front of the building. As she walked, trying to be silent, which was impossible on this gravel, she looked toward the front of the store and saw the smashed glass and the huge opening in the door.

She wanted to continue toward the street, but her

heart kept telling her that this was partially her fault and maybe someone needed help.

After all she reasoned, if she hadn't been hitching a ride, these maniacs wouldn't have picked her up. If they hadn't picked her up, she wouldn't have stabbed one of them and they wouldn't have stopped at this store. It was all totally crazy, but she was part of this ugly chain of events like it or not.

Beverly walked over to the broken door, carefully climbed through the opening and what she saw horrified her. Produce and other boxes were strewn all around the place. She saw a light coming from the back of the store and was drawn to it.

It appeared to be a door. As she started toward it, she saw a great deal of blood on the floor and it looked like something had been dragged through it toward the back.

She listened as hard as she could but heard nothing. Obviously someone was in trouble and, as frightened as she was, she continued through the door into what appeared to be a warehouse full of store supplies.

Once through the door, she saw more blood on the floor. There were more drag marks that made a path of blood ending at a large freezer door. There was no way she wanted to see what was inside that freezer, but she had come this far and she had to know.

Beverly grabbed the large handle on the freezer door, held her breath, counted to ten and pulled the door open.

She jumped when the freezer's automatic light came on. She couldn't believe what she found.

There were three people inside. A woman and a young man were sitting on the freezer's floor. The woman was crying and holding the head of an older man in her lap.

The woman looked up at Beverly, with tears in her eyes and said, "Can't you leave us alone, haven't you done enough?"

Beverly was confused. Why was she looking at her like that? Then it came to her. Here she was with her black leather jacket, looking like one of the bastards that had done this terrible thing.

"No, No!" she cried, "I'm not one of them. They kidnapped me, but I got away and I've been hiding. Please, let me help you."

Martha looked at Beverly and, through her tears, said, "Call 911! Get an ambulance! Use the phone in the front next to the cash register. Hurry, Hurry please!"

Beverly asked them, "Where are we, I don't know where to tell them to come."

Pete said, "Just tell them the "Farm Fresh" store, in Marietta, out on The Four Lane. They'll know where to come."

Beverly ran to the front of the store. She found the phone by the register and dialed 911.

"This is 911. Is this an emergency?" said the voice on the other end of the line.

"Yes, yes, "Beverly screamed. "Send the police and an ambulance. There's been a robbery and someone was shot. We're at the McCord's "Farm Fresh" store in Marietta on The Four lane. Please come quickly!"

The 911 voice said, "Help is on the way. What is your name, please?"

Beverly wasn't sure why she did it, but she just said, "Please, hurry," and she hung up the phone.

Just then she heard tires screeching and gravel being thrown up in the parking lot. She knew that 911 couldn't have responded that quickly.

She thought to herself, "Oh no, they've come back for me!"

Chapter 25

Detective Sullivan

Mike Sullivan was a tough cop, but he was fair. Twenty-nine years on the force and he should have pulled the plug four years ago.

While he hated shift work, it was better than his present "24 hour on-call" duty. At least you could plan your day or your night, as the case might be. Except, of course, on those rare occasions when he had to work extra time on a case, or, got volunteered for some special detail.

Well, he had worked hard to become a detective and this was part of the price you had to pay for the gold shield.

He and his wife, Anne Marie, were sitting in the den of a comfortable little bungalow that they called home. It was located in a small suburb of Macon, called Unionville. They had just finished watching one of his favorite movies, "Dog Day Afternoon". Mike thought it was one of Al Pacino's best performances and had watched the movie at least ten times.

It always amused Mike at how really stupid the characters in this movie were. Mike actually lived in the world that was being portrayed in this film, and he knew that this portrayal was much more true to life than most people, who didn't live in this world, thought.

As the credits rolled down the screen, they turned to each other and, without having to speak simply nodded, meaning that it was time to "Hit the Hay".

He and Anne Marie had just crawled into bed and turned out the light when they heard the harsh ring of the bedside phone. With a groan he reached over and pulled the receiver from the hook and placed it to his ear.

The familiar voice of Sergeant Bill Rowan told Mike that he was needed at the emergency room of Macon's Northside Hospital.

There had been a robbery and assault at a Citgo station in Pope's Ferry. The attendant had been rushed to Northside, after a "Good Samaritan" motorist had called 911.

Mike kissed Anne Marie on the forehead and said, "I'm off again. I'll call in the morning if I don't get back before then."

When Detective Sullivan got to the hospital, Wally Higgums was fading in and out of consciousness.

After about two hours of drinking coffee, fending off reporters and sitting at Wally's bedside, Mike was able to ascertain that there had been two bikers involved. One of them had a fetish for snakes, based on the tattoos on his forearms.

He also learned that the robbers had taken a gun from Mr. Higgums, which made everything a bit dicier. Chains, knives and tire irons were bad enough, but guns, that was a whole other thing.

Mike had been shot once, during his twenty-nine

years, and still experienced discomfort in his left hip when it rained.

He always remembered the last statement made by the lieutenant who trained him at the Police Academy.

On the final day before they graduated, the lieutenant had reviewed all of the training that had occurred in the last six months. *Protect and Serve. Do not draw your weapon unless deadly force is required. Treat all citizens the same.*

"But", the grizzled, old lieutenant had said in as serious a voice as possible, "Make sure that you and your partner go home for dinner tonight, no matter what!"

Well, after a short stay in this very hospital, Mike and his partner had made it home to dinner the night he was shot.

The "perp", on the other hand, had not.

Chapter 26

Johnny felt at one with the Porsche and put it through its paces every chance that he got. The closer he got to his dad's little grocery store, the more concerned he got, and the more worried he became the harder he pushed the Porsche.

What would normally have taken about fifteen minutes only took nine.

He knew something was terribly wrong when he saw the glass from the broken front door all over the parking lot.

He spun the Porsche up to the front door with no regard for what the glass might do to his tires.

Releasing the trunk latch, he jumped out of the car and opened the trunk. He reached in and pulled out a pearl handled Colt 45, one of the matched set in the case, along with a full clip of ammo. He jammed the clip into the handle and pulled the slide back sending the first shell home and putting the 45 on "full-cock".

Without hesitation, he climbed through the broken door and couldn't believe what he was seeing. He was scared, shocked and angry, but he remembered the training his father had given him. He held the Colt pointing straight up, in his right hand, with his left hand supporting the handle.

Seeing no movement in the front of the store, he made his way to the back.

As he approached the storeroom door he shouted anxiously, "Mom, Dad! Are you ok? It's me Johnny!"

Beverly had run back to the storeroom and told the McCord's that the gang had returned.

Pete said, "I heard it too, but I didn't hear any motorcycles, are you sure it's them?"

At that moment they heard movement in the front of the store. Pete began to look for something, anything to defend them with. He uttered a great sigh of relief when he heard the unmistakable voice of his big brother shouting at them from the other side of the door.

He hollered back, "Johnny, Johnny, it's me Pete. We're back here by the freezer. Dad's been shot, Hurry."

Johnny put the 45 on safe and ran to the freezer. His dad was lying still with his head in his mom's lap. Pete was standing in front of the freezer door with a strange girl in a black leather jacket.

He dropped to the floor, beside his mother and father and put two fingers on his father's neck. He said, "I feel a pulse, we need to get an ambulance!"

The strange girl said, "I already called 911. They should be here in a few minutes."

Pete said, "Johnny, it was a biker gang. They broke in and shot dad. They took Carol and Gloria with them."

Beverly said, "I think they took one of your cars."

Pete said, "I know where they're going. They said something about "Red Top"."

Johnny said, "Where in the hell is Red Top?" Pete replied, "It's a state park in Cartersville, up on Allatoona Lake.

There's a mountain there called "Red Top". It's only twenty minutes or so from here.

We can catch them, if we hurry. The girls must be scared to death."

Beverly said, "I know how they feel. Those bastards kidnapped me, but I got away. It's my fault that they stopped here. Please let me help."

Johnny said, "The best way for you to help is to tell us everything you know about them and then stay here to help my mom with dad. You can fill the police in when they get here."

Beverly said, "There are four motorcycles, all Harleys. The leader is a big guy they call "Bear". His bike has a stuffed bear hanging on the sissy bars. The other guy is called "Snake". You can't miss him or his bike. He has snakes tattooed on his arms and a snake painted on his gas tank. I don't know who the others are, but, there are two other guys and three girls."

Pete said, "Dad fought like hell. I think two of the guys are hurt pretty badly and one of the girls is dead.

The big guy had a gun. He and dad fought over it. It went off and got her right in the face. It must have been the Snake guy's girl, because he went ballistic and shot dad. They were gonna shoot mom if we didn't get in the freezer. But, that's when they took Carol and Gloria. This girl came in to help after they left."

"What's your name, and how are you involved in all of this?" asked Johnny.

"My name's Beverly, and it's a long story", she answered.

Johnny looked at his mom and said, "Mom, we'll

find Carol and Gloria. Beverly, here, will stay with you and dad."

Johnny and Pete went out the back door and saw that their dad's Caddy was gone. They ran around to the front of the store to the trunk of the Porsche, which was still open.

Johnny reached in and grabbed a Ruger replica of a German Luger. He grabbed a box of 9mm parabellum shells and two extra clips. He gave them to Pete. He also grabbed a box of 45 shells and gave them and two empty clips for the Colt to Pete.

"Load these clips while I drive."

Johnny closed the trunk and they both got in the Porsche. With a squeal of tires, Johnny spun out onto The Four Lane and headed north toward I-75 and Cartersville.

Chapter 27

Max and Kurt

Max and Kurt Stremler might have bitten off more than they could chew.

They had driven their 78' Dodge Eldorado Sportsman all the way from Chicago. They were on their way to St. Petersburg with a sack full of cash, ready to make a big coke buy.

They both carried S&W .38s in the belt holsters behind their backs. These boys weren't terribly worried about spending a night in the woods.

This seemed like as good a place as any to stop for the night. The sign had said, "Red Mountain State Park – Campsites Available – Next Left".

Well maybe "next left" didn't mean the same thing in the "hicks" as it did in "Chicagoland" because after turning left and driving for about ten minutes, the road, if you could call it a road, was fizzling out.

Other than the illumination from their headlights, it was pitch black and the foliage was scratching the finish of their year old motor home. They figured they had made the proper turn since they had seen two bikers fly past them and turn left at the same place.

The bikers hadn't turned back, so they were sure that the campground must be up ahead.

When the road veered to the right, they could see the area opening up somewhat. Sure enough, their headlights revealed three sizable tents.

As they pulled the motor home alongside the tents they saw the two bikers just walking from their motorcycles toward one of the tents.

Max turned to his brother and said, "Am I dreaming or do those bikers have tits?"

Kurt said, "Maybe we got lucky, you think?"

Max rolled down his window, stuck his head out and hollered, "Hey ladies, could you help out some fellow campers? I think we're lost."

Shelley and Linda looked at each other. "This is not cool," thought Linda. Bear and the others couldn't be that far behind and things were already complicated enough.

Shelley walked over to the motor home and checked out the two occupants.

She had noticed the Illinois license plates and said, "You guys are kinda far from home aren't you?"

Max said, "Yep, we're heading for the sunny south, got another six or seven hours to go, thought we'd spend the night in this campground."

By then, Linda had come up next to Shelley and said, "This ain't the campground, it's the next exit up."

Max thrust forward a six-pack of Coors Light, with one can missing. He showed it to the girls and said, "You gals want a cool one?"

Before they could answer, both men opened their doors and got out of the Dodge. Kurt said, "Yeah, looks like you got a cozy little place here."

The girls could see that both of these men were

well put together and they didn't like the way the conversation was going.

Linda said, "Our friends are gonna be here in a few minutes and they ain't gonna like you guys being here, why don't you just turn around and head back out the way you came in?"

"Feisty little broad, ain't you," said Max. "We thought we could keep you and your girlfriend company out here in the scary woods, until your friends show up."

Shelley reached into her jacket and pulled out a straight razor. She looked the two men in the eye, unflinchingly, and said "Get the fuck out of here, if you know what's good for you."

Max reached behind him and withdrew his .38 from a belt holster. He pointed it at Shelley and said, "So you do wanna play, doncha? Unless you plan on shavin' something, you better drop that razor!"

Shelley quickly dropped the razor to the ground.

Max looked at Kurt and said, "Check em' both out while I keep them covered." He waved the Smith & Wesson threateningly back and forth from Shelley to Linda.

Kurt said, "It'll be my pleasure, really." He pulled Linda away from Shelley and grasped both of her hands behind her back with his massive left hand. He began to frisk her, with his free hand, from the bottom of her stretch pants upward. When he got to her breasts, he looked at Max, laughed and said, "The only weapons she's got are these, but, no doubt they could hurt a guy."

He pushed Linda back in front of Max, motioned for Shelley to come to him and said, "Next."

Kurt found a switchblade in Shelly's leather jacket pocket. He pulled it out and pressed the release button. A lethal looking six-inch blade appeared. He stuck the blade hard into the trunk of a nearby tree and with one sideways flick of his wrist, broke the handle from the blade. He shoved Shelley toward the tent and waved for Linda to follow her. He said, "Let's see what other goodies they have in the tent." Max turned to Kurt and said, "I'll keep an eye on these two. Why don't you take a look inside the tent?"

Kurt nodded and unzipped the front flap of the tent. He lit his cigarette lighter, stooped over and disappeared inside the tent. Max heard a click and saw a light come on in the tent. Kurt reappeared at the opening and said, "Come on in ladies. Let's get comfortable."

When Max followed the girls into the tent he ducked his head to avoid banging into the portable, rectangular, fluorescent lamp hanging from the top of the tent's center pole. The light from the lamp revealed four inflated mattresses with open sleeping bags lying on top. There was also a portable Boom Box on one of the sleeping bags.

Kurt said, "I checked it out. There ain't no more surprises waiting here for us. They must have carried all the scary stuff in their pockets."

"Very cozy," Max remarked. Let's don't waste any time. Why don't you take off them clothes and let's see what you got."

Linda thought, "I need to stall for time, just long enough for Bear and Rick and Snake to get back. Then we'll see who's gonna fuck who."

She turned toward Max, with her most seductive smile and mewed, "Why don't you give a girl a chance to warm up to the idea. How about a couple of those silver bullets you showed us? I'll turn some music on for us."

She reached over and turned on the radio. Kenny Rogers was singing "Lady", in his unmistakable, gravelly voice.

Linda squealed, "Oh, that's my favorite song!" and she turned it up louder.

Kurt said, "I thought you told us your boy friends were on the way. We wouldn't want to be interrupted now would we?"

Shelley chimed in, "They are coming, but we told you a little fib. They aren't due to get here 'til about eight in the morning. That gives us plenty of time."

Max said, "Go ahead Kurt, bring in the beer. There's an extra six-pack in the fridge, why don't you grab it, while you're there? It'll be more fun if the ladies are relaxed."

Kurt climbed out of the tent and was making his way to the motor home when he realized too late, that something wasn't right.

Chapter 28

Bear and Ricky had hung back about five miles behind the Caddy. They didn't want to bring any undue attention to the car and what it contained.

They knew how cops just naturally took a second look at motorcycles and they wanted to get to the lake as quickly and quietly as they could.

"Tough luck for Phil and Rachel, but that's the way it goes," thought Bear. "If that little bitch hadn't stabbed me, none of the rest of this shit would've happened. He shoulda' left her ass standing on the side of the fucking road! But, who knew."

They would have to dump the bodies someplace where they wouldn't be discovered for a while.

He would let Snake have his fun then they would close up this campsite, which had been home base for the last week, and head to Tennessee. They'd only gotten a lousy two hundred bucks from the Citgo station. He had expected a bigger score on a holiday at a beer & wine place.

Well, the two hundred would have to tide them over until they put some distance between themselves and "The Peach State".

He noticed that Ricky was wobbling on Snake's bike.

Bear thought, "If he drops that bike, I'll leave his ass where he falls. If I don't, Snake will tear him apart."

When he saw the sign for Red Top, he started feeling a little better. He thought, "We'll dump the bodies, have some fun and get a good night's sleep. I guess we'll have to do the two bitches too. What's the difference? They can only hang you once!"

As they pulled up behind the stopped Caddy, Bear saw Snake running back toward them, signaling for them to shut the bikes down.

Snake said, "I don't know what the fuck's going on, but there's a camper blocking the way. I see the light on in your tent and they got music playing. The other bikes are up by the tent, so the girls are here, but what's the deal with this motor home?"

Bear replied, "Just chill out man, we're gonna find out what the fuck's goin' on!" At Bear's direction, they took up positions around the tent with Bear off to the right side of the front. He was just about to signal Ricky and Snake with his lighter, when this guy came out of the tent stooped over. Bear saw the gun sticking out of his belt at the small of his back and decided now was his best chance.

Chapter 29

Kurt saw the car that was pulled up right behind their motor home. He reached around his back to grab his .38.

Before he could get to it, he felt his hand being grabbed and at the same time he felt a powerful arm lock around his throat and squeeze.

He tried to scream, but nothing came out. The arm kept on squeezing him tighter and tighter and for Kurt, the tough monkey from "Chicagoland", that was the night the lights went out in Georgia.

Bear could hear the neck snap and he let the body fall slowly. Kurt was dead before he hit the ground!

Bear had watched the guy start toward the Dodge and then stop abruptly. As he tried to grab his gun, Bear had moved in. The guy never knew what hit him.

Bear stealthily returned to his side of the tent and signaled the others by lighting his lighter. Snake cut the back of the tent open and Ricky did the same on the left side. As soon as Bear heard the sound of canvas being cut, he barged in through the front flap with the Browning nine in his hand.

Chapter 30

Detective Sullivan decided to call into the night desk and report what little information he had gleaned from the semi-comatose Walter Higgums.

When he got hold of the desk sergeant, Sergeant Rowan, he was advised that a 911 call had just been received.

He said, "Mike, I know you're a ways from Marietta, but we just got a call from a store called "Farm Fresh" out on The Four Lane. It sounds like it might be your guys."

He went on to fill Mike in on the pertinent facts. He said, "Marietta PD is on the scene and they're talking about motorcycles and a guy with snakes on his arms. It's getting worse. Mike, they shot a guy and there's blood all over the place. They also stole a car from the guy who got shot and kidnapped his twelve-year-old daughter and pregnant daughter-in-law. They need you out there right away."

Mike said, "I know exactly where it is. When I worked cases out that way, I've occasionally stopped there for coffee. You need to get Atlanta PD's chopper to pick me up at Northside Hospital. I'll be on the front lawn. Tell the locals not to do anything 'til I get there. I figure I can be there in twenty minutes on the chopper. It would take me an hour and a half to drive, even if I ran the siren. I'm afraid we don't have that kind of time to waste. I've got a good buddy at Marietta PD and I'll call him now to get a spare unit to meet me at the scene." "Ok Mike, I'll get my guy working on that chopper right now."

"Bill, these guys are bad actors and it looks like it's gonna' be a long night. Give Annie a call for me. If I call she'll just want to know the details and I don't want to get her any more worried than she is normally.

Tell her I'm at a robbery scene and I'll call her as soon as I can. I'm on my way to the front lawn. Tell those guys to hustle!"

Chapter 31

Pete knew exactly where Red Top was located. He had driven past the entrance many times, but had never actually gone into the park.

Johnny was driving as fast as he could safely go, while at the same time, he kept looking for his dad's Cadillac.

As he mulled the recent events over in his mind, he recalled the news reports that he had seen on TV and heard on his car radio.

He glanced at his brother and said, "Shit, I heard about these guys on the news. These sons-a-bitches robbed and beat a guy down in Pope's Ferry.

The news guy said he was mumbling something about snakes. I'll bet it's the same assholes that robbed us. If we see the bikes or the Caddy, we'll recognize them."

At that moment Johnny saw a sign that told them that Red Top was at the next left turn.

As Johnny began to slow down for the turn, Pete said, "No, not here. It's a little confusing, the entrance is actually up a ways on the left by a little souvenir stand."

Johnny hit the accelerator and about a quarter of a mile further down the road he spotted the closed souvenir stand that Pete had mentioned.

They turned left, onto the park access road and saw a guard station. He pulled up and stopped.

The guard slid his Plexiglas window open and said, "Can I help you boys?"

Johnny replied, "Yes sir, we're trying to find our friends. They should have come in here within the last thirty minutes. They're driving a 1978, green Cadillac convertible."

The guard replied, "I don't recall a Caddy convertible coming in. Are you boys staying the night? It's $2.00 per person if you are."

Johnny said, "No sir, we just need to see them for a minute. Can we take a look?"

The guard wrote down their license number and waved them in.

Chapter 32

All the way, since they left the "Farm" store, Snake kept warning Carol and Gloria to stay down and keep quiet.

Carol knew that Gloria was terribly uncomfortable and was worried about her baby.

The last five minutes were the worst. They were bumping up and down on some rutted back road, but finally the car stopped.

Again, Snake had reminded them both not to move and he got out of the car, closing the door very quietly.

Realizing that the only help they were going to get was from each other, Carol wiggled around until she was back to back with Gloria. She began to work on the tape that bound Gloria's hands.

After about five minutes, Snake had not returned to the car and Carol had managed to get one of Gloria's hands free. Gloria pulled the tape from her own mouth and then she pulled the tape from Carol's.

Just then they heard the low rumble of motorcycles and Gloria quickly replaced the tape loosely over her mouth and Carol's. She put her free hand behind her back and they both froze.

The sound of voices came through the open window and Carol was sure she recognized the voice of the big man that her father had fought at the store. She couldn't hear what they were saying, but the very fact that they were speaking in whispers led her to believe that they were worried about something.

She could hear music coming from in front of the car. Her hopes began to rise and she prayed that there was someone here who could help them.

After a few minutes, she heard footsteps returning to the car and her hopes sank again.

But, they didn't stop at the car! She could hear them more clearly now. The big one was giving the others orders.

He said, "You go around by that tree and Snake, you get behind the tent. I got the gun, so I'm going in the front. When I click my lighter on, cut the tent and go in."

By the time he had finished his instructions, they were well past the car, heading toward the music.

Gloria must have heard the conversation, as well, because she had begun pulling the tape off of their mouths once more and then started to free her other hand.

Carol said, "We gotta' get out of here while we can. Get this tape off of me and we'll make a run for it."

Gloria said, "I don't know about a run. I don't feel very well; maybe you should just leave me and go for help."

Carol chided her, "There's no damn way I'm leaving you. These bastards don't care that you're pregnant. We're going together."

She pushed the back of the front passenger's seat forward, reached over and quietly opened the door. Fortunately the interior light switch was off and they were able to get out of the car unnoticed.

They saw another vehicle parked in front of the Cadillac, but it was too dark to make out what it was.

Carol put her arm around Gloria and they began to walk slowly down the dirt road, hoping it would lead them out of this nightmare.

Chapter 33

When Mike arrived in Marietta in the police helicopter, the local boys in blue had already blocked off The Four Lane both east and west of the McCord's "Farm Fresh" store.

The helo landed in the eastbound lane and Mike jumped out onto the road, keeping his head down as he hurried out from under the menacing blades.

Mike's friend Sergeant Paul Robbins, from the Marietta Police Department, was waiting for him with a patrol car ready for Mike's use. He let Mike know that Mr. McCord had been rushed to Emory-Adventist Hospital in Smyrna about six miles away.

He explained that Mr. McCord had been hit twice, but was holding his own.

"He's one tough s o b," he told Mike. "He must have put up one hell of a fight. It looks like a war zone in there. We kept Mrs. McCord here so you could talk to her, but as you can imagine, she's anxious to get to the hospital to be with her husband.

There's also a young gal here who can give you more information than Mrs. McCord can, and you ain't gonna believe her story. They're both in there." He pointed to the patrol car.

Mike looked into the police car and saw a young girl in her late teens, sitting in the back seat. He saw a middle aged woman in the front passenger seat and assumed it was Mrs. McCord. Mike went around and slid into the driver's seat.

He reached over and gently took Martha's hand in his. He said, "Mrs. McCord, I'm Detective Mike Sullivan and I can assure you we are going to do everything possible to get your girls back safe and we're gonna' make these bastards pay for what they've done to you and your family."

Martha gave his hand a little squeeze and said, "This has been the worst day of my life Detective. Please help us and let me go to my husband as soon as possible."

Mike said, "Sure ma'am, I understand. Here's what were gonna' do. I'm going to drive you to the hospital right now. You can tell me all you can remember on the way over."

He turned and looked at the girl in the back seat and said, "You're Beverly right?" Beverly nodded and Mike continued, "Just hold on back there and listen to what Mrs. McCord has to say. After we get her to the hospital, you and I can talk about what you know."

Martha tearfully related the events of the day to Mike. He stopped her every now and then for clarification. As they pulled up to the emergency room of Emory-Adventist, she was explaining how her two sons had taken off after the intruders.

She told Mike that they were headed for Red Top State Park up on Allatoona Lake. She said that the first police on the scene had gotten a description of Roger's car and had put out an "all-points-bulletin".

After walking Martha into the emergency room, Mike and Beverly got back in the police cruiser. Mike said, "Right now, we don't need to go to the scene.

I want to get to Red Top immediately. I'll call another car to meet us on the way and you can go with them."

Beverly said, "No, please don't do that. Let me go with you. I can tell you a lot more about these creeps and I want to be there when you get them."

Mike said, "It's against my better judgement, but we have to get there fast. Just make sure you listen to me and do everything I tell you to do, no questions asked!"

Beverly agreed and as they raced north toward Cartersville, she told the detective everything that had happened. She provided as many of the details as she could recall.

She began with her father's attack and filled in everything between then and now.

Mike listened intently and just kept shaking his head.

Chapter 34

Max thought he had heard a thud; right after Kurt had gone through the front of the tent. He perked up his ears to try and hear over the music. He grabbed his gun and pointed it toward the front of the tent.

He heard a ripping sound to his right. He spun to the right and saw someone bursting through a large hole in the tent. Whoever it was came in right in back of one of the girls. He didn't hesitate. He fired three times.

The girl went down hard, with the first shot, and the guy behind her took one in the throat and one in the chest.

The guy had a shocked look on his face, but then again so did Max, an instant later, as the nine-millimeter slug hit him in his temple just above the left ear.

Linda screamed as the dead bodies of her best friend Shelley, her boy friend Ricky and this stranger piled over her on the sleeping bags.

Bear and Snake rolled the bodies off Linda and pulled her to her feet. She was screaming hysterically and was covered in blood.

Bear grabbed her and shook her saying, "Shut up, shut up we need to get out of here now! Somebody must have heard all these shots." He looked at Snake and said, "There's no time for clean-up. We need to go now! Get his gun; I got the other guy's. Check their pockets for wallets and keys. We'll take the motor home."

Snake whined, "What about our bikes?"

Bear growled, "Screw the bikes, this has gotten

totally out of control. We need to get out of this state fast, and the motor home is our best chance."

They grabbed the keys and wallets from both dead bodies and the three of them jumped into the motor home.

Then Bear said, "Oh shit, the girls in the Caddy! Go get them and bring them back here. You can pull the Caddy into the woods while I turn this thing around."

Snake jumped back out of the motor home and ran to the Cadillac. When he looked in the back seat and realized the girls were gone, he said, "Son-of-a-Bitch!" He cranked up the Caddy's engine and pulled it off the road and down an embankment. He climbed out, threw the car keys into the woods as far as he could, and jumped into the open door of the motor home as Bear was pulling it alongside where the Cadillac had been. He hopped into the co-pilots seat and said, "They're fuckin' gone."

Bear hollered back, "We can't worry about that now. Let's just make some time out of here."

Chapter 35

Johnny and Pete shook their heads at each other. They had driven through all the campsites, past all the markers and gravestones from battles long since fought. They had paralleled the train tracks and gone half way round Allatoona Lake, or at least it seemed so.

Pete said, "They're not here Johnny. No way could we miss Dad's Caddy and the motorcycles."

Johnny had a thought and he shared it with his brother. "What about that little dirt road that I almost pulled into?" No guard to check on them there."

Pete responded, "Let's try it. We're getting nowhere fast here."

Johnny pushed the accelerator to the floor and only slowed down when they came to the guarded gate.

He thanked the guard and explained that they hadn't located their friends. The guard gave them a brisk salute and wished them a good day.

When they got out of earshot, Pete said sarcastically, "Yeah, we're having a great day already, what we need is more of this."

Johnny swung the Porsche right onto the highway and floored it again. They covered the quarter mile in about ten seconds flat. Johnny spied the red dirt road and they fishtailed as he swung the car between the two pine trees that guarded either side of the road. He cranked the engine up and they sped up the bumpy track. After about five minutes of roller coaster riding, they crested a hill in the road and saw headlights bearing down on them from the other direction.

Pete yelled, "Slow down Johnny, they're coming straight at us. I don't want to play "chicken" in this dinky little car."

Johnny did slow down and fully expected the other vehicle to do the same, but it kept on coming at them.

Johnny screamed, "They're out of their fucking minds! They must see us, why don't they slow down?"

As the oncoming vehicle got closer to them, Johnny realized that it was much bigger than the Porsche. There wasn't room for both of them on this piece of shit road. He flashed his headlights furiously. But it quickly became apparent that these folks, whoever they were, weren't about to stop.

He said to Pete, "They're either drunk or crazy, either way I got to get us off this road."

He pulled the Porsche to the right, as far as it would go. It got stuck up in the heavy brush and would go no further.

He and Pete had the same thought at the same time, "Get the hell out!" They opened the doors and jumped out of the car. They slammed the doors shut and made a leap into the brush.

No sooner had they landed sprawling in the bushes, than the motor home sideswiped the Porsche and kept right on going.

Johnny cried out, "Would you look at that, those bastards tore up my Porsche with a damn motor home!"

They heard the motor home's groaning as it tried to go airborne each time it hit a bump in the road.

Johnny got up, brushed himself off and walked back to his car with trepidation. It looked as though the heavy brush had cushioned the front of the car, but the left rear wheel was broken off at the axle. They wouldn't be driving this anywhere tonight.

They reached into the wounded Porsche and grabbed their guns and extra shells. Johnny popped open the glove box and retrieved a flashlight from its depths.

He said, "We've come this far, let's walk up and see what they were in such a big hurry to get away from."

They had walked for approximately twenty minutes when Pete pointed off to the side of the road ahead and said, "Look, isn't that's dad's car up there?"

Johnny shone the flashlight in the direction Pete was pointing and the beam bounced back as it illuminated the unmistakable green fins of his father's Cadillac. They ran over to the car and peered inside. The keys were missing and it was obvious that the car had been driven purposefully into this ditch.

Pete bent over, near the back of the car and picked up some strands of duct tape. He said, "It looks like somebody freed themselves from this tape. Maybe the girls got away!"

They looked farther up the road and saw a group of tents. One had light coming from it and they could hear the blare of a country-western song seemingly emanating from the tent.

Chapter 36

It was a difficult hike for the girls. Carol and Gloria wondered if this dirt road would ever lead to civilization. Gloria was now able to walk without Carol's help, but at a very slow pace.

Carol kept turning around to see if their absence had been discovered. She was constantly looking to the left and right for a place to hide if they saw or heard anyone coming after them.

They had heard what they thought were gunshots, but that had been at least half an hour ago. Since then all had been eerily quiet and the darkness was overwhelming.

When, at last, they caught a glimpse of moving lights ahead and then saw an eighteen wheeler passing from left to right, in front of them, they knew they were only moments away from a real road.

Carol said, "Gloria, I know this is hard on you, but we have to hurry. We can flag down one of these cars or trucks and get away from here."

After another few minutes they had finally made it to the highway. They looked left and right, in hope of seeing a car and also to decide which way they should go.

With no real sense of direction to guide their decision, they arbitrarily turned to the right. Even though it made the walking more difficult, they moved into the tree line and paralleled the trees to insure quick access to cover should it become necessary.

They had covered about a mile and hadn't encountered any traffic at all.

There weren't any mileage markers or signs to give them a clue as to where they were or where they were headed.

Gloria stopped to catch her breath and Carol ventured out to the highway surface to see if she could see anything helpful.

As she looked to her left, she couldn't see anything that told her where they were or which way they should go. She wished she had her watch, but she had taken it off back at the store, while preparing for bed.

She thought to herself, "If I had my watch I could tell how long we have been driving. Once the sun comes up, I could figure out which direction we're going."

She turned to the right and could just make out the silhouette of what was either a speed limit sign or maybe, she sighed, a sign with information about where they were.

It was then that her ears detected the sound of an approaching vehicle. She turned back toward the lightening sky and she could see that someone was coming.

She turned toward Gloria and yelled, "Come on. I see something; it looks like a van or a RV. I'm gonna' flag them down.

I think we finally found our way out of here.

Chapter 37

Linda was still in a state of total panic. Ricky and Shelley were both gone. She knew she was freaking out and she needed something to calm her down.

She had brought Shelley's purse with her and was frantically rooting through it to locate pills she knew Shelley had. She found the small prescription bottle whose label indicated that it contained Oxycontin. The bottle was almost full, so she swallowed four pills as if her life depended upon them.

Snake was pulling clothing out of the small closet at the rear of the motor home. One of the pairs of slacks, he was appraising, slipped from the hanger and onto the floor of the closet.

When he reached down to pick up the slacks, Linda heard him exclaim, "Looky here, hey looky here, look at what I found!"

He stood up and turned around. In each hand he was holding a leather, business type briefcase.

He said, "These things are heavy. What were these assholes collecting... Rocks?"

Snake walked up behind Bear and leaned over the edge of the driver's seat. He was so close that Bear could feel his breath on his ear.

Bear snarled, "Get the fuck away from me, I'm trying to drive this boat!"

Snake moved back from Bear and lifted the two briefcases out to the side where Bear could see them with his peripheral vision.

He said, "I don't know what's in these, but you know how it was when we was kids at Christmastime. We always opened the heavy presents first and I'm about to open these."

Before he could say anything else, Bear exclaimed, "I don't fucking believe it. You think you found something? Well take a look at what I found trying to hitch a ride up ahead!"

Chapter 38

As the motor home started to slow down and slip off onto the shoulder of the road, Carol grabbed Gloria's hand and squeezed it so hard that it hurt.

She squealed, "We're going home Gloria, we're going home!"

The motor home's front windshield was tinted a dark greenish color and Carol couldn't see the driver, but she hoped it was some nice family who would understand their plight and take them home or at least to some safe place. She knew that most serious campers had car phones and she was already mentally composing, what she would say to both her mom and the police.

The motor home came to a full stop. When the side door opened and the girls saw who stepped out, they knew that their nightmare, rather than being over, was just beginning.

Snake, holding a revolver in his hand, sneered at them and said, "We missed you bad girls. Why don't you c'mon and just get in here? ....It's ladies first, unless you'd rather make another run for it, but I don't think the little chubby girl is gonna get very far."

Both girls knew they wouldn't be able to escape. Not alive anyway.

Well, where there was life there was hope, and with that thought in her mind Carol said to Gloria, "Let's just do what he says."

With what little bit of courage they had remaining,

Carol and Gloria climbed up on the step to the motor home's entrance and went inside.

Snake followed them in, shut the door and pushed the girls back to the sleeping area. He told Bear to take off and he pointed to the bed across from where Linda was sitting.

"Both of you sit down there and don't cause any more trouble", he snarled at them.

He asked Bear for the other .38 and placed the pistol into Linda's hand. He said, "Watch these two, carefully. It looks like we got our insurance back."

He then turned his attention back to the two inviting briefcases he had found.

The motor home had gone only a few miles when Carol despairingly glanced out of the side window by the bed where they were sitting. She couldn't believe their totally unfair lack of timing as she saw a police car, with red lights flashing, speed right past them in the other direction.

She thought to herself, "Whose side is God on, anyhow?"

Chapter 39

By the time Beverly had finished relating the events of the past twenty-four hours to Detective Sullivan, he had become fully convinced of what he'd already suspected. He didn't yet know the background of the perpetrators, whether it was bad or real bad, but he knew that if they hadn't crossed the line before now, they had vaulted way past it this time.

He asked Beverly if she wanted to call her home to see what the situation was. With a wry smile she told Mike, "No news is good news."

Mike let out a chuckle and Beverly said, "What's so funny?" Mike replied, "I'm sorry my dear, but it's been a long time since I heard that phrase. As a matter of fact, it was a coded message between my old partner and me. We agreed that if one of us was in a tight spot, and had the opportunity to talk to the other one by phone, but were being overheard by bad guys, we would try to work that phrase into the conversation. It was to be understood as an explicit request for help, no questions asked.

Mike had become so engrossed in their conversation, and so focused on getting to Red Top State Park, that he really didn't take any notice of the innocuous motor home that passed them going west.

Mike slowed the patrol car down and turned off the red flashing lights, as they approached the entrance to the park.

They hadn't even gotten to the guard gate, when a

guy in a State Park uniform came out of his little air-conditioned guardhouse and approached them.

Mike rolled down the window to ask the guard about the Caddy and the motorcycles.

Before he had the chance to say anything, the guard piped up, "You must be a mind reader, cause I was just getting ready to call when you pulled up."

Mike replied, "Why, what's the trouble?"

The State Park guard, who identified himself as Winchel Froman, said, "I've been getting complaints from some of our campers about hearing shots being fired. The first couple of complaints didn't really get my attention, because they couldn't be sure it wasn't a car backfiring. But I just had a couple of tent-campers from a little west of here, come by to talk to me.

They said there was no doubt about it, they heard gunfire and they said it wasn't rifle fire it was pistol fire. These guys were both NRA types and they assured me they could tell the difference.

It's probably just some guys, with a little too much to drink, plinkin' at their empty beer cans. But with this many folks complaining, I'm not taking any chances." Then he added, "By the way, why are you here?"

Mike said, "Winchel, I need you to go ahead and make that call. Here's my card. Get hold of Sergeant Paul Robbins…. Hold on, lemme have that card back." He took back the business card from Winchel's still outstretched hand, pulled a pen out of the plastic holder in his shirt pocket, turned the card over and wrote down a name and a phone number.

"This is Sergeant Robbins' direct number. He's with the Marietta Police Department. Ask him to send a couple of units up here right now. Tell him I said it was urgent! Now where did you say those shots came from?"

Winchel pointed back down the access road and said," I think your best bet would be to go back down to the highway, turn right and go a quarter mile. You'll see a small, red clay road on your right. Take that road and go back about two miles. I know there are some bikers camping back there. I didn't see them, but I've heard the bikes goin' in and out of there for the past week or so."

Mike said, "Did you say bikers?"

Chapter 40

Johnny and Pete approached the tent cautiously. They both had their weapons drawn, loaded and cocked.

It was not yet dawn and they still needed Johnny's flashlight to find their way. They looked at each other as they came upon the body of a big man. He was lying on the ground about fifty feet in front of the tent where the music was playing.

The man was lying on his side and there were no wounds that were apparent from where they viewed the body. They couldn't see any blood, but as they rolled him carefully over onto his back, they could see that he was dead.

He was dressed in street shoes, khakis and a short sleeve shirt. He was clean-shaven and looked to be in his late thirties or early forties.

Johnny put his index finger to his lips and motioned for Pete to follow him to the tent. What they could see through the tent's front flap was enough to nauseate them both. They held back the sick feeling that was rising in their throats and slipped into the tent.

There, three more bodies presented themselves in all their bloody horror. Pete recognized two of them and said, "Johnny, these two", and he pointed at Ricky and Shelley, "were at the Farm store. Dad broke this guy's wrist with a baseball bat…. and she was there too", he said, pointing at the girl in the bloody leather jacket.

"I don't have a clue who this guy is, but he looks a lot like the guy layin' outside."

They were both extremely relieved not to find Carol and Gloria among this carnage.

Pete looked at Johnny and said, "Maybe the girls did get away. Let's get out of here and see if we can find them."

Johnny climbed out of the tent with Pete right behind. He slipped his Colt 45 into his belt, wishing that he had brought a holster. Pete followed suit with his Ruger and they began to survey the area.

The first thing that came to their attention was the four, obviously abandoned, motorcycles.

Johnny said, "Didn't that girl, Bev, say that there were four bikes?"

Pete responded, "Yeah, she did. I wonder how they got out of here."

Johnny immediately replied, "That fuckin' motor home. No wonder they were in such a hurry to get out of here. Do you think they still have Carol and Gloria?"

"I don't know," said Pete, "But with the duct tape we found and all, I think we need to keep looking."

Johnny and Pete agreed to continue the search and walked behind the three tents where they found a path leading deeper into the woods.

They looked at each other quizzically and Pete said, "Let's try it." After about fifteen minutes of following the path, they were too far away from the campsite to either see or hear the police car pull up in front of the three tents.

Part Two

Rome, Georgia

Chapter 41

Snake was just sitting there on the floor of the motor home. He was staring in amazement at what was lying in his lap. He had wrestled with one of the briefcase's locks for the last fifteen minutes until he had managed to half cut, half pry the two latches off with his switchblade.

More money than any of them had ever seen and the good news was that it was all in tens, twenties and fifty dollar bills. He grabbed a handful of the bills and crawled on his knees until he got right behind Bear. He threw the bills up in the air so that they floated down on Bear's head and into his lap.

Bear yelled, in a startled voice, "What the shit is this?" As he took one hand off the steering wheel and grabbed a handful of the bills, he nearly ran the motor home off the road.

He saw a small restaurant coming up on his right. It probably wasn't open yet, but all he wanted was a place to pull over. He swung the motor home into the parking lot of the restaurant, pulled around to the back and stopped.

As he turned to ask Snake about the money, he saw him busily trying to pry the latches from the other briefcase. Snake saw Bear turn toward him and he grabbed the first briefcase and slid it toward Bear.

Linda could see all the activity in the front and said, "What's going on, why the hell are we stopping?" Snake responded, "Linda baby, we're fucking rich." And he threw a handful of fifties back at her.

Carol and Gloria didn't have any idea what this was all about, but at least it was keeping everyone's attention away from them.

Bear was leafing through the bills like a dealer at a casino. All he needed was a green eyeshade to fully look the part.

After a few minutes he stopped counting, held a wad of bills up over his head and said, "I only counted this much and I'm already at twenty thousand bucks. I don't know what the fuck those guys were doin' but they sure as shit weren't collecting rocks."

Bear thought for a minute, and then said to Snake and Linda, "This is a whole new fuckin' ballgame. The first thing we have to do is to get some regular threads and then we gotta dump this motor home. No tellin' who'll be lookin' for it, but you can bet your ass someone will be. And with this much dough on the line, I don't want to be anywhere near this thing when it gets found!

Here's what we're gonna' do. We just passed I-75 and I saw a sign for I-411. It's just up ahead. It'll take us in to Rome.

Linda, you can take some cash and go into one of the malls. You can buy us all some "normal looking" clothes. Make sure you get some hair coloring for your hair; I think you'd look good as a redhead.

Make sure you buy some scissors and shaving gear for us. I know it's summer, but get us a couple of light-weight jackets or sweaters; something to cover these tattoos."

Linda and Snake looked at Carol and Gloria. Then they looked at each other, both of them thinking the same thing.

Snake put it into words. He said, "Bear, what are we going to do with these two here?" and he pointed his thumb back at the two girls sitting quietly on the bed.

Bear replied, "I thought about that. We could dump them, but they already know too much. They're gonna' be a pain in the ass, but I want to hold on to them until we put a lot of miles between here and where we're goin'.

And since you asked, it's gonna be your job to see that they don't give us any more trouble. I want them both alive and healthy, at least for now. So don't screw around with them until I say it's ok. You catch my drift?"

"Yeah", said Snake, "for now."

Bear looked at the dashboard clock and said, "It's only 4:30. Even if I creep along, it won't take us more than two hours to get to Rome. We can't afford to get pulled over for driving too slow. Everyone needs some sleep so we'll stay here until just before eight o'clock. This place doesn't open 'til ten and neither do the malls."

Chapter 42

Johnny and Pete had spent over two hours searching for the girls.

Since everything seemed to indicate that their abductors had split the scene, they yelled out the girls' names hoping that they had gotten away and were hiding.

Both of them were hoarse as well as depressed.

Pete said, "We gotta' go back and get help. The more time we waste out here the farther away we're getting from the girls, whether they're on their own or not. Maybe they found help and they're already on their way back home."

Somehow, Johnny didn't believe this and he was pretty sure that Pete didn't either, but it was time to go for help. Just maybe he or Pete knew something that would assist the police in finding the girls.

As they approached the top of the trail and neared the campsite, they could see and hear a lot of activity going on.

When they got close to the back of the tents, they saw what appeared to be every police car in Georgia, not to mention a whole slew of ambulances. They all had their warning lights flashing which, had it still been dark, would have lit up the sky like last night's fireworks.

The sun was just beginning to peek out above the tree line and even if Johnny hadn't looked at his watch, he'd have known that it was after ten o'clock in the morning.

As they emerged from behind the tents they were greeted by two serious looking police officers who had their service revolvers in their hands.

They ordered Johnny and Pete to put their hands on their heads.

Johnny was taken aback until it occurred to him what they must have looked like. They had semi-automatics in their belts and they were walking casually into the midst of a violent murder scene.

One of the policemen turned his head toward the closest police car and yelled, "Detective Sullivan, over here! We got something over here!"

Mike Sullivan had been standing next to his patrol car and speaking into the mike on the car's police radio. He was providing the person at the other end a full description of what he had found at the scene, from the motorcycles in front of the tents and the wallets from the dead bodies that had been found in the trunk of the Cadillac.

Beverly was standing alongside the Detective, as per his instructions when they first arrived at this slaughterhouse. When Mike heard his name being called out, he turned toward the tents and so did Beverly.

When she saw Johnny and Pete she grabbed Mike's arm and said, "Detective Mike that's not the bad guys. They're Mr. and Mrs. McCord's sons. Remember, I told you about them."

During the drive from Marietta, Beverly had

informed Mike that Johnny and Pete had gone after the bikers and that they had armed themselves.

Mike looked at Beverly and said, "I'll handle it, but you've got to understand that these police officers don't know those boys from Adam."

By the time Detective Sullivan had gotten to where Johnny and Pete were being held, they had already been disarmed and cuffed.

He told the two officers, "These boys are ok. They're actually a couple of the victims. Just hang on to their weapons and leave them to me. We'll sort out the firearms question later."

Pete rubbed his wrists to remove the sting of the handcuffs. He said, "Thanks a lot. That was starting to hurt."

Mike pointed to Beverly and said, "You need to thank that young lady over there. She's the one who recognized you both."

The three of them walked over to where Beverly was standing.

She said, "Did you find anything?"

Johnny said, "We didn't find the girls. We thought that maybe they had gotten away from those guys, because we found duct tape on the ground by dad's car. I guess they didn't, though, if they haven't contacted anyone by now."

Detective Sullivan looked at the boys and said, "Tell me what happened when you got here."

"I think maybe the most important thing that happened was getting sideswiped by a motor home on our way in here," said Johnny. "Yeah" said Pete, "Now we kinda' think that maybe the bikers were in that motor home and that they might still have the girls."

Mike explained, "We added up the dead bodies and compared them to the bikes over there.

Based on Beverly's information, we came up three bikers short, two males and one female. They had to have some kind of transportation out of here. You may just be right about the motor home. Can you describe it?"

"It all happened pretty fast", said Johnny. "I know it wasn't very big, maybe eighteen to twenty feet long. It looked pretty new. What'd you see Pete?"

"Yeah, I agree on the size. "I'm also fairly certain that I saw a "Dodge" emblem on the hood. Either that or that's just what I had to do to avoid being run over by it."

"There were two unaccounted for dead guys here, who looked like they could be related. You know, brothers or maybe cousins," Mike explained. "They're both on the way to the morgue now. As soon as we print them we'll get their prints off to the feds. Maybe they can shed some light on them. Maybe connect them to the motor home."

Chapter 43

Bear started up the motor home and pulled back out into the busy, morning traffic. He figured that if he drove slowly, but not too slowly, they should arrive at the mall just about the time that it was opening. This would avoid their looking conspicuous by being parked on a mall parking lot when it was closed.

He turned his head to the side and said, "Hey Linda, come up here and get in the co-pilot's seat. I need to talk to you about something."

Snake wasn't concerned. He guessed that Bear had something to say to Linda that these girls shouldn't hear. Bear would fill him in later.

Linda got off the bed and passed Snake on her way to the front.

She smiled at him in a totally laid back manner, now fully under the soothing calm of the Oxycontin. She said, "See ya' wild man. "Bad News" needs me."

When she had settled herself into the seat next to Bear, she said, "What's up boss?"

Bear lowered his voice and said, "First of all, lay off those fuckin' pills. I need you to have your whole head into this, at least for the next few hours." He asked her if she had a valid driver's license. She told him that she did.

Then as an afterthought she added, "I've also got Shelley's and with a little change of my hair, I could pass for her."

Bear told her he would drive around and try to spot

a used-car lot while she was in the mall. He wanted to find one that had the kind of car he was looking for and whose salespeople were used to making cash deals.

He told her to buy the stuff they had talked about, then find a ladies room at the mall and change her clothes and her hair.

He said, "Dump all of your old stuff and make your hair look like Shelley's.

I don't care how much you spend... we got plenty. Just make sure you act like you belong in the stores you choose and don't buy any jewelry or shit like that. It'll just bring attention to you. Try to spend a little bit at each store so it doesn't add up to too much in one place."

Just then they saw the large mall on their left. Bear drove up to the red traffic light and flipped his flasher on to signal for a turn into the mall parking lot.

When the light turned green, he swung the motor home into the access road to the mall. He was pleased to see that there were a bunch of cars already on the lot. This would insure that they wouldn't stand out like a sore thumb.

At one corner of the mall he saw a "Denny's" restaurant. It had a large window facing the parking lot.

He explained to Linda, "When you're finished in the mall, go into that Denny's and wait for us. Order yourself breakfast and sit by that big window. If you get finished, before we get back, just sip on some more coffee. I'll park the motor home right there in that spot close to the window. Keep looking for us.

When you see us, order some coffee and donuts or toast or whatever they have, to go.

Find out what the girls in the back will eat. I don't want them to get sick on me. Once we pick you back up, I'll drop you off a block or two from the used car lot and tell you what car to buy. Do you comprende all this?"

Linda assured Bear that she could handle it and said, "You know how I love to shop, big guy. This is gonna' be fun."

He said, "Yeah, well don't make it so much fun that you ain't waitin' by that window when we get back! I won't be more than two hours and even that may be too long to spend in this motor home."

Linda got up and climbed into the back. She went to where Carol and Gloria were sitting and spoke to them as if they were long time friends on vacation together.

She said, "This is gonna' be a long day girls. What can I get you for breakfast?.............. How's coffee and donuts sound?"

Gloria decided there was no point in starving herself and she knew her baby definitely needed food. She said, "I can't have coffee" and she pointed to her stomach. Then she added, "If you can get me a few small cartons of white milk and a couple of orders of toast and butter, it would help."

Linda said cheerfully, "You got it." Then she turned her gaze to Carol and said, "what about you hon', you don't have a bun in the oven do you?"

Normally Carol would have smiled at this kind of

talk, but all of this was far from coming anywhere close to being funny.

She simply said, "No, I don't, but you can get me the same thing you're getting for my sister-in-law, thank you."

Linda said, "Oh isn't that sweet, a Sister-in-Law. You're gonna be an aunt. Ok milk and toast it is."

Linda returned to Bear and said, "Alright, I'm ready. How 'bout some cash."

He counted out fifteen hundred dollars and gave it to her. He pulled the Dodge up to the mall entrance and let her out.

He was pleased to note that the small group of people, who had been waiting at the entrance for the mall to open, was now breaking into two lines and beginning to file in through both of the mall's front doors.

Snake shouted, "What the fuck about me? I'm hungry as hell!"

Bear growled back, "Just chill asshole. I already ordered for us."

As soon as he saw Linda walk through the mall entrance, Bear drove away. He got back on I-411 and headed west toward Rome. After a mile or so he saw what he had been trying to find.

He pulled into a "Mobil" station and parked next to a public telephone booth.

By then, Snake had picked up all of the bills that had fallen on the floor and had begun a serious count. When he had finally broken the two latches on the second briefcase, he'd been ecstatic but not surprised to see a mirror image of the contents of the first briefcase.

Bear opened his door. But before he got out of the motor home he looked at Snake and warned, "Don't take your eyes off them girls. You can finish counting when I get back. I won't be but a minute."

Snake nodded in acknowledgement and stopped counting; making a mental note of how much he had already counted.

So far, he was up to one hundred and eighty five thousand dollars.

Bear got out and closed the door. He walked over to the phone booth and picked up the local Rome phone book that was hanging from a chain next to the phone.

He had planned on taking the whole book, but he didn't feel like screwing around with the chain. He flipped to the yellow pages and found the "Used Car Lots" section.

There were only two pages of used car listings so he carefully tore them out, folded them and stuck them in his pocket. He returned to the motor home, got in and drove off.

With a smirk on his face, Snake resumed his cash counting.

Bear drove with one hand and unfolded the pilfered yellow pages with the other. He was humming, "let your fingers do the walking...."

His eyes were drawn to an ad that was outlined in a bold rectangle. It was headed "ABC Auto Sales".

"Wow, that's original", he quipped, primarily for his own enjoyment.

The console, between the two front captain's chairs, was equipped with a portable Motorola phone.

He lifted the handset and was greeted with a dial tone. Fortunately for him, the previous owners hadn't bothered to password lock the phone.

He punched in the seven-digit number of "ABC Auto Sales" and heard the phone ringing on the other end.

A pleasant sounding female voice greeted him. "ABC Auto Sales, Good morning. If you're alive, we can help you drive. My name is Sandy. What can we put you in today?"

Bear responded, "Well Sandy, I'm just tryin' to figure out how to get to your lot."

"Certainly sir, where are you coming from?"

Bear answered, "I'm on I-411 just east of Rome."

"No problem sir, you're only about twenty blocks from us."

She went on to say, "If you'll come west on 411 for six or seven traffic lights. Look for Main Street. There's a Jack-in-The-Box on the left and a Sears' appliance store on the right. Go to the next light. That'll be Lanier Drive. Turn left and go down three blocks. We're on the left side at 377 Lanier. You can't miss us. Look for the big ABC sign with the yellow smiley face."

Bear asked her to repeat the directions as he made his mental notes. Then he said, "Ok, see you in a bit."

He heard Sandy say, "And what is your name sir?", but he hung up the phone as if he hadn't heard her.

He knew that it should only take about ten minutes to get there from where they were located, and he didn't want anyone expecting them. He drove to within three blocks of the used car lot and found a place with no parking meters. He pulled over to the curb and shut off the engine.

There was a "Piggly Wiggly" food store two doors down and it had a Coke machine out front. He told Snake to give him one of the fifties and to watch the girls. He asked if they wanted a cold soda and the girls said that they would rather wait for the milk. Snake told Bear to get him a regular coke.

Bear had quit smoking about a year ago. When cigarettes got to a dollar a pack he quit. The desire never went away and now that he was wealthy he thought, "Screw it!"

He walked into the "Piggly Wiggly" and up to the cash register.

As he stood there, waiting to be served, he calculated that it had been about twelve hours since he last stood in front of a cash register. He thought to himself, "A lot of shit's happened since then."

It never occurred to Bear to feel compassion for any of the victims of this spree of crime. He didn't even really care about Phil or Ricky or Shelly or Rachel.

As a matter of fact, he actually felt that things were much less complicated now. "And….", he thought, with a smile on his face, "I'm a rich man!"

The clerk had to repeat himself. He said, in a somewhat loud voice, "Can I help you?"

Bear was startled. He realized that he had gone off for a moment. He had to watch that.

He replied, "Yeah, gimme a couple a packs of Pall Mall regulars, and some change for the Coke machine out front...... and throw in a couple of books of matches."

Then he added, "And these." He placed a box of twelve "Hostess Twinkies" on the counter that he had retrieved from the display case in front of the cash register next to where he was standing.

The clerk pulled out two packs of cigarettes and laid them on the counter, next to the box of "Twinkies".

Bear handed him a fifty-dollar bill.

The clerk said, "Don't you have anything smaller? I just opened up and I don't have a lot of change."

Bear replied, "Too bad, pal, that's all I got."

With a muted sigh, the clerk opened the register and handed Bear two twenties, six singles and fifty-four cents in change. He said, "The Coke machine takes singles."

Bear picked up the "Piggly Wiggly" bag in which the clerk had placed the "Twinkies", cigarettes and matches. He walked out to the Coke machine and bought four regular Cokes. He figured he and Snake would easily polish off four Cokes between them.

He climbed back into the motor home, pulled a coke and two Twinkies out of the bag and tossed the bag to Snake.

He decided that he had killed enough time for

Sandy and the eager salesmen at ABC to figure he was a "no-show".

He drove the motor home to 377 Lanier and parked across the street from the Smiley Face sign.

Bear slowly surveyed the lot, from his seat, to see what they had.

He saw a blue 1972 Chevrolet Caprice station wagon and he thought, "That will do the trick. Plenty of space to sit and room in the back for the camping gear. He strained his eyes to make out the price that had been written on the wagon's windshield with a bright, orange marking pen.

It promised, "**A Bargain at Only $ 2,995**".

Bear thought, "I don't give a shit what it costs, but Linda needs to haggle them down to twenty seven fifty. Otherwise they'll remember the dumb broad who paid full price."

With that in mind, he cranked up the motor home and headed back to the mall.

Chapter 44

Johnny asked Detective Sullivan if he would call a tow truck for the Porsche.

Mike told him that tow trucks were on the way for his Porsche, his father's caddy and the four bikes.

"But", he told Johnny, "Both the cars and the motorcycles will need to be taken to the crime lab to be checked for evidence. The Porsche is our best bet for identifying the kind of motor home they're using.

We should be able to get a make and model from the paint left on the side of your car when they hit you. That sideswipe may turn out to be a blessing in disguise.

Once we finish going over what you boys know, I can have one of these officers drive you back to Marietta."

Then he turned to Beverly, who had been listening intently, and said, "And what about you, young lady, do you want to go back home to Dublin?"

Beverly replied hastily, "No, I really don't. I'm part of this thing and I'd like to stay around here to help in any way that I can. Plus, I really haven't made up my mind whether I want to go home or not."

Johnny offered, "Detective Sullivan, Bev really tried to help my family back at the Farm store. If it's all right with you, and if she wants to, she can stay with us until all of this is over."

Mike thought about it for a minute and then said, "What do you think, Beverly, is that what you want to do?"

Beverly didn't have to think about it. With all that had happened, she was already beginning to feel like a part of the McCord family and somehow she trusted Johnny and Pete completely.

She said, "Yes, that would be great!"

Mike said, "I need for you to stay close to a phone in case I need you or in case the girls try to call you. Do you have a number that you can give me, where the girls would be likely to call if they get the chance?"

Pete said, "I guess the Farm store is out, but we could go to our house. Even though we had the fire, the front of the house is ok and we can open all of the windows to air out the smell of smoke."

Johnny said, "We need to get to the hospital to be with mom and dad. If you can just get us home, Pete and I can take shifts at the hospital using mom's car and I know mom would like to see Bev."

Mike took out his notebook and wrote down the address and phone number as Pete recited it to him.

When he was sure he had gotten all the helpful information he could get from the boys and Beverly, he called over one of the officers who had taken the boys into custody earlier.

He said, "Denny, this here is Johnny McCord and his brother Pete and this is their friend Beverly. Kids this is Officer Broderick with the Marietta PD and he's here to help you."

Pete said, with a smile on his face, "Yeah, I think we already met."

Detective Sullivan said, "Denny, these youngsters

and their family are having a tough time of it. I'd appreciate it if you would take them home. They live in Marietta."

Then he added, "Under the circumstances, I think we can forget about the weapons thing. When you get them home, you can return their guns to them."

Officer Broderick said, "Whatever you say, Detective. Sergeant Robbins instructed us that you're the boss on this case." He looked at his three wards and said, "If you're all ready, we can go now."

Johnny looked sheepishly at both Detective Sullivan and Officer Broderick and said, "There is one other thing.", and he told them about the gun collection in the trunk of the Porsche.

Mike laughed and said, "Well we sure as hell don't want that stuff lying around, do we?

Denny, help them load all the other stuff into your patrol car and take it to the house with them."

Officer Broderick said, "Ok boss", and to Johnny, Pete and Beverly he said, "Let's go."

They got into the police cruiser and drove over next to the Porsche. They got out and transferred the gun collection from the Porsche's trunk into the trunk of the patrol car. Then they hopped back into the police car and headed back to Marietta.

Chapter 45

When they pulled back into the mall, Bear parked exactly where he had told Linda he was going to park.

He noticed that the blinds had been drawn shut over the restaurants large picture windows. He figured it was to keep the bright sunlight from bothering the patrons.

Just as he was about to go and look for Linda, he noticed one of the blinds being spread apart. He could see enough of the face peering between the slats to recognize that it was Linda looking for them.

He looked back at Snake and said, "We're on, she saw us. By the way, are you finished counting yet?"

Snake slid up behind Bear, keeping one eye on the girls, and whispered, "You bet your ass. I counted it all three times. There's exactly two hundred forty eight thousand, four hundred and fifty bucks here."

Bear let out a long, low whistle and said, "A quarter of a million George Washington's. Partner, we're in the fuckin' "Big Time" now. Guess what? No more knockin' off gas stations. In fact, we can buy a damn gas station with all that dough."

Snake replied, "Not me man, I'm gonna get me another Harley, but this time it'll be custom made."

Bear said, "You can do whatever the fuck you want, but I'm stayin' away from bikes for a while."

As he spoke to Snake, he watched out of the windshield and saw Linda exiting "Dennys". She had large white bags in both hands.

He was somewhat surprised to see that she hadn't

changed her hair, but he would never have recognized her in the clothes she was wearing, unless he had seen her face.

Snake pushed open the door and took the bags out of her hands.

She explained, "I couldn't carry everything at once, so I left the clothes and stuff inside. Let me go get it, I'll be right back." Then she did a slow pirouette and said, in a sultry voice, "How do I look?"

Snake said, "Great, you look great. Now just go get the other shit and let's get outta' here."

Linda's big smile turned to a frown and she retorted, "You know what Snake, you're a real asshole!"

And with that she hastened toward the restaurant to retrieve the other packages.

When Linda returned with the clothing and sundries that she had purchased for them, Bear had her sit up front once more. He asked her how she had made out with the fifteen hundred bucks. She told him that she still had around two hundred left.

He said, "Fine, keep it." He then handed her another stack of bills, mostly fifties, and said, "There's three grand here."

"I found the car we want and they're asking just under three for it, but that's bullshit. I want you to wheel and deal with them. Anything you can save is yours."

Bear told Linda about the used car lot he had found and described the station wagon to her.

He said, "Make sure the engine sounds ok and make them check the oil and tires. Be damn sure they fill up the tank. Act like a hard-ass. Tell them that's part of the deal."

Then he said to her, "You ain't taking any more of them pills, are you?"

She assured him that she had not and that, other than being a little mellow, she was cool.

He said, "Now be careful what you say to these jerks. The address on your license says Atlanta, so they'll figure you still live there.

They won't know that you got divorced two years ago and haven't been back since. Let em' keep thinking you still live in the same place. Tell them you're visiting your sister, here in Rome, and that she dropped you off to get a car, after you had to junk your old one."

Linda acknowledged that she understood what he had said and he cranked up the engine.

When they got to within a block of the lot, Bear pointed to an available parking space on the other side of the street.

He said, I'm gonna drop you off here, then I'm gonna' do a huey and park right there. When you get the wagon, pull up next to me and I'll follow you.

Go northeast on 411 and slow down to let me pass. Then follow me until I find a good spot to dump this baby. Then we can make the switch.

You shouldn't be more than an hour, with the paperwork and all, but you need to hustle cause we're probably startin' to run out of time."

Bear pointed up the street to the "smiley face" sign, to make sure she knew where the lot was.

Linda put the cash in her purse, opened up the door and got out.

Once Linda was half way to the auto lot, Bear checked the street both ways. Seeing that he had plenty of leeway, he made a U-turn and slid smoothly into the parking spot he had selected.

He told Snake to give him a cup of coffee and whatever else was in the "Denny's" bag to eat.

Snake had already let the girls take the milk and toast and while they sat quietly eating, drinking and contemplating their fate, he and Bear drank coffee and ate pastries.

Chapter 46

Detective Sullivan watched the police cruiser as it took off back down the dirt road. Now that Beverly and the McCord boys were on their way home, he could place all of his concentration on the problem of finding his quarry.

He looked at his watch and saw that it was after eleven. Anne Marie would be worrying about him, no matter what Bill Rowan had told her, so he decided to check in with her first.

She answered on the second ring.

"Hi honey. Did Bill call you last night?" he said in a tired voice.

"Yes," she responded "and I've been worried about you ever since he called. Are you ok?"

"I'm fine babe, just a little tired. I caught a real bad case this time, lots of victims, way too many."

Anne Marie chastened him, "You need to get some sleep or you're not going to be much help to anyone!"

"I will honey. I'm just about finished at this crime scene. It looks like we have three scenes on this case so far. I'm on my way home. I need to take a nap and get cleaned up. I should be there in about two hours. I can call everything in, from the car radio, on my way home.

I could eat about a half dozen eggs and a bunch of bacon when I get there."

Anne Marie said, "I'll get everything ready. Just give me a yell when you're about fifteen minutes out, and it'll be on the table when you get here."

Mike said, "I can smell it already. Thanks Annie, I love you. See you shortly."

After she returned his love and told him to be careful, they both hung up.

On his way out, Mike checked in with the leading officer at the scene. He let him know that he would touch base with him in a few hours.

He instructed the officer to call him, immediately, if there were any breaks in the case.

Mike pulled out of the park and began the long drive back to Macon. He pulled a big cigar out of his pocket humidor and stuck it between his teeth. He knew he wouldn't smoke it because, number one - this wasn't his car and number two - he never allowed himself the full pleasure of this nasty habit until the case was over. He did, however, enjoy chewing on it.

He picked up the cruiser's radio microphone and contacted his office in Macon. He brought them up to speed on all he had discovered, dwelling at length on the suspected Dodge motor home. He gave them the hazy description the boys had provided and apologized for the lack of detail.

While he knew they couldn't just stop every motor home they saw, he wanted to know if any similar vehicle had been reported stolen or involved in any crime or accident.

He told them to look for one that had damage to the front left side.

"If you spot one like that", he instructed, "keep it in sight and call me immediately!"

Mike added, "These perps are armed and dangerous and they probably have two young girls as hostages. I know that's a real bad combination, so tell our people to be careful for their own sake as well as that of the hostages."

He asked his people to check with the coroner's office and determine when they expected to get back any fingerprint information on the six bodies that had been recovered.

He told them that he was particularly interested in the two men with empty holsters attached to their belts. He felt that they were probably the owners of the motor home and he wanted to find out more about them, like why did they have guns and who had the guns now?

Mike was pretty convinced that he already knew the answer to the last question!

Chapter 47

The St. Petersburg Connection

Ramone was more agitated than concerned. The German brothers from Chicago had never missed an exchange before, and he figured they must have hit some road construction. It seemed like the State of Florida was always tearing up I-75 to make it bigger.

He had heard from Max around midnight. Max said that they would be grabbing a few hours sleep at a campground, in some Georgia State park, called "Red Top". He had told Ramone that they would get an early start and should be at the meeting place by noon.

It was now pushing one o'clock and Santino, Ramone's partner in the cocaine business, had suggested that they should place a call to the German's mobile phone.

Ramone retrieved the phone number from a piece of paper that he had stuffed in his wallet. The word "Germans" was written at the top and below that were two phone numbers. Next to the first number was the word "Home" and next to the other was the word "Mobile".

With Santino anxiously looking on, he punched in the number listed next to "Mobile" and listened to the phone as it began to ring.

After five rings he heard a click and the recorded message that followed, "This is your AT&T mobile operator. The party you are trying to call is presently unavailable. Please leave a message when you hear the tone."

Santino said, "What's the deal?"

Ramone replied, "No answer. Maybe they stopped to take a piss. I'm gonna wait ten more minutes and try again."

Santino walked over to the table where they had laid out the six bags of white powder. He picked them up, one by one and placed them into a briefcase that was also sitting on the table.

He looked at Ramone and said, "I don't like this shit. We've already been here too long. When you get them, tell them to meet us at the other place."

Ramone checked his watch and saw that fifteen minutes had elapsed since the first attempt to contact the Germans. He picked up the phone and pressed the "redial" button.

The phone rang again and after the third ring he heard a totally unfamiliar voice growl, "Yeah, what?"

Chapter 48

As she walked the last few paces to the auto lot, Linda made up her mind. She needed to begin covering her tracks right now.

When she turned toward the shack that ABC used for an office, a bald headed man who looked to be in his thirties, walked briskly toward her with a big toothy grin on his face.

"And just how can we help you today, little lady?"

It always irked Linda when people used the word "we" in these circumstances. She had the urge to do a complete turn around, ostensibly looking for the missing person or persons who made up the "we".

Today was not, however, a good day for her to be a smart-ass. She hoped that nobody would remember her with sufficient clarity to provide a good description to the cops.

Linda just smiled and said, "I'm looking for something that I can drive to work and take the kids back and forth to their swimming classes."

"Well, you came to the right place. My name is Manny and I'm sure I can put you into the perfect ride. Sounds like you're looking for a van. Am I right?"

"Actually," Linda responded "I don't think so. My sister has a van and I tried to drive it. I never could get comfortable; they're too big for me."

"Well," the bald man replied, with undeterred enthusiasm, "How 'bout a station wagon?"

Linda perked up and said, "That would probably

work. But, you have to understand that I really don't know a darn thing about cars and I need one that's dependable."

She was sure that she had detected a glint in his eye at her response. It seemed to say, "Another dumb blonde, I can feel a big commission on this one."

With the glint in his eye still apparent, He said, "Well let me show you this one, little lady. It's the top of the line.

A "Chevrolet Caprice" with all the bells and whistles.... and we just lowered the price on it this morning." With that, he put his hand on her upper arm and gently directed her toward a blue station wagon.

Linda thought, "That was kinda stupid to tell me. The only reason you'd lower the damn price is cause it ain't moving." But, she resisted the temptation to blurt out her thoughts and continued to play the game.

"And what is your name, little lady?" said the bald man. "After all, if we're going to do some serious business, I can't keep calling you *little lady.* Am I right?"

Linda said, "Li......Shelley, my name is Shelley." She corrected herself as fast as she could.

"Pardon me, I didn't catch that." Manny said.

Linda smiled and replied in a slow casual voice, "Shelley, it's Shelly Moran." And she held out her hand for him to shake.

Manny nodded and grasped her extended hand. It didn't appear that he had become suspicious since, without a pause, he continued to describe the features and benefits of this "must have" automobile.

Manny opened the driver's door for Linda and she slid in behind the wheel. He went around and got into the front passenger's seat and went on to describe how the "Climate Control", stereo and power equipment worked.

Linda knew that she had to get this deal moving, so she came right to the point.

She said, "Manny, this really looks like it could be the perfect car for me, but truth be told, I can only spend about twenty-three hundred."

She really didn't expect this offer to fly.

Manny lost some of his enthusiasm, as he realized that he wasn't going to score as big a check as he had hoped. "But," he thought, "A sale is a sale." And Manny hadn't made a sale today. He figured he should give this deal the old "college try", so he made a counter-offer.

"Shelley, the very best I can do is twenty-six hundred on the road."

Shelley paused for effect then said, "If you can show me that all the oil and stuff is filled up and give me a full tank of gas, you got a deal!"

Manny's spirits lifted somewhat. It really was a pretty fair deal all the way around, and at least he would break the ice with his first sale of the day.

He extended his hand to Linda, to seal the deal and said, "I'll have my associate take the wagon around the corner to the Texaco station.

They do our mechanical work for us. They'll check the oil and transmission fluid, grease her up for you and put in a full tank of Premium gas. It's on us.

We aim to please. You and me can go inside and get the paperwork done. By the time were finished she'll be back here and ready to go. Can I see your driver's license?"

As they walked to the front door of the sales office, Linda reached into her purse and carefully pulled out the State of Georgia driver's license that had Shelley's photo and data.

She handed it to Manny and casually commented, "Please don't look at my picture, it's terrible and I've dyed my hair since that was taken."

Manny took the driver's license out of her hand and said, "No problem Shelley, I get this all the time. I know how all you gals never look like the photo on your licenses. Gotta keep changing your looks to keep the hubby interested, am I right?"

Chapter 49

He was startled when he heard the mobile phone ring. He hadn't given the number to Linda, so it wouldn't be her calling.

Snake said, "Ain't you gonna answer it?"

Bear growled back, "No, you dumbass, why the fuck would I answer it?" Snake just shrugged and took another sip of coffee.

Carol whispered to Gloria, "How are you doing?"

Gloria put her hand in front of her mouth and responded in as quiet a voice as she could, "I'm ok, considering. We've got to figure a way out of here and we better do it while there are people around. If they get us back to the woods, they're not going to let us go."

Carol said, "I know. We can identify them. We have to be ready at the first chance we get."

"Snake looked back at them and snarled, "You girls better keep your lips zipped. I know you're back there hatching some kinda plan. Don't even think about it! The only way you're gonna get outta this is to just chill and do what the fuck we tell you to do!"

Bear was considering the mobile phone. It occurred to him that maybe Linda did write the number down, just in case something went wrong. Well, if it rang again he would answer it.

About ten minutes later, the phone rang again.

He let it ring twice, and then he snatched it from the cradle, put it to his ear and growled, "Yeah, what?"

By now he had fully expected that it would be Linda on the other end.

He bolted upright when instead he heard a heavily accented voice say, "What the fuck you mean, what's up? Who in the hell are you man and whatchu doin on this line?"

Bear had built up a real hatred for Hispanics, during the five years he had lived in Los Angeles.

He turned to Snake and said, "Sounds like some fucking "spic" to me. Probably a wrong number, I think I'll fuck with him."

Ramone had heard every word. He motioned for Santino to put his ear next to the phone and listen. Then he spoke into the phone, with a menacing voice.

He said, "No man, this ain't no wrong number and you really don't want to fuck with me! Now put Max or Kurt on the line."

"So that was their names," thought Bear. He pressed the phone closer to his mouth and whispered, "They ain't ever comin' to the phone again. That's what they get for hangin' around with "spics"!"

Santino was enraged. He grabbed the phone from Ramone and screamed, "Where's our fucking money, you cocksucker?"

Bear just smiled and hung up the phone.

Snake said, "What the hell was that all about?"

Bear laughed and replied, "I don't know. Sounds to me like a couple of "beaners" lost some money."

Chapter 50

Johnny sat in the front of the police cruiser, next to Officer Broderick. Beverly and Pete sat in the back seat. They had been filling Officer Broderick in on all the details of their nightmarish experiences.

Denny Broderick had kept quiet and let them vent. He knew they were going through a lot of stress. What with their dad in the hospital with two bullet holes in his chest and their sister and Pete's wife kidnapped, Denny thought they were holding up pretty damn good.

When they finally got to the part where he had confronted the boys at the tents, he said, "Sorry 'bout the cuffs boys, but we can't afford to take any chances when we see hardware like you were both packing."

Johnny said, "We understand. I don't envy you your job. I guess it's not easy to tell the good guys from the bad guys."

Denny decided this might be a good time to interject a friendly warning.

He said, "Yeah, you got that right. And I would sure hate to see the good guys become the bad guys. You three have every right to be upset, but you've got to leave this to the police."

"Remember," he said, "Detective Sullivan is as good as they come and we're all behind him. If you get any more bright ideas about helping, I strongly recommend that you run them past Mike first. We've got enough on our plates now and the last thing we need to be doing is worrying about the three of you."

Johnny's face flushed slightly, at what the officer was saying.

He said, "Well, in the heat of the moment, all we were thinking about was saving the girls. I guess we could have made things worse."

Officer Broderick replied, "I might have done the same thing, in your shoes, but I've been on the job long enough to know that when you're personally involved you don't always think straight. You really could do the girls more harm than good."

Pete suggested that they all go to the hospital. They could visit their mom and dad, get her car and house keys and then one of them could get her car and drive it back to the house to wait by the phone.

Beverly interjected, "Could we make a quick drive-thru at "Mickey Ds". I don't know about you guys, but I'm starving."

Denny said, "Fine, there's one right up ahead. I could stand a cup of coffee myself." Then he turned and smiled at them and added, "And maybe even a donut."

As sad and concerned as they all were, they still couldn't help laughing at Officer Broderick.

He said, "That's good. You have to keep your hopes up and think positively. If we all work together, we'll get everybody safely back home."

Pete said, "Yeah, I know. But I can't stop thinking about how scared they must be. If something happened to my wife and baby and to my little sister, I don't think that I would want to go on living."

Beverly grabbed Pete's hand and said, "Don't talk like that Pete, they're going to be all right. I just know it."

They arrived at Emory-Adventist Hospital with bags of burgers, coffee and cokes. Johnny was sure his mom would never leave his father's bedside and she probably hadn't eaten anything since last night.

Officer Broderick told them that he would stick with them until he was sure that they had gotten the keys to the house and the car. He would then take one of them to get their mother's car.

They walked up to the emergency room admitting desk, and were told that Mr. McCord was out of surgery and had been placed in a private room.

The receptionist pointed to the right and said, "Room 117, in the Intensive Care Unit, through those doors and down the hall."

Getting a nod from the police officer, she asked them all to sign the "Visitor's Log". When they had completed this necessary procedure, she buzzed the automatic doors that allowed them access into the ICU.

They followed each other down the long hall, lit by the overhead fluorescent lights recessed into their egg crate fixtures.

When they got to room 117 they stopped. Johnny carefully opened the door and they all made their way quietly into the room.

Martha was sitting on a chair next to Roger. He appeared to still be sleeping off the effects of the anesthesia. She was holding his hand in one of hers and brushing the hair back from his forehead with the other.

When Martha heard them enter the room she looked up and smiled a very tired smile.

In a low voice she said, "Dad's gonna be ok. It was touch and go there for a while, but he pulled through. Thanks to Beverly, we got him here just in time. Now tell me about Carol and Gloria. Are they ok?"

Officer Broderick moved over beside Martha and said, "Hello ma'am. My name is Denny Broderick. I'm with the Marietta Police Department. We haven't located the girls yet.

There's a chance they got away and are hiding in the woods. We have over fifty people looking for them right now. There's no indication that they might be hurt, but we just don't know. It is possible that they are still being held by these criminals and we are tracking down every lead we have to find them."

Then he took out his business card and offered it to Martha.

He patted her gently on her shoulder and said, "I'm going to leave you folks alone now. If there's anything I can do, please don't hesitate to call. As soon as we know anything more, we'll get in touch with you."

He added, "We've asked that one of you stay at your home, round the clock, to answer the phone in case the girls call. If we hear anything we'll call your home. Whoever is there can relay any news to you here at the hospital."

"Do you have the keys to the house and your car? I'm going to drive one of the boys back to the "Farm" store to get your car."

Martha reached over to the room's covered air conditioning unit that was located against the wall, under a large picture window that looked out on the hospital grounds. She picked up her purse, reached inside and found her keys. Johnny walked over and took the keys from her hand.

He reached down, kissed his mother on the head and said, "I love you mom. Tell dad that I love him and I'll be back in a little bit."

He turned to Pete and Beverly and said, "I'll take the first shift. You both stay here with mom and make sure she eats something."

He asked his mom for a pen and paper, which she retrieved from her purse and handed to him. He wrote down the phone number for the hospital, noted the room number as well and put it in his pocket.

"As soon as I hear anything, I'll call you right away." he told them.

Then he emptied one of the McDonald's bags of all but a couple of "Big Macs"; some french fries and a coke. He folded the top of the bag closed, looked at the policeman and said, "I'm ready to go now, if you are?"

Denny Broderick nodded his head and they left.

Chapter 51

Santino's face had turned blood red. He slammed the handset down so hard that it cracked the base of the phone.

He screamed, "Dumb fucking Germans. They can't even stop for a rest without something going wrong! I don't know, man, it sounds to me like they got ripped off. I think they're fucking dead!"

Ramone said, "We can't let this go. Our people ain't gonna' be happy when we show up without the cash. How the hell are we gonna get it back?"

Santino held up his hand with the palm facing Ramone. He waved it in a "stay back" motion and said, "Let me think man, just let me think!"

He went to the table and closed the briefcase that held the drugs. Then he walked over to the Camaro, opened the trunk and put the briefcase in the hidden compartment under the custom speaker system. He slammed down the trunk lid and went back and sat on the edge of the table.

Looking down at the floor of the huge garage, he began to think out loud seemingly not acknowledging that Ramone was even there.

"They could be anywhere. We don't know when they got to the Germans, or where. It had to be after midnight, but when? That's over thirteen hours ago, they could be six hundred miles away from Georgia by now. How in the hell are we gonna find them?"

Ramone had been listening, intently, to what Santino was saying. He knew better than to interrupt him.

Santino didn't have any friends, not even Ramone. He would cut off your balls as soon as look at you. You definitely didn't want to get on his wrong side.

When Santino finally stopped talking to the floor, Ramone said, "I got an idea, man."

Santino responded, "Ok, let's hear it."

"What about the phone company? They gotta know where we just called, don't they? How else can they bill us for the call?"

Santino looked at Ramone, with what appeared to be newfound respect.

He said, "You know, man, you ain't so dumb as I thought you was."

He picked up the broken phone, hoping that it would still work. He breathed a sigh of relief, when he pressed the handset to his ear and heard the dial tone. He pressed "0" for operator.

After a few rings, a voice on the other end said, "This is the AT&T operator, how may I help you?"

Santino found his most casual and friendly voice. He said, "I wonder if you could help me. I just phoned my friend on his car phone and after I hung up I realized that I needed to call him again. But you see, the thing is, I had his cell phone number on a piece of paper and the daggone dog grabbed it."

"I think he ate it and I don't know the number off the top of my head. Can you help me?"

The operator let out a chuckle and said, "Well, you

know I'm not supposed to do this, but I've heard a lot of stories and this one is so ridiculous that it must be true.

You sound like a nice person. Let me see what I can do. What is the number you are calling from and how long ago did you make the call to your friend?"

Santino gave her the information and then he held his breath.

The operator said, "Hold on please."

After about a minute, she came back on the line and asked, "Would that be the call you made to Rome, Georgia?"

It was all Santino could do to stay calm. He couldn't believe his good fortune. He had been trying to think of a way to ask her for the location of the call, without it sounding too suspicious. She had taken care of that problem for him.

He replied, "Yes, that's the call. I just hung up five minutes ago."

Then the operator asked him to identify the owner of the cell phone.

Without any hesitation, he said, "Stremler, Max Stremler."

She responded, cheerfully, "That's the one," and she gave him the cell phone number, which matched the one he was looking at on the piece of paper in his hand.

Santino said, "I really appreciate your help. It's real important that I get hold of Mr. Stremler."

She said, "You're welcome. Thanks for using AT&T and watch out for that dog. Goodbye."

Santino hung up the phone, more carefully this

time. He slapped Ramone on the back and said, "Yeah man, you did it! We know where they were five minutes ago. Rome, fucking, Georgia.

Where's that picture you took of Max and Kurt when they were here six months ago? If you remember, they was standin' in front of the motor home. We need that photo to find them."

Ramone said, "I got it in my wallet, but what are we gonna do now? Rome is a good six hours from here?"

Santino said, "Unless these assholes are really stupid, they know they have to dump the motor home. As far as they know, we could be calling the cops right now. If we find the motor home, we got a chance of picking up their trail."

"Unless they already had another car, they're gonna have to get one. Hey man, if we don't find them we will call the cops. If we can't have the money, I ain't lettin' these bastards get away with it either."

Chapter 52

As Manny was counting the cash that Linda had given him, she was gazing out of the front window.

Her newly purchased Chevy wagon was being pulled up in front of the office. The price and other advertising had been cleaned off the windshield and the car was sparkling in the sunlight, from a recent washing.

Manny said, "Twenty-six hundred, right on the nose."

He slid the temporary registration in front of her and said, "You should receive your permanent tags and registration in about two weeks. The temporary tags that we put on are good for thirty days. If you have any problems, give me a call," and he handed her two of his business cards.

He pointed to another document and said, "This here's a ninety day "full" warrantee. Anything at all goes wrong and we fix it free!"

He added, "Well little lady............oh, I mean Shelley, if you don't have any questions, I think that about does it. Let's go get you a car."

They left the office and walked out to the station wagon. Linda could still see the water dripping off the undercarriage from the car wash.

Manny reached through the driver's side window and retrieved the keys from the ignition. They had been placed on a key ring that had an "ABC Auto Sales" pendant hanging from it as well.

Manny handed these keys to Linda, along with a second set also attached to an ABC pendant. He smiled and said, "You can never have enough advertising. Am I right?"

Manny opened the wagon's door for her and held out his hand. Linda shook the proffered hand and put the extra set of keys in her purse. She slid behind the wheel and turned on the ignition. Manny carefully closed the door for her.

With a final exchange of waves, Linda slowly pulled out of the lot and turned left to find Bear.

"Well" she thought, "That went pretty well. I got the car, made another four hundred on the deal and didn't have to use my own name."

She slowed down, as she pulled alongside the motor home.

As she approached, she could see Bear's face reflected in the side view mirror. She knew that he had seen her coming.

She looked, casually towards the motor home and saw him point his finger forward, indicating that she should keep going.

In her rear view mirror, she could see the motor home pull out into the sparse traffic, two cars behind her.

As they had agreed, she headed northeast on I-411. As soon as she got out of the downtown Rome area she slowed to let the motor home pass.

Bear thought that he remembered seeing a rather large automobile graveyard, on the way into Rome. He figured that, if he could find it again, it might be the perfect place for the switch.

Sure enough, about ten miles out of Rome, he saw an old, dilapidated sign that said, "**Ray's Junkyard and Auto Parts**". It was a big hand with the index finger pointing to the left.

He pulled the motor home over to the side of the road and stopped on the shoulder. Linda followed behind him in the station wagon.

He got out of the motor home and walked back to the wagon. Linda rolled down the window and Bear laid both of his forearms on the roof and stuck his head inside.

He said, "You did good. This will do fine." He turned his head toward the high fence on the other side of the street and said, "See that old junkyard. It looks like it's closed down. At least that's what I'm hoping. Go up and get in the motor home and keep an eye on those girls. Tell Snake that if I don't drive back out of there, in ten minutes, he should drive the motor home through the gate and meet me. I'll be waiting for you in the wagon."

Linda agreed, got out of the wagon and went forward to the motor home. Bear slid behind the wheel of the wagon, adjusted the power seat and mirrors and pulled away from the curb.

When Linda got into the motor home, she began to explain what Bear had said when Snake interrupted her.

He said, "Yeah, he told me before he went back to see you. Here, take this gun and keep an eye on the girls. I think they need to use the shitter, but they was embarrassed. Let 'em do what they gotta do, but watch them!"

Linda went back to where the girls were sitting and said, "If you have to use the crapper, you better do it now. Once we switch to the station wagon, we're not gonna be making any pit stops."

Then she pointed to Gloria and said, "You go first and when you're done she can go, but no tricks!"

Chapter 53

Mike hadn't been this tired in a long time. It really started to hit him on the drive back to Macon. He turned the air on full blast, but he kept the driver's side window down anyhow, hoping that the sound of the wind rushing past would help keep him alert. He often wished that cars still had wing windows like they had in the fifties. You could get a nice breeze to blow right at your face.

He kept trying to build a mental bridge from all of the elements he had gathered so far about this case, but there were so many missing pieces that the bridge kept falling down.

Based on Beverly's story, it was pretty clear as to how and why the events, up to and including the break-in on "The Four Lane" had occurred. What he didn't understand was the mayhem at the campsite.

More importantly, unless they got lucky with the motor home, he didn't know how they were going to pick up the trail of the perps and, assuming they still had them, the two girls.

Mike knew from experience, that when this much violence happened, life didn't count for much. The longer it took to find the girls the less chance they had of surviving this ordeal.

As he pulled the police cruiser into an empty space in front of his home, he could see Anne Marie standing behind the screen door, anxiously awaiting his arrival.

He had called her about fifteen minutes before, to let her know that he was almost home.

He parked the car and locked his holstered Smith & Wesson in the glove box.

When he got close to the front door, his nostrils were filled with the pleasant smell of the breakfast that had been prepared for him.

Anne Marie just shook her head and said, "Michael... honey, you look terrible!"

He knew she was concerned because that was the only time she ever called him Michael.

She gave him a big hug. Then they walked, arm in arm, to the kitchen where he plopped down on a chair in front of his oversized, "Detective Shield" coffee mug.

He loosened his tie and sipped on the soothing brown nectar. Anne Marie placed a large plate, piled high with scrambled eggs and surrounded with strips of bacon, in front of him.

While he wolfed down his breakfast, he took the opportunity, between bites, to explain what had gone on since he left her alone in their bed.

Mike was always careful not to relate any of the "gory" details to Anne Marie.

While he elaborated on his descriptions of the McCords and Beverly, he simply stated that Mr. McCord had been shot and some of the "bad guys" had been killed, when it came to the violence part of the story.

Mike glanced around the "Early American" kitchen and his gaze came to rest on the "Rooster" framed clock, hanging on the wall. It was now three fifteen in the afternoon and he had been up for thirty-three hours straight.

He took a last sip of coffee, then stood up and gave Anne Marie a peck on the cheek.

He said, "Thanks for breakfast, hon. I really needed that. Now what I need is to get some rest." He didn't say "sleep" because, with all of the images racing through his head, he feared that sleep would be impossible.

Pulling off his tie and unbuttoning his shirt, he headed for the bedroom. Anne Marie walked with him and collected each article of clothing as he handed them to her. When he got to their bed, he sat down and reached over to set the alarm clock for six thirty P.M.

"I'm sure I'll hear the phone, if it rings, but please wake me up if I don't," he said.

Mike was asleep before his head hit the pillow, and he never would have gotten the phone call if she hadn't been there to answer it for him.

Chapter 54

Snake gave it a full fifteen minutes. When the wagon had not reappeared in the entrance to the junkyard, he cranked up the motor home and headed in after Bear.

About fifty yards into the property he saw a high, chain-link fence that surrounded the property for as far as he could see. There were two closed, swinging gates prohibiting their access into the yard proper. A large, rusted sign was wired to one of the gates.

It warned, "No Trespassing – Private Property!"

As the motor home approached the gates, they swung open as if by magic. There, inside the gates, he could see Bear waving them to enter. He was pointing off to the right to tell Snake to pull the motor home behind the wagon. Snake pulled over and stopped. Once more he admonished Linda to watch the girls.

He got out of the motor home and joined Bear by the front gates. Bear had already swung the gates closed and was re-wrapping a long chain around them, to secure the entrance.

Bear picked up a "Master Lock" that had been lying in the road. It was totally corroded with rust and the locking mechanism appeared to be sprung from the many blows it had sustained.

Bear said, "I used the tire iron on this bitch. I don't think it's been opened for years." He slid the lock back through two links of the chain and turned it so it would appear to be locked.

Snake said, "Did you scope this place out?"

Bear responded, "Yeah, the most recent junker I could find was a sixty two and a half Ford Falcon Sports Futura. I haven't seen one of them in a long time. I guess nobody's used this place for over ten years. It's fucking perfect!"

He told Snake to follow him and they both returned to their respective vehicles.

As Snake followed Bear deeper into the junkyard, he was amazed at the thirty-foot piles of rusted junk. There were trucks and buses and every imaginable style of automobile.

The road surface that was, in fact, a field that no longer could sustain greenery wound between and around these piles of derelicts.

It appeared that back when it had been thriving, the junkyard had been very carefully arranged. Chevys were piled on Chevys; Fords on Fords; Mopars on Mopars and so on.

After about ten minutes of winding around these piles, they arrived at the motherlode.

In front of him, Snake could see motor homes stacked in rows, not on top of each other like the cars, but side by side.

Bear stopped just in front of an open space that was located between two rusted motor homes. He got out of the station wagon and signaled for Snake to join him.

When Snake got to his side he told Bear, "They'll never find this thing in here. I'll get the girls out and pull it in that space."

Bear said, "Not yet, we still got things to do first. We're gonna spend the night here.

You and me got some shavin' to do and Linda needs to dye her hair. We need the motor home's bathroom to do all of that."

"You need to take the wagon and find a place that sells camping equipment. You can shave and change clothes when you get back. That way anyone who might see you now, ain't never gonna recognize you later."

Snake said, "Gotcha, wild man."

Bear handed Snake a list that he had written on one of the empty McDonald's bags. He told Snake to get a thousand dollars from one of the briefcases to buy the listed camping supplies.

Snake said, "Why don't I just take one of the briefcases with me in the wagon, and you keep the other one here with you?"

Bear knew what Snake was suggesting, but he didn't want a confrontation with Snake. At least not now!

Bear said, "Ok, but keep the damn thing hidden in the storage compartment under the floor in the back of the wagon. Take the money out now. You don't need to be rooting through that briefcase, on some fucking mall's parking lot! And since we're gonna spend the night, bring back some food and beer. Get milk for the girls and I think Linda said we were out of toilet paper. No reason for things to get nasty."

Snake smiled and went to the motor home to collect one of the briefcases. He asked Linda if they needed anything that wasn't on Bear's list.

Linda told Snake to get a couple of bags full of canned goods, along with a bunch of snacks.

She said, "Get chips and pretzels and stuff and don't forget to get a small, two burner stove and some propane.

We're going camping again and we may not be able to stop on the way. And safety matches get a couple of boxes of them."

Snake snapped back, "We ain't fucking married, quit sayin' shit like you're giving me orders!"

Linda said, "Look asshole, if you want to eat just get the stuff, if you don't then forget it!"

Snake said, "Yeah…yeah," and he picked up the pen from the console of the motor home and added to the list on the bag. He thought to himself, "How in the fuck did Ricky put up with this bitch? Well her time would come."

He said, "Just don't forget……"

Linda finished the sentence for him, "Watch the girls, I got it! Like where in the hell are they gonna go?"

Snake replied, "Well they got away once and I don't need to be chasing around in this dump, looking for them tonight."

He jumped down from the motor home, got into the wagon and headed out to shop.

Bear came into the motor home and said, "I'll keep an eye on them while you take care of your hair. Then I need you to cut mine. It's time I start looking like just another family man."

Chapter 55

When their home phone rang, Anne Marie knew it wasn't Mike's office calling. They would have used Mike's private line.

The voice on the other end said, "Hi, this is Johnny McCord, can I speak to Detective Sullivan?"

Anne Marie answered, "Hello Johnny, I'm Mrs. McCord. Let me see if he's awake."

She put down the phone and went to the bedroom. Mike was snoring loudly, as he always did when he was overly tired.

She shook him gently and said, "Mike... Mike, there's a call for you." Mike awoke with a start and quickly sat up in the bed. His hair was all mussed from the pillows and his mouth was dry.

Through somewhat glassy eyes, he looked at Anne Marie and said, "What did you, the phone?...... Did they say who it is?"

"It's one of the McCord boys. "Johnny," he said his name was."

"Alright, I'll take it in here. Would you hang up the other phone, please?"

She returned to the kitchen and as soon as she heard Mike say Hello, she hung up the extension.

"I know you said you would call if you heard anything, but mom is really worried and she asked me to phone you."

Mike replied, "That's ok Johnny, I understand, but, I haven't heard anything, one way or the other.

I was just getting ready to check in with the crime lab to see how they're coming along. Once I get anything at all I'll definitely call you. How's your dad doing?"

"I just spoke with Pete and he told me that dad is coming out of the anesthesia. He seems to be doing ok. In fact, that's another one of the reasons I called. I'm getting ready to drive over to the hospital and Pete and Beverly are going to come back here to babysit the phone. But I'm worried that there won't be anyone here for about an hour. Can you do anything to cover this line?"

Mike answered, "Yes, there sure is. I can contact the Phone Company and ask them to forward any incoming calls to my office. Make sure that Pete calls me as soon as he and Beverly get to the house. We can decide what else to do about the phone, then. As soon as we hang up, I'll make the arrangements, so wait about fifteen minutes before you leave for the hospital. By the way, what's your dad's room number?"

Johnny told Mike the room number, assured him that he would hang around for fifteen more minutes and then hung up the phone.

Mike pressed down the phone hook until he got a fresh dial tone. He called the Phone Company and got hold of the supervisor. He identified himself and explained the situation.

The supervisor put Mike on hold until he could call Police Headquarters to confirm Mike's identity.

He returned to the line in less than five minutes and

said, "Done." Mike thanked him and pressed the hook once more to get a new tone.

He dialed the Crime Lab's number from memory and asked to speak to whoever was handling, what had now come to be known as, "The Four Lane" case.

A familiar female voice came on the line.

"Hello, this is Angela Sabatino. To whom am I speaking?"

Mike answered, "Hi Angie. This is Mike Sullivan. I'm hoping that you have something for me on all that trouble out at "The Four Lane" and up at "Red Top". Whatta' ya' got for me?"

"Oh, hi Mike, this is a bad one, isn't it? I've got six people, plus myself, working the case as we speak. All the DOAs have been printed and the data has been sent to the Feds. We're lifting prints from the Caddy and the motorcycles, as well. Once we match them all up, we can try to pare it down so it begins to make some sense.

I took it on myself to send a technician with a print kit to Emory-Adventist Hospital. I figured we better print all the good guys to help us exclude their prints from the stack."

Mike said, "I see that, as usual, you're right on top of everything Angie and I appreciate your help. What can you tell me about the paint scrapings taken from the Porsche? I've got that down as my number one lead in locating the motor home."

Angela asked Mike to hold on while she checked on the status of the paint check.

After a brief silence, she returned to the phone and

said, "I think we can help you out there, Mike. We just finished cross-checking the paint samples against our motor home database.

My people were able to pin it down to one of two years, but it's the same basic vehicle. It's either a nineteen seventy-seven or a nineteen seventy-eight, Dodge "Eldorado Sportsman".

The book shows it as twenty feet, six inches in length. This one has a "two-toned" paint job. The cab and the roof are a cream color and it's a medium blue color everywhere else.

The only other thing I can tell you, for sure, is that it's missing the left, front headlight assembly. We picked most of that up off the ground, at the scene."

Mike asked her to get that information off to dispatch immediately.

He said, "That's the best information we have so far, maybe we can get lucky." Then he added, "And Angie, please give me a holler, just as soon as you get anything back on the fingerprints or the motorcycle registrations."

Angela assured Mike she would and said goodbye.

Mike decided to see if a couple of the Marietta guys could meet him at Northside Hospital. He had left his own car there and he really wanted to get it back. It had all of his "stuff" in it and who knew, maybe he'd get to light up his cigar.

While he was at the hospital he wanted to check in on Wally Higgums and see if he had recovered sufficiently to provide a better description of his assailants.

They hadn't found any "snake" tattoos on the dead bodies and that told Mike that at least one of the major bad guys was still out there.

The prints would help them to I.D. the dead perps. But, unless they got additional hits on the prints or the bike registrations yielded something pretty quickly, identifying the dead guys might not be much help in the short run.

Mike wanted dearly, to get those girls back safely. He got on the phone and called Sergeant Robbins.

Chapter 56

Santino looked at Ramone and said, "Here's what we're gonna do. First, we need to stop by my pad and pick up some extra firepower. Then I'm gonna call Mr. Rodriguez and tell him that the Germans had some trouble with their motor home.

I'll tell him I decided it was better for us to drive to Georgia and do the deal there, than to wait for them to get the motor home fixed. If he buys that, it should give us another forty-eight hours."

Ramone asked, "What the fuck are we gonna do if we don't find those bastards and get the money by then?"

"Well, then I guess I'll just have to come up with another plan.

C'mon, let's straighten up here and get going."

Ramone backed the black Camaro out of the garage and into the alley. Santino took a quick look around garage, especially the area by the table. He wanted to be damn sure they hadn't left anything behind.

Once he was satisfied that it was clean, he walked out to the alley, used the remote to close the garage door and jumped into the front passenger seat of the Camaro.

He turned to Ramone and said, "Crank this mother up! We need to get to going, like right now."

Ramone held his watch out in front of his face and said, "It's two-fifteen now. By the time we stop at your place, grab something to eat and drink, even if I punch it, it'll take us about ten hours. That ain't gonna get us there 'til after midnight."

"With all the "shit" we're gonna have in the back, we'd be a helluva lot safer hangin' around the speed limit.

That'll still get us there by two or three. And we ain't gonna' find nobody in the middle of the night, anyhow."

Santino replied, "Yeah man, you're right. Just get us to my pad. Once we load up and get this thing onto I-75, I'll have to do some serious thinkin'."

Chapter 57

Snake drove the wagon back to the same mall where Linda had shopped earlier.

As he pulled up to the mall entrance, he said to himself, "Yeah, son-of-a-bitch, I knew it was here!"

While they had been waiting for Linda, he thought he remembered having seen a sign that told him there was a "Sunny's Surplus" in the mall.

Snake loved Sunny's Surplus stores. They had lots of cool Army type stuff and he figured they would have all the camping supplies that were on his list.

"On the way back to the dump I'll stop at a fast food place, maybe even a Mini-Market" he thought with a chuckle. "I'll get the chow there."

Linda had finished coloring her hair and was waiting for it to dry. She was a little irritated with herself for not thinking to get a hair dryer, when she bought the red dye.

"Hell," she thought, "it's hot enough out that it shouldn't take very long to dry." This would especially be true, considering the fact that she had hacked off about six inches of her hair before she applied the coloring.

When she emerged from the small bathroom, Bear did a double take and said, "Who in the hell are you? With them new clothes and that hair, I don't think your own mother would recognize you now. Since you're all warmed up, why don't you cut my hair and trim my beard so I can shave without cutting my own throat?"

Linda told him to sit on the edge of one of the beds and she began to cut his hair.

He looked at Carol and Gloria and said, "Watch this girls, this is gonna be the new, improved Bear. Who knows, if I like the way I look, I might even let you both go free tomorrow."

Carol and Gloria wanted to get their hopes up, but they didn't believe him for a second.

Snake hadn't encountered any problems. He had gotten everything that had been on the list and then some.

He added three canteens along with a nine-inch Bowie knife and scabbard for himself.

After returning to the wagon and loading all of the supplies, he sat down in the front seat and carefully unwrapped his new toy.

He gingerly drew his thumb and index finger down the razor sharp blade and thought, "You're my baby. And that's what I think I'll call you...... (Baby)."

In the same way that a normal person might handle a baby, he lovingly slid the menacing knife into the newly acquired scabbard and threaded the scabbard onto the belt of his jeans.

On the way back to the motor home, he found a small, corner grocery store. He went inside, with the large knife still hanging against his hip. He referred often, to the list he was carrying and when he was finished he had bought enough to fill three groceries bags.

Throughout the thirty or so minutes it had taken

him to gather all of the items on the list, no one had even given him a second glance.

As the clerk smiled and handed him his change, Snake couldn't help thinking, "Don't you just love the South?"

After leaving the grocery store, he pulled into an Exxon station, topped off the gas tank and then drove back to the junkyard.

Chapter 58

Mike Sullivan checked his watch. It was eight thirty-five PM. He had been hanging around Walter Higgums' hospital room for over an hour. Wally appeared to be in a deep sleep and Mike decided to let him sleep and instead stretch his legs.

He left Wally's room and walked down the hall to the nurse's station.

The head duty nurse told Mike that Mr. Higgums had been medicated for pain and probably wouldn't be coherent until the next morning.

While she was talking to Mike, her phone rang. She picked up the receiver and listened for a few seconds, and then she looked up at Mike.

She said, "Detective, it's for you," and offered the handset to Mike.

It was the hospital's front lobby. The voice on the other end informed Mike that there were two Marietta police officers waiting for him at the front entrance.

Mike said he'd be right down and handed the phone back to the nurse. He said, "Thanks, I'm going to be leaving for home now. As soon as Mr. Higgums is alert enough to have a conversation, please call me at this number." And he handed her his card.

She taped the card to the front of Wally's chart, with a note that Mike should be called as soon as Mr. Higgums regained consciousness.

Mike thanked the nurse, again and headed for the elevator.

When Mike got to the revolving door, in front of the hospital's main entrance, he saw the Marietta PD cruiser.

He could make out the familiar profile of his friend, Sergeant Robbins, leaning against the cruiser with an unlit cigarette dangling from his lips.

Mike approached the police car and said, "Hey Paul, I didn't think you'd be coming."

Paul, who was in casual street clothes, turned to Mike, smiled and said, "No problemo. I thought we could grab a cup of coffee and exchange some thoughts before I drive the loaner back."

Mike said, "Sounds good to me. Why don't you tell the officer to go ahead back home? I've got your patrol car parked right over there next to mine."

He pointed at the two cars only about twenty-five yards away.

Paul Robbins sent the cruiser back to Marietta and rejoined Mike.

He said, "This is your neck of the woods, buddy..... Why don't I follow you?"

Mike tossed Paul the keys to the Marietta cruiser and told him to follow him to an all night diner, which was only about ten minutes away.

When they got to the diner, they grabbed a booth back in the smoking section. The waitress brought them menus and asked for their drink order. They both ordered coffee and she went to get it.

Paul lit up the cigarette that he had been dry smoking and pulled an ashtray in front of himself.

He took a small, black notebook from his back pocket and said, "Let's compare notes. Whatta ya say?"

Mike began, "I just left the guy from the Citgo station. He's still out but it looks like he'll be ok, except for a few stitches and a bad headache. Probably won't get any more out of him 'til tomorrow."

Paul made a note on his pad and interjected, "That's victim number one," then he continued, "I stopped by Emory-Adventist, on my way over here, and it looks like Mr. McCord will pull through. He's gonna be laid up for at least a week, even if everything goes well."

Mike said, "That's victim number two. I'm waiting for a call from the feds on any matches from the prints on the Caddy and we're checking the Motor Vehicle Administration for ownership I.D. on the bikes."

Paul commented, "That should pin down the four drivers of the motorcycles and tell us which two are still out there. The other two dead guys from Red Top, are still a mystery. Hopefully we'll get hits on their prints as well."

Then Mike summed it up by saying, "That leaves us with the three biker gals, one of which is still alive and kickin'. Unless she left some prints, she may be the only one we can't identify. And most importantly, it leaves us with the two kidnapped girls."

Paul said, "Yeah, that's victims three and four!" Then he closed his notebook and returned it to his back pocket.

Mike looked at Paul and said, "You know the Dodge motor home is the key. They either have to keep running in it or steal something else. Now that the description is all over the news, my guess is that they'll dump it and steal another vehicle."

Sergeant Robbins picked up on what Mike was saying and he responded, "We'll keep looking for the Dodge, but let's get all units to report directly to us on any stolen vehicles, anything stolen since noon today."

Mike agreed and asked Paul to take on the responsibility for getting that message out to all units right away.

As Paul pulled out his portable phone to call it in the waitress returned with the coffee.

She said, "What are you guys gonna have?"

They looked at each other, shook their heads and Mike said, "All we needed was the coffee, thanks, and we won't be needing refills, so just leave the check please."

The waitress nodded her head toward a man, over on the grill, preparing flapjacks.

She said, "The manager, Mr. Walker, saw you pull up and he said to tell you that the coffee is on the house."

Chapter 59

After four hours on the road, Ramone and Santino made a pit stop.

They visited the men's room and got some fresh coffee, then filled up the gas tank and hit the road again.

Santino was taking a turn at the wheel and Ramone was scanning through the radio stations. They were close enough to Georgia, to begin picking up the bigger Atlanta stations.

What they heard on the newscast made them both sit up and listen.

It seems as though there was a major crime spree happening in the Atlanta area. It included the deaths of six people and the kidnapping of two others.

Motorists were being told to be on the lookout for a late model Dodge motor home. The motor home was described as medium size, two-tone cream and blue color with damage to the left front headlight assembly.

The newscaster stated, "We have been advised by Detective Michael Sullivan of the Atlanta Police Department, to warn anyone who might see this vehicle to report it to the Atlanta police immediately. The occupants are considered "Armed and extremely dangerous", and no one should attempt to approach the vehicle or its occupants."

Santino said, "Get that photo out! Wasn't the German's motor home white and blue?"

Ramone opened his wallet and, excitedly, pulled out the picture.

He said, "Just like they described it, the son-of-a-bitch is cream and blue!

I don't know what we're getting' into, but there ain't no way anyone coulda' got that motor home from the Germans, unless they iced 'em first."

Santino said, "What the hell was that detective guy's name,…… something Sullivan? That might come in handy. Don't change this damn station. Maybe they'll say his name again. Get out something to write on and make sure you write it down"

Chapter 60

Bear had finished changing into the clothes that Linda had gotten at the mall. He looked in the mirror and tried to remember the last time he had seen himself in regular clothes. He couldn't.

Ever since he was sixteen, he had been wearing biker clothes and long hair. By the time he was eighteen, he had already quit school and left for California with his friends. That had been fourteen years ago.

The last time his hair had been cut was during the two years he had spent in the California Correctional Institution for Men in Chino. He had fallen in with one of the L.A. gangs and had gotten two years for aggravated assault, for helping the gang demolish a local poolroom and put some of their customers in the hospital.

That was where he met Snake. Snake's real name was Kyle Louis Billings and he was doing five years for armed robbery. He had immediately gotten close to Bear, because a punk like Kyle needed a bodyguard in jail.

They had been released within thirty days of each other, first Kyle and then Bear. Kyle had been so impressed with Bear that he decided to get his own nickname. He hung around L.A. pushing drugs and made enough money to get his arms and fingers tattooed.

By the time Bear got out, Kyle had officially become "Snake".

Bear didn't have to try very hard to convince Snake, who was originally from Dayton, Ohio, to leave L.A. and go back with him to Georgia.

It had taken over a year for them to steal and hustle their way to Georgia. Once they arrived they rented a small trailer home, which provided them the address to get driver's licenses.

They managed to get enough cash together to buy motorcycles and started to put together their gang.

The gang had done very well, until two days ago. Now the seven were down to three and Bear thought that it couldn't have worked out better.

He still had to think through the how, but there was no doubt in his mind that he wasn't going to share the quarter of a million with anyone.

Bear walked out of the motor home and lit up a Pall Mall. He was trying to decide which part of his name, "William Robert Masterson", he would use in his new life, when he saw the headlights of the wagon coming around the corner.

"Bob," he thought, "Bob Masterson, That'll work."

Snake hopped out of the car and walked up to the motor home. He had to look twice to convince himself that it really was Bear.

He said, "Well hot damn, ain't you pretty!"

Bear stuck out his hand and said, "Hi there, Kyle, Bob Masterson, nice to meet you. Now let's get the fucking tent up!"

Snake pulled a large four-person tent from the back

of the wagon and together they pitched it next to the motor home.

Bear called Linda out of the motor home and said, "Snake and me are gonna stay in there. You three girls can stay in the tent. I want Snake to cut his hair and get into his new clothes before we head out of here.

Get the young girl to help you put the sleeping bags and shit in the tent. I'll keep my eye on the pregnant one while Snake cleans up."

Linda went into the motor home and told Carol and Gloria what was happening. Carol went with Linda and they started putting the sleeping gear in the tent.

Chapter 61

After waiting a good twenty minutes, Johnny left the house and drove to the hospital. By the time he arrived, it was after visiting hours.

The nurse at the front desk recognized Johnny and told him that he could go in to see his dad for a few minutes, but then he, Beverly and Pete would have to leave. She explained that they had made arrangements for Mrs. McCord to stay overnight with her husband.

When Johnny got to his dad's room, Pete and Beverly were ready to go. Roger was awake and happy to see Johnny. He asked whether they had any news about the girls and Johnny told them no. They spoke for a few minutes and then Johnny kissed his mom & dad, as did Pete, and the three of them left.

On the way back to the house, they stopped at the "Farm" store and surveyed the damage. There was yellow crime scene tape all around the store and he assumed that the police department must have put up the plywood covering the broken front door.

Johnny made a mental note to thank Marietta's finest for securing their property. While it remained a crime scene, he knew that they would not be allowed to enter the store. Well, that was the least of their worries right now.

Pete was becoming very emotional and he said, "Johnny, I'm going crazy here! We have to do something to find the girls, but I don't know what."

Beverly said, "Pete, I know you're upset but there's

really nothing we can do except stay calm and keep in touch with Detective Sullivan." Johnny nodded his head and said, "Beverly's right. We'll stop and get something to eat and then go back to the house for a good night's rest. That way when we do hear something, we'll be able to do whatever we need to do."

Beverly held her arms down at her sides her index fingers pointing to her clothes and with a frown she moaned, "I have to do something about this. I've been in these same clothes for two days and I'll bet I look as grungy as I feel." Johnny replied, "There's a Target store in the mall down the road. You can get just about anything you want there." Then they left the store and drove to the mall.

Beverly bought a new pair of jeans, a blouse and some underwear. Then they stopped at a local diner on The Four Lane and got something to eat.

While they were waiting for their food to arrive, Johnny used the pay phone to call Detective Mike's home. Anne Marie answered, explained that Mike was on his way home, and would let him know that they had called. She would tell him to call them at their mom's house if he had any news.

By the time they finished eating, they had all commented on how exhausted they were and they drove straight to the McCord home to sack out for the night.

Chapter 62

Santino and Ramone listened to the car radio as they continued toward Rome. When the news came on again, there was no mention of the policeman's name.

Santino smacked the steering wheel and said, "Well, that ain't gonna help us." Ramone replied, "I don't think they're gonna hang on to that motor home. Now that the cops have a description of it, they would be begging to get caught. Hey, the bastards have plenty of dough, our fucking dough! They'll probably just buy a car for cash somewhere.

It was now approaching seven p.m. and the last sign they saw told them that they were only ten miles from Rome, GA.

Santino saw a sign for a Motel 6 at the next off-ramp and he told Ramone, "There's nothing we can do tonight so let's get a good night's sleep and an early start in the morning.

After checking into the motel, they went out and found a McDonald's. They loaded up on Big Macs, fries and sodas and returned to the motel.

Santino said, "You could be right about them buying a different ride for cash. How many people do that and how many auto places can there be in this little town?" Ramone reached under the nightstand that separated their beds and pulled out the Rome "Yellow Pages" book.

He opened it to "Autos, Used" and said, "Not many, as a matter of fact, there's eight of em."

Santino said, "Let's start with the first one and work our way through the list. What's the first one?" Ramone flipped the phone book around and sat it on Santino's bed so he could read the ads. The first one read "ABC Auto Sales", open 7am to 7pm, seven days a week. Santino tore out the two pages of auto sales ads and put them in the fold of his wallet.

Ramone looked at the time on the clock radio and noted that it was almost 10pm.

"We're gettin' up early tomorrow so I suggest we catch some shut-eye", Santino grumbled.

Chapter 63

Carol and Linda unloaded the sleeping bags from the station wagon and carried them to the tent. Linda was thinking about all that had happened since yesterday and she thought to herself, "I didn't sign on for all this shit. Things have gotten totally out of hand and I need to find a way to get myself out of this."

Linda glanced at Carol and for the first time she noticed how pretty she was. Carol saw Linda looking at her and got worried, she said, "Did I do something wrong?"

Linda replied, "No, I was just wondering how old you are." Carol breathed a little easier and replied, "I'll be thirteen next month." Linda was totally taken aback at this. She said, "Girl, you could have fooled me, I thought you were at least sixteen."

As they continued to spread out the sleeping bags Linda, once again, thought to herself, "This kid is only twelve years old. Damn, this is all wrong!"

Just then Snake looked into the tent and called Linda outside. He told her that Bear wanted her for something in the motor home. He said with a very noticeable sneer, "I'll keep an eye on this one 'til you get back."

Linda didn't feel comfortable leaving Carol alone with Snake, especially after what she had just discovered, but this was not the time.

Linda started for the motor home and saw that Bear was smoking a cigarette about twenty feet away from the door.

He motioned for her to come over to where he was waiting.

He turned his back to the motor home and said, "Something ain't right with the pregnant girl. Go in there and find out what the deal is."

When Linda entered the motor home, she could hear Gloria whimpering. She was sitting on the bed holding her stomach in both hands. Linda went back and sat down next to her. She said, "Is it the baby?" Gloria nodded her head and said, "I don't feel well. You have to let me get to a hospital."

Linda thought this over for a moment then told Gloria, "We're leaving here early tomorrow. Once we get out of Georgia, I'll convince Bear to let you both go. Just try to hang in there."

Gloria hoped that Linda was telling her the truth and that she and Carol would be far away from this nightmare before anything else happened to them or the baby. She reached over and took Linda's hand in her own and said, "Please get us out of this, before it's too late."

Linda patted Gloria's hand, pulled her hand free then got up to go and tell Bear the situation.

Chapter 64

As soon as Linda left to find out what Bear wanted, Snake pulled open the tent flaps, went inside and closed the flaps behind him. Carol was standing there holding the last sleeping bag in her arms as if it offered some protection against what she feared was going to happen.

Snake walked over to Carol and pulled the sleeping bag away from her saying, "Let me help you with this." He had been checking her out ever since he first saw her at the "Farm" store and he decided that this was the time to make his move.

Carol was wearing a men's button-up shirt and Snake was staring at her breasts. He pointed at her shirt and said, "Why don't you show me what you got." Carol was terrified and began backing up. But there was no where for her to go. Snake pulled his new Bowie knife from the scabbard and showed it to Carol. She could see the blade glistening from rays of the setting sun that were coming through the space between the tent flaps. He said, "Hard way or easy way, don't matter to me?"

Carol began to sob and she said, "Please don't hurt me." He answered, "Oh, I wasn't gonna hurt you. This here's", and he moved the knife from one hand to the other, "for your girlfriend. You give me what I want and I won't use this on her."

Carol had never been so scared in her life. There wasn't any doubt in her mind that this monster would hurt Gloria. In fact, she had become convinced that, barring a miracle, neither one of them would ever get out of this alive. She made up her mind that she would do whatever she had to do, in order to buy more time for that miracle.

Carol began undoing the buttons on her shirt, from the top down. After the shirt was fully opened, Snake pointed the knife at her and said, "Now the bra." Carol undid the hook on her bra, then took off her shirt and slid both straps over her arms.

First Snake just stood there and gazed at Carol's breasts. Then he took the bra from her hand, put the knife back into the scabbard and reached out to touch Carol. She thought that she could do this but she now realized she could not and let out a scream!

When Bear heard the scream, he went over and looked into the tent. By now, Snake had thrown Carol on the sleeping bags and was trying to open her jeans.

Bear began laughing and said, "Snake, you are a sick shit, but you gotta do what you gotta do." With that he backed out of the tent still laughing.

Chapter 65

Just as Linda was leaving the motor home to relate her conversation with Gloria to Bear, she heard Carol scream. When she got there, Bear was backing out of the tent laughing. She said, "What's happening?" Bear replied, "Snakes just having a little fun with the chick."

Without hesitation, Linda screamed, "That "chick" is only twelve years old. You can't let him do that, plus we've got problems with the other girl. We need to drop them off somewhere out in the boonies the first chance we get."

He went back inside the tent and grabbed Snake by the collar. He pulled him off the girl and pushed him outside of the tent. Snake bellowed, "Get the fuck off of me!" He started to reach for his knife and Bear grabbed both his hand and the knife in a vice-like grip.

Bear screamed in Snake's face, "Calm down asshole, you need to keep your mind on business! Get your shit together so we can get the hell out of here!"

Linda got between Snake and the tent and said, "C'mon Snake, if you want it that bad you and me can get it on."

Snake was totally pissed off and he replied, "Fuck that, I ain't in the mood anymore. Get the other bitch out of the camper. I'm gonna cut my hair and I don't need any more distractions."

With that he and Bear went back to the camper and told Gloria to go out to the tent with Carol and Linda.

Bear followed Snake into the camper and patted him

on the back. He said, "Calm down you crazy bastard, let's just get out of here tomorrow and once we get to where we're goin' we're gonna get rid of the chicks for good, all three of them.

Snake said, "Yeah, let's face it, Linda ain't getting with the program. I don't trust her and a two way split beats the hell out of a three way." Bear nodded in agreement and said, "We are gonna lose them so far back in the hills of Tennessee, nobody's ever gonna find them. Once we get there, I don't give a shit what you do to them, before we bury them."

Chapter 66

Linda was totally freaked out! After helping Gloria to sit down on one of the sleeping bags, she managed to calm Carol down. She found that she was dying for a smoke. She told the girls to sit tight and she walked back to the camper to bum a cigarette off Bear. As she approached the door of the camper, she heard the discussion between the two men.

She quietly backed away from the motor home and stood behind the tent, where she couldn't be seen. She thought, "Those bastards! I guess I knew from the time we found all that money, that they were gonna find a way to screw me out of it, but I didn't think they would kill me. I need to come up with a plan, between here and Tennessee."

She hadn't signed on for all this bullshit. Knocking over a gas station was one thing, but kidnapping and mayhem was never part of the plan. The last thing she ever thought, when she hooked up with Ricky, is that she would end up fighting for her life. She decided that, if she could, she would find a way to help Carol and Gloria and she knew it was time to talk to the girls. Three heads were better than one and Linda figured she would need all the help she could get, if she was to get out of this mess alive and with the money.

Linda went back to the tent and sat down across from the girls. She pressed her index finger against her lips, motioning the girls to keep quiet.

She began by saying, "I'm gonna try to help you get

out of this, and I'm gonna need your help to get us all away from those two."

Carol and Gloria turned and looked at each other. They were confused at what they had just heard and were reluctant to get their hopes up. After all, this girl had been in it since the beginning.

Linda could see the questioning look on their faces and said, "I know you gotta be wondering why the change of heart. Well let's just say that finding all that money has changed everything. Bear and Snake have no intention of sharing it with me and they won't be leaving any witnesses. That means all of us!"

The girls nodded to indicate that they understood what Linda was telling them. Carol whispered, "What can we do?"

Linda replied, "I don't know, but we need to be ready to take advantage of any opening we see. I'm not gonna lie to you, even though I didn't hurt anyone myself, the cops will consider me just as guilty as the others. I'll try to get us all out of here, but I'm gonna need that money to get my ass out of the country."

Gloria said, "We could care less about the money, just get us out of here. I don't know how much longer I can hold on."

Linda said, "Is there anyone who can help us who won't call the cops?" Carol said, "Pete, my brother, he will do whatever it takes to help me and Gloria. If you can get something to write with, I'll give you the phone number for the store, back in Marietta and my mom's house. He's bound to be at one of those two places sooner or later."

Linda left the tent and went to the camper. Snake was busy cutting his hair and Bear was counting the money again.

Linda asked him for a cigarette. When he gave her one, she went to get her shoulder bag for her lighter. She always kept a pencil and pad inside her bag. Then she lit the cigarette, put the bag over her shoulder. While contemplating her next move, she returned to the tent.

Chapter 67

Santino reached over and punched the alarm button on the clock radio. It was 6:00am and time to get going. He swung his legs out of the bed and reached over and yanked the pillow out from under Ramone's head.

Ramone jumped up and grabbed for the pistol he always kept on the nightstand next to him. It wasn't there.

It was then that he saw Santino grinning at him and realized where he was. He shook his finger at Santino and said, "Hey man, you shouldn't do that, you might get shot."

Santino, who was holding Ramone's pistol in his hand, said, "What are you gonna shoot me with, your dick?"

With that they both laughed and Santino said, "Come on; get your greasy ass out of bed. It's time to find our money!"

They checked out of the motel and headed toward Rome. About a mile and a half down Rt. 411, they found a Waffle House. They both agreed they were hungry and they pulled into the restaurant.

As soon as they had gotten coffee and ordered breakfast, they began to plan what they were going to do.

Santino asked Ramone if he still had the "fake" Detective's badge he'd purchased at a novelty shop in Miami.

When Ramone pulled it out of his pocket and

showed it to him, Santino said, "Ok, we're gonna tell these used-car dealers that you and I are part of the task force working on this big crime spree we heard about on the radio. Your name is Detective Ramirez and mine is Detective Cruz. Just flash the badge fast and hope nobody looks at it too closely."

Ramone nodded and said, "Yeah, right but this could take all damn day! Why don't we use the pay phone outside and see if we can't cut down on some of the legwork?"

Santino reached into his pocket and pulled out the two yellow pages he had taken from the motel room. He handed one of the pages to Ramone and said, "You go outside to the phone booth and I'll use the one back by the rest rooms. It'll go quicker if we split it up."

Santino got the waitresses' attention and when she came over to their table, he asked for the check and two coffees to go. He told her he would be at the pay phone in the back.

Ramone had already gone out to the phone booth, in the parking lot, and had started calling the listings on the second page. They began with "Silver Fox Used-Cars".

When Santino got to the pay phone he realized that he didn't have any change. He went back to the cash register where his waitress had just finished putting lids on the two paper cups of coffee and was completing the sales check. He paid the check and got two dollars worth of change.

Chapter 68

When the phone rang at ABC Auto Sales, Sandy geared herself up for another day at the "salt mines" and conjured up her best happy, sexy sales voice. "ABC Auto Sales, Good Morning. If you're alive, we can help you drive. My name is Sandy. What can we put you in today?"

Even as she repeated the words, Sandy thought how she was sick of this line. Maybe she and Manny could come up with something better. She knew that if she had to keep saying this stupid line, she was going to barf.

The voice on the other end of the line was somewhat gruff. It had both an official sound as well as a hint of an accent. It said, "Hello, let me speak to the manager!"

Sandy responded, "I'm sorry, but the owner won't be in until about nine. He always stops for breakfast with his local merchant buddies on Friday morning. Is there something I can help you with?"

Santino paused for a second then said, "My name is Detective Ray Cruz. I'm with the Major Crime Unit and we need some information. Maybe you could help us." Sandy really knew she should wait for Mandy to handle this, but this sounded like it might be exciting and her curiosity got the better of her. She said, "What is it you need to know Detective?"

"I'm sure you've heard about the robberies and killings, in this area, over the last couple of days. Well we're checking out all of the used car lots around here.

There's a good chance that the people involved in these crimes will be switching vehicles, since the one they were using has been identified and reported all over the news."

Sandy said, "How are you going to know if it's the right one? A lot of cars and trucks get sold around here every day."

That's true, but we don't think that too many are paid for in cash and we know that these folks have plenty of that", replied Santino. "How about it, have you made any cash sales yesterday or today?"

Sandy remembered the young girl who had purchased the Chevy wagon yesterday, but she was a local mom with kids. Sandy was concerned that she might unnecessarily get her involved in a mess if she said anything. On the other hand, if this really was a cop, she could get herself into a lot of trouble by lying….. "That was it!" she thought, "How do I even know this guy is a cop?"

"Detective, we did sell a car for cash yesterday, but to be perfectly honest, I'm not comfortable giving out any more information on the phone. How do I know you are who you say you are?"

Santino had expected that this might happened and went along with the play. "Sandy, you are one hundred percent right in being cautious. You never know who might be trying to get information from you or why. My partner and I will stop by your office within the hour and show you our I.D. How about giving me the directions to your lot?"

Sandy explained exactly where they were located and hung up the phone. She hoped that this wouldn't be one of Manny's long-winded, story-telling breakfasts. She wasn't sure how much she should tell the Detectives and she would feel a lot more comfortable if Manny got to the office before they arrived.

Chapter 69

Mike Sullivan was awakened by the sound of rain pattering on the bedroom window. Anne Marie had gotten up earlier without disturbing his sound sleep. The pleasant smell of fresh coffee was tantalizing. He went into the bathroom and threw some water on his face. He grabbed a hand towel from the rack and was drying his hands as he walked into the kitchen.

"Good Mornin' beautiful." He said, as he accepted the steaming cup she offered. "Looks like we got a little summer rain to help cool things off some." Sitting down at the kitchen table, he reached for the sports section of the paper that Anne Marie had gone out in the rain to get for him.

She leaned over, gave him a peck on the cheek and said, "I love the smell of a summer rain, but you know it'll all be gone by noon and the humidity will be awful."

Mike checked his watch and realized that he had slept in 'til almost ten. He didn't know if it was due to the sound of the rain or if he was just that tired. He got up and went to the phone. He dialed the desk sergeant's number and waited until heard Sergeant Gifford's familiar voice. "Hey "Giff", Mike Sullivan here. Have you heard anything from Angela on this Four Lane thing?"

"Morning Mike, I understand you had a busy night, but to answer your question, yes. I talked to the crime lab a few minutes ago. They identified the bikers who got taken out at the McCord's "Farm Fresh" store."

The girl, with the nine-millimeter slug in her face was a Rachel Lee Brevard. The biker who took the hit from the baseball bat was a Philip Charles Gorman. They both had driver's licenses on them. They're local, small time, Georgia trash, mostly misdemeanor stuff. Both of them have drug use problems and Gorman did eighteen months for burglary. We didn't have any paper on the four bodies taken from Red Top, but Angela ran their fingerprints and came up with an I.D. on the dead girl.

Her name was Shelley Ann Moran. This one is definitely interesting. She's also a local Georgia gal with a few small drug possession busts, but here's the interesting part. We checked her out at the Motor Vehicle Administration and found out that she bought a car yesterday. Now, answer this one for me. How does a dead girl buy a car?" Mike almost dropped his favorite coffee mug when he heard the news.

"Damn Giff! Maybe we finally caught a break. Do we know where the car was bought?"

"Hold on Mike, I have it right here. I was just getting ready to call them. Here it is. It's ABC Auto Sales up in Rome. The number is 747-1594. Got it?"

"Yep, I'll give them a call myself right now. I'll touch base with you when I'm done."

Chapter 70

Sandy saw the Camaro pull onto the lot and watched as Manny got himself in position to greet the new prospects. As the two Latino men got out of the Car, Manny felt the hair on the back of his neck bristle. There weren't many Latinos in this neck of the woods.

Santino didn't hesitate. He pulled the "fake" badge out of his pocket, flashed it at Manny and said, "I'm Detective Cruz and this is Detective Ramirez, we spoke to someone here named Sandy, about an hour ago concerning an investigation we are on. Who are you?"

Sandy had filled Manny in on the phone call from the detective and while it might have explained the appearance of these out-of-towners, he was still somewhat ill at ease.

"I'm Manny Goldberg and I am the owner of this lot. Sandy is my assistant and she told me to expect you. Why don't we go into the office and see what we can do to help the police department?"

As they entered the office, Santino looked at Sandy and said, "You must be Sandy. We spoke earlier on the phone."

The office was small as would be expected for a small town used car lot. Sandy's metal desk was backed up by filing cabinets and faced across the room to a much larger desk made of cherry hardwood, which obviously belonged to Manny. A medium sized safe sat on the floor next to his desk.

There was a straight-backed chair sitting next to Sandy's desk.

In front of Manny's desk, there was a low circular table with Car & Driver magazines stacked neatly on top. There were three padded chairs arranged around the table. Behind Sandy, on top of the filing cabinets, were two coffeepots each full of hot, fresh brewed coffee, one regular and one decaffeinated.

A large picture window covered the wall behind Manny's desk. It offered a full view of the auto lot and the driveway into the property.

Sandy stood up from her desk and stretched out her hand toward the table and chairs. "Why don't you sit here, would you care for a cup of coffee?" she said.

Ramone, who to this point had not spoken, said, "We are kinda in a hurry, how about just giving us the information on the car you sold for cash yesterday."

Manny sensed that something was not right. Both the accent and the tone of this man's voice caused him concern. He said, "Would you mind if I took a closer look at your credentials? A businessman can't be too careful. Am I right?"

Ramone and Santino took a quick glance at each other and nodded. Santino reached around his back and pulled a pistol from a holster in his belt. As he aimed it at Manny, Ramone withdrew a switchblade from an ankle sheath, flipped it open and grabbed Sandy from behind. He said, "We want that information now! Show her we mean business." With that, Santino shot Manny twice in the chest and once in the head.

Sandy couldn't believe what she was seeing and began to scream. Ramone pressed the blade to her throat and whispered in her ear to be quiet. "Now, where is the information we want?"

She tried to control herself and find some way out of this. Pointing to the safe she said, "It's in there, but only Manny had the combination."

Chapter 71

When the phone rang at ABC Auto Sales, it startled all three people in the room. Ramone was still holding Sandy with his knife to her throat. Santino had just finished closing the blinds behind Manny's desk and putting the "**Out-To-Lunch, We-Will-Be-Back-At**" sign in the window of the door.

Santino looked at Sandy and said, "If you don't want to join your boss, you better do exactly what I tell you! Now, answer the phone with the speaker and keep your eyes on me."

Sandy knew they were serious and she would do anything she could to try to get out of this alive. She nodded her head and stammered, "Anything you say." She pressed the answer speaker button and said, "ABC Auto Sales, Good Morning. If you're alive we can help you drive. My name is Sandy. What can we put you in today?"

As she was repeating this hated phrase, she could see Manny's body lying on the floor. She couldn't help thinking that no one would ever be helped to drive by Manny again.

A man's voice at the other end, somewhat tinny through the speakerphone, said, "Hello Sandy, this is Detective Mike Sullivan with the Macon Police Department. I need to ask you some questions."

Santino immediately remembered the name from the radio news. He slid next to Sandy and whispered,

"Answer his questions and don't let on that anything is wrong."

Trying to control her fear and sound as calm as possible, Sandy said, "How can I help you Detective Sullivan?

Mike explained to her that someone claiming to be a local woman, who the police knew to be deceased, had purchased a car at ABC's lot, yesterday. Then he asked her if she recalled a woman customer, who said her name was Shelley Ann Moran.

Sandy looked at Santino for direction and he whispered, "Go on tell him everything you know."

Santino thought to himself, "This might work out better than we hoped."

Sandy answered the Detective. "Yes, she bought a blue 1972 Chevrolet Caprice station wagon and she paid for it with cash."

"Alright, Mike replied, that's good. That agrees with the MVA record. I'm going to ask the local Rome police to follow up with you, since I'm in Macon. Was anyone else there when you sold the car?"

"Yes my boss, Mister Goldberg. He actually made the sale, but he's not available right now."

Mike said, "Well try to contact him and let him know that we need to talk to him as soon as possible. Will you be there for the rest of the afternoon?"

Sandy looked at Santino and he nodded yes.

"Yes, she answered", and she hoped it was true; "I'll still be here."

Chapter 72

By 8:00 am, the wagon was packed up. The two briefcases, with the money, were safely stowed in the back with the spare tire. Linda, Carol and Gloria were in the back seat and Bear was driving.

Snake had wanted to burn the motor home to destroy as much evidence as possible. Bear told him he was stupid to think that the cops didn't already know who they were and besides the smoke and fire would just draw more attention to where they had been and in what direction they might be headed.

As was always the case, Bear won the argument, and they were now on the road toward Chilhowee Mountain in Tennessee. They had left Rome on Rte. 411 and woven their way North and East. When they crossed the line into Tennessee, Bear somehow felt more at ease. In another hour or so they would reach the Rte. 72 cutoff and be "headed for the hills", the Smokey Mountain kind.

Bear had been camping in this area a few years back. He knew that they could easily lose themselves in the heavily wooded area of Chilhowee Mountain. Once they were there, he and Snake would take care of the three girls.

Snake, on the other hand, would be a little trickier. Bear had already decided there was too much money at stake to trust a partner. If he was going to get away clean, he needed all the money and what he didn't need was Snake.

Part Three

Into Tennessee

Chapter 73

The Bear

Even for July, it was extremely hot. You could say that it was comfortable for neither man nor beast.

Normally, this fast running stream would have been considered "lukewarm" at best. But on this particular day, he found it to be quite refreshing.

He had walked all night foraging for his next meal and up until now he had not met with any success. His keen eyes focused on the passing waters, searching for any sign of edible movement.

He watched the water bubble, as it came into contact with the small rocks and larger boulders, causing it to turn white as it flowed into them then back to clear as it successfully navigated around them. His sensitive ears would alert him to any dining potential in the surrounding woods. His paws were fully submerged and he found the effect to be quite pleasant. Every now and then he would lower his head into the cooling waters.

His skull would measure twenty-one on the "Boone and Crockett" scale.

It was the middle of the afternoon and he really would have preferred to be sleeping. Usually, he would hunt in the evenings and after dark, but the hunger pangs in his stomach won out over his normal instincts.

The sound of buzzing, and all that it promised,

became an overwhelming temptation, which ultimately lured him away from this pleasant place.

The "Ursus Americanus" or Black Bear, as he was more commonly known, slowly began to move his four hundred and fifty pounds away from the stream and closer to the enticing, familiar sound.

The tree that held this afternoon's delicacy was surrounded by thick foliage that extended for twenty yards in all directions. The bees that had stayed behind to guard their treasure were no match for the heavy fur that protected him from their anger. The few stings he might get, on his unprotected nose, would be well worth the reward. Without any hesitation, he stuck his nose into the hive and began to curb his hunger at the expense of all their hard work.

Chapter 74

Mike called information and got the number he needed. The voice on the other end said, "Rome Police Department, Desk Sergeant Foley speaking."

Mike identified himself and brought the sergeant up to speed on the situation. He asked if they would send someone over to ABC Auto, to take a statement from a girl named Sandy and her boss, a Mr. Goldberg.

Sergeant Foley said, "You're Mike Sullivan, right? Paul Robbins and I work cases together quite often. I'm Ted Foley. Say "Hi" to Paul for me the next time you see him.

Mike, we've all been keeping a lookout for these biker bastards. Let me get right on it and I'll put out an APB on the car." Mike thanked Foley and asked him to call him at home, once his people had interviewed the folks at ABC Auto.

Officer Pat Flynn was hot and bored. It seemed like the heat would never let up, but that was par for the course in Rome at this time of year. He had pulled radio car # 4 into the Texaco station at the corner of I-411 & Main street to get a coke and to take a quick smoke. He sat in the car, with the door open, to minimize the effect of his cigarette smoke. From this position, he could see up and down 411 for two blocks in either direction.

At that moment, two things happened at the same time. He heard Sergeant Foley's voice over the radio asking if any cars were close to downtown.

As he picked up the mike to respond, he observed

a black Camaro turning right onto I-411 from Lanier. Officer Flynn saw the car run through the stop sign, at the corner, making no attempt to slow down.

Simultaneously, he turned on the "bubblegum" light on top of the cruiser and responded to the radio call. "Sergeant, this is car 4. I'm at 411 & Main and I'm about to get a stop-sign runner."

"Pat, unless that runner is driving a 1972, blue, Caprice wagon forget him. We have a lead on the motorcycle gang killings and I want you on it right away."

"No, Sarge, he isn't. It's a '78 black Camaro. Where do you want me to go?"

The sergeant barked, "ABC Auto Sales on Lanier and report back to me right away."

Pat Flynn put the coke in a cup-holder attached to his window, tossed the spent cigarette butt in the general direction of a trash can and pulled out onto I-411. The Camaro was just then passing Pat's patrol car and he noticed that the tag was out-of-state. This made him doubly pissed.

Pat murmured under his breath, "This is your lucky day, asshole. I better not see you in my town again"

Chapter 75

Santino saw the lights on the cop car begin to flash and said, "What the fuck is this?" He told Ramone to slow down, and they both put their guns between their legs.

As the police car passed them, they could both see the scowl on the face of the cop. But to their relief, he raced right past them. "Quick! Wheel into this Texaco station and let's top off the tank. We got some drivin' to do."

Ramone pulled the Camaro in next to the pump and got out of the car. He filled the tank with "High Test" and paid the attendant with cash. As he pulled back out onto the road, he asked Santino where they were going.

Santino looked at him and said, "We need to get as far away from here as fast as we can. We know what the assholes that have our money are driving, but we got no idea where they are. I think we should let the law do the legwork for us. This Detective, Mike Sullivan, seems to know the most about this and we know something about him."

Ramone looked at Santino quizzically and asked, "What do we know about him?"

Santino smiled and answered, "We know he lives in Macon. We're headed south."

Chapter 76

Since the bedroom area of the house was pretty messed up, Johnny, Pete and Beverly placed blankets and pillows on the living room floor, and that's where they slept.

Fortunately, the hall bathroom was undamaged. Beverly took advantage of that fact when she awakened before the boys. It felt great to be able to take a long, hot shower and put on some of the new, fresh clothes she had bought.

Johnny and Pete slept in 'til almost 11:00am and she had resisted the temptation to wake them up any earlier. She knew that they were both tired and needed all the rest they could get for the day ahead.

The smell of fresh coffee rousted Pete from his sleep and he poked Johnny in the side, to get him up.

They followed their noses to the kitchen and when they got there they saw that Bev had arranged three place settings, and was pouring the coffee into their cups.

She looked at them with a smile and said, "The frying pan is heated up. Do you want eggs or pancakes?"

Pete and Johnny looked at each other and in one voice replied, "How about both?"

As they ate breakfast they went over the events of the past two days. "Was it only two days?" Beverly thought. It seemed like forever since she had slammed through that screen door!

Pete took a sip of coffee and said, "The worst part is the waiting, the not knowing. I want to do something, but what?"

Beverly reached out and put her hand on Pete's hand. She had gone through a lot these last two days, but she knew it was nothing compared with what Pete was dealing with. She could only imagine how fearful he was for his sister, his wife and the baby.

Johnny said, "I know, Pete, this sucks, but all we can do now is wait for a call from the girls or from Mike Sullivan."

Almost as if he had willed it to happen, the phone on the kitchen wall began to ring.

Johnny jumped up from the table and grabbed the phone and said, "Hello." He couldn't help thinking, "Let it be the girls!" It wasn't.

"Hi Johnny, it's Mike Sullivan." Johnny sighed in disappointment and responded, "Hi Mike. Please tell us some good news."

"Well I can't say it's good or bad, but we think we have a lead on the vehicle they are driving now. It seems as though they switched to a blue 1972 Chevy Caprice wagon. They've probably dumped the camper by now. I've got the Rome police checking it out for me and I'll get back to you as soon as we know more."

"Rome! Where the hell are they going?

Mike said, "I know, it's frustrating. We've alerted the North Carolina and Tennessee State Police to be on the lookout for the wagon. Just stay put! Call me if you hear from the girls."

Johnny thanked the detective and hung up the phone. He noticed that the clock on the kitchen wall had just passed noon.

Chapter 77

Just as he had remembered, Route #129 took them to Foothills Parkway. Once he got there, Bear found an old dirt road and took it to the end. It was completely wooded and well hidden. It ran right along the edge of Chilhowee Lake.

Linda had been paying close attention to where they were. If she got the chance to run, she wanted to be sure she knew the way out.

Gloria was virtually passed out for the whole trip and Linda was really concerned for her and the baby. In no way did Linda consider herself a saint, but, she hadn't signed on for any of this and it was all just going downhill as the hours passed.

It had taken a little longer than Bear had said it would. It was 1:00pm when they arrived and when they got out of the wagon, the heat hit them like a blast furnace.

Linda told Bear that they should open all the windows and let Gloria lie down in the back seat, while they set up camp.

Bear said, "I don't give a shit. She ain't gonna be much use to us anyhow and as long as I've got the car keys, she ain't goin' anywhere." Then he grabbed Carol by the arm, pulled her out of the back seat and said, "There ain't nothin' wrong with you. Get your ass out of there and help."

The four of them unloaded the station wagon and Carol and Linda began to set up the tent.

Since they no longer had the benefit of the station wagon's air conditioner, both Bear and Snake removed their jackets and immediately felt relief from the heat in their thin t-shirts.

Snake went over to a tree that had a substantial trunk and was located very close to the edge of the lake. He began passing the time by throwing his knife, "Baby", into the tree trunk. He missed it much more often than he hit it.

After his last miss, as he bent over to pick the knife up, he cocked his head to the side and saw Carol reaching up to attach the front of the tent to the tent pole. He quickly became bored with knife throwing and his mind drifted, once again, to his fixation about what a sweet piece of ass she would be.

He decided that he wasn't going to wait much longer to find out and if Bear tried to stop him again he would be ready for him. Snake picked up the knife and decided that he could wait until the tent was up. It didn't hurt to be comfortable.

Linda had secured the back of the tent and was standing to the side, out of the sight of Bear and Snake. She whispered to Carol, "Don't look at me, just keep doing what you're doing and listen!"

Carol had noticed that Snake was ogling her and she was becoming even more concerned than before.

Linda said, "When I bought the car, they gave me two sets of keys. Bear has one set, but I still have the other. Here's the hard part. I don't know if we can both make it to the car without them stopping one of us, but

I promise I'll get Gloria to a hospital and send help for you if you don't make it."

Carol paused for a moment and considered what Linda was saying. While she was in fear for her own life, she knew that Gloria had no chance to defend herself.

Carol thought that if Linda could at least get Gloria away from these monsters, she could live……..or die with that.

She nodded to Linda and whispered, "How do we do this?"

Bear had been busy piling up logs to build a makeshift table for the propane stove. He saw Snake screwing off, as usual, throwing his stupid knife into a tree. He thought, "The asshole thinks he's fuckin' Daniel Boone."

He was just about to say something to Snake, when he heard Carol say, "I want to go and check on my sister-in-law."

Bear turned to face her and said, "Bullshit, you stay in the damn tent where I can keep my eye on you." He turned his head in Linda's direction and said, "Hey, go check on the little bitch in the car!" Linda smiled at Bear thinking, "This is my chance," and said, "No problem, boss."

Bear looked over at Snake and said, "I gotta take a shit, keep your eye on the girls." He grabbed a roll of toilet paper from the supplies and disappeared into the deep foliage.

Snake watched as Linda walked toward the wagon,

which was parked about twenty-five yards away from the center of the campsite.

When they first arrived at the camping area, Bear had turned the wagon around and backed in to what served as a parking space to make it easier to unload.

He had also considered the possible need for a quick escape and if that situation arose, he didn't want to have to turn the station wagon around.

As Snake watched Bear go into the woods, he looked over at the tent and decided he had waited long enough. With the knife still in his hand, he moved to the tent, opened the flap and slipped inside.

Linda watched Snake go into the tent. Quietly, she opened the back door of the wagon and grabbed her purse. As she retrieved the second set of car keys from the depths of her purse, she turned to Gloria, smiled and put her finger to her lips. "Shhh," she said, "We're getting out of here now."

She could see Gloria's face brighten at this news. As weak as she was and as bad as she felt, Gloria's spirits were immediately lifted. Then, just as quickly, the look of concern returned to Gloria's face and she whispered, "But, what about Carol?"

Chapter 78

Having eaten his fill of the glorious honey, the bear began to lumber on through the woods. All of his senses told him that there was a larger body of water ahead and he knew that meant fish.

As he moved through the woods, he also became aware of certain sounds that were different from the normal sounds of the woods. Human sounds!

Since it was still daylight, he decided to wait until dark, before investigating. He found a particularly dense growth of foliage and moved to the middle of it. He reclined on the soft grass and closed his eyes.

While he rested, his keen ears stayed alert for any sound that might require his immediate attention and it wasn't long before he heard something of interest.

Chapter 79

As Officer Flynn pulled onto the lot at ABC Auto Sales, he instinctively knew something was wrong. The big, front window blinds were closed and it was the middle of the day.

He drove as close as possible to the front door. His suspicion was only increased when he saw the "Out-to-lunch" sign displayed in the window of the front door. The arrows of its clock were pointing to 1:00 o'clock. It was only 10:45 and why would they go to lunch when they knew he was coming?

Pat took out his service revolver and got out of the squad car. He walked to the front door and tried the handle. It was unlocked. He pushed the door open quickly and put his other hand on his revolver to achieve a firm, two-handed shooting stance.

There were no lights on in the office, but the sunlight streaming through the open door was all that was necessary.

Pat had been on the force for twelve years, but had never seen anything like this!

Sandy Bennett was a nice girl. She was only a year younger than Pat. They had gone to Coosa High School together. When Pat was nine, he had been very ill. He was held back a grade and he and Sandy had actually graduated in the same year.

Sandy had married a fellow named Paul Bennett right after graduation.

Paul went off to Vietnam in 1972, like thousands of other young kids. But Paul never made it back home.

"Sandy was a great gal, everyone liked her", Pat thought. "She didn't deserve this."

Pat checked for signs of life from Sandy and Manny Goldberg. Finding none, he carefully backed out of the office in order to insure no further contamination of the crime scene.

He holstered his weapon and reached through the open window of the patrol car for his radio microphone. Depressing the "talk" button he said, "This is Officer Flynn in car 4."

Sergeant Foley's familiar voice replied, "Go ahead Pat."

"Sarge, it's really bad. We got two dead, Sandy Bennett and Manny Goldberg. I need some help out here and I need it right now!"

At first there was utter silence on the other end. Pat could visualize Sergeant Foley trying to contain his anger. Finally, in a low measured voice, he heard Foley say, "Son of a Bitch Pat! Stay with them until I get the coroner and forensics out there. I'll send another car to help you check for witnesses."

Chapter 80

Linda started walking toward the wagon and Carol went inside the tent. For once, Carol hoped that Snake would follow her into the tent. She planned to distract Snake just enough to provide Linda with the time she needed to get Gloria away from here.

Sure enough, Carol heard footsteps coming toward the tent. Within seconds, she saw Snake stooping over and entering through the tent flaps.

She was all the more petrified when she saw the ugly sneer on his face and the knife in his hand, but she had bought into this plan to save Gloria and she wasn't about to back out of it now.

Snake walked up to her so that his chest was almost brushing her face. He looked at her and said, "Well it looks like we finally got a little quality alone time." He lifted the hand that held the knife and flicked the blade against the top button of her blouse. "I've been looking forward to this ever since we left Marietta. I want to see what you've got hiding under there. You can start with this button!"

Carol's plan had been to push past him and run into the woods, but he still had the knife in his hand. With tears beginning to flow down her cheeks, she pointed at the knife and said, "You don't need that, I'll do whatever you say and I won't give you any trouble. Just don't hurt me."

Snake laughed at her, sheathed the knife and said, "Sure, just make sure you give me a good show.

Carol backed up a step and with her hands shaking, slowly began to unbutton her blouse. As the last button was unfastened, her blouse spread apart revealing her bra. It was the kind that clipped in the front. Snake decided that this time he would open it himself. He made a guttural sound and reached out to unhook the clasp. Carol was looking directly at Snake's face and could see that he was not even aware of her stare. His greedy eyes were transfixed on her breasts.

As he anticipated what was to come, he was surprised to find out that it wasn't what he had been looking forward to.

Carol heard the station wagon's engine come to life a few seconds before Snake realized what was happening.

She could see the initial confusion on his face and hoped that this just might be the chance she was waiting for. Probably, she thought, it would be her last chance.

The glaze went out of Snake's eyes and he began to curse. He spun around and rushed out of the tent, knocking down the front tent pole on his way out.

Carol followed closely behind him pushing the falling tent out of the way, to avoid becoming trapped. She watched as he ran toward the station wagon, pulling out the .38, that he taken from the dead man at Red Top. He began to fire it at the moving car.

Carol saw that there was deep brush to the left of where Snake was running and she quickly ran off in that direction.

Chapter 81

After dispatching the coroner and the crime lab unit along with two other patrol cars to ABC Auto Sales, Sergeant Foley dialed Mike Sullivan's home phone number.

Mike was helping Anne Marie clean up the breakfast dishes and trying to decide whether or not to go into the office. He was still pondering this decision, when the phone rang.

He quickly dried his hands, tossed the dishtowel onto the drain board of the sink and grabbed the ringing phone. "Mike Sullivan here."

"Mike, this is Ted Foley up in Rome. I've got some bad news for you! I sent a car over to check out your lead from ABC Auto and, when he got there, it looked like a slaughterhouse! He found Sandy, the girl you spoke to, and her boss Manny Goldberg both dead."

"Whoa, Hold on Sergeant, what the hell's going on here?"

"I don't know, Mike, but the girl's throat was slit and Goldberg was shot execution style. Somehow this doesn't look like the work of any motorcycle punks."

Mike sat down on a kitchen chair shaking his head. He was totally thrown off by this information and didn't know what to say to Ted.

"Detective, are you still there?" Mike realized that he had created a pregnant pause in the conversation and quickly replied, "Yeah Ted, sorry, I'm still here but I'm kinda at a loss for words. Why would the bikers come back, wouldn't they be long gone by now?"

"That's the way I read it too Mike, but I don't believe in coincidence. There's got to be a connection."

"Did your guys find any witnesses?"

"Not yet. In fact I just sent the team out to do just that. I only had one man on the scene and I told him to stay put at the crime scene."

Now it was Mike's turn to hear dead air on the line. Sergeant Foley was recalling his conversation with Officer Pat Flynn, when he had first given him the call.

Finally, he broke the silence and said, "Mike, this may be way out in left field but, when I first gave this call to my patrol officer, there was something he said. It didn't seem important, at the time, but now I can't help wondering."

"Go with your gut, Ted. That's what we do... right?"

"Ok, Mike, here's the deal. My guy, Officer Pat Flynn, was parked only a few blocks from ABC Auto. He was sitting at Main Street & I-411. He had a good view of the corner of I-411& Lanier. Lanier is the street that the auto lot is on. Anyhow, Officer Flynn observed a black Camaro running the stop sign at Lanier & I-411. The Camaro would have been coming from the direction of ABC and whoever was in it was obviously in a big hurry. This could only have been minutes after you and I talked about your call to Sandy Bennett. Shit! Mike, he was going to pull the Camaro over and I told him to let it go."

"You know, Ted, if they are the ones who did it

and they're professionals, you just may have saved that officer's life."

"As soon as we hang up, I'm going to get hold of Ted. I'll find out if he remembers anything else. It's time to share this with the State Police and ask them to involve Tennessee & the Carolinas as well. Let's face it, we don't know who they are, why or if they did it and we've got no damn clue as to where they're headed."

"Well Sergeant, before you called, I was trying to decide whether or not to go into the office. Now I don't think there's any question about it. I'm headed in right now. This way I'll be able to monitor any buzz from the state boys. Give me a call if you get any additional information and I'll do the same for you."

Mike grabbed his wallet and car keys and gave Anne Marie a hug. He told her that things were getting complicated and he needed to get to the office. As he was reaching for the front door, the phone rang. Anne Marie picked up the phone and addressed the voice on the other end. Mike turned around and looked at Anne Marie. She said, "It's for you", and she extended the hand holding the phone to Mike.

Chapter 82

Linda slid the key into the ignition and turned, praying that the wagon would start. She knew it would only be a matter of seconds before Snake and Bear would react. Looking into the rearview mirror, she saw Snake running toward them and pointing a gun. She also saw Carol running off to her left. Gloria was now sitting up in the back seat and she saw Carol. She screamed, "Don't leave her, please!"

Linda's first impulse was to get out of there as fast as she could, but at the last moment, she couldn't bring herself to leave Carol to the fate she knew would befall her, if they left her behind.

Without any further hesitation, Linda slammed the gearshift into reverse and floored the accelerator.

Snake was still screaming and cursing as he continued to shoot at the rear window of the wagon. He realized, too late, that instead of pulling away from him, the station wagon was getting larger and larger as it came directly at him. He was totally unprepared for this and before he could react, the back bumper of the wagon smashed into him.

The blow lifted him off his feet and tossed him like a rag doll. The only reason he didn't land in the lake was that his body had no trouble hitting the tree that his new knife could not.

Linda slammed on the brakes, pulled the transmission into drive and, once again, jammed the accelerator down, this time moving the station wagon forward.

Finally, they were going to get away from this place, away from Bear, away from Snake and away from all of the killing!

Chapter 83

Bear couldn't believe what his ears were telling him. He had just finished taking a much-needed crap and was pulling up his pants when he heard the gunshots.

Hurriedly, he shoved in his shirt, hooked his belt then reached over and picked up the Browning 9mm that he had left lying on the ground while he did his business.

Rushing out into the campsite he tried to take in what was happening. The first thing he saw was Snake sprawled out next to the tree by the lake. He didn't appear to be moving. He wheeled around and looked toward where he had parked the station wagon. It was gone!

He was confused because he could feel the keys in his right-hand pocket. Then it occurred to him, "Two sets of keys, she had two sets of keys, Son-of-a-bitch", he screamed.

Everything seemed to be falling apart. He couldn't even trust Snake to watch the girls for ten minutes without fucking up. Now the girls were gone, the wagon was gone and so was the money.

He ran past Snake and the tent and onto the dirt road where he had parked the wagon. After running about thirty yards, he could see that the road turned off to the right. He could just see around the corner of the road and he spotted the red brake lights on the wagon. They had stopped!

He realized that he was too far away to get off an

accurate shot and he couldn't see anything specific to shoot at. He decided to cut through the brush and try to get in front of them.

He thought, "That fucking Linda, I'm gonna make her pay for this. I'll make them all pay!"

Chapter 84

All of the commotion caused him to grudgingly forego his nap and roll up onto all fours. His natural tendency was to move away from these kinds of noises. The only noise that sounded somewhat familiar was the cracking sound that he heard.

He had heard this kind of sound, in the past; when tree branches had been broken off by a strong wind.

But these cracks were much louder and disturbed his ears. As he turned to leave this place, he felt a sudden pain in his shoulder and it burned. Bees had stung him many times, but his thick fur had always protected him. Occasionally, he had been stung on the nose and that had hurt. ………..This was much worse!

He pulled himself up to his full height, balancing easily on his two hind legs. This put his head and eyes over seven feet above the ground. He was now able to see clearly over the vegetation and into the clearing just in front of the lake. As he turned his massive head he both saw and heard something moving rapidly through the underbrush. Wild with pain and anger, he returned to all fours and took off after his prey.

Chapter 85

Carol kept the dirt road to her right and fought her way through the thick underbrush. As she ran, she tried to button her blouse. She didn't dare to turn around and look back in fear of stumbling. She knew that if Snake caught her he would kill her.

She stayed in the underbrush until she saw the road turn off to the right. She worked her way back to the road and looked back toward the campsite. She saw the station wagon coming up the road toward her position.

As the wagon passed her, she could see that Linda was driving and Gloria was looking out of the window from the back seat. Carol jumped out into the road behind the wagon, frantically waving her arms in the air and screamed, "I'm here, I'm here!"

Gloria saw Carol standing in the road, now about twenty yards behind them and she grabbed Linda's shoulder as hard as she could. "Stop!" she wailed, it's Carol. Please stop!"

Linda immediately slammed on the brakes, reached over and pushed open the front passenger's door.

Carol ran toward the open car door as fast as she could. She was just about to grab hold of the door when she heard an angry, familiar voice shout, "Where the hell do you think you're going?"

Chapter 86

Even though he was a big man, Bear was very fast. He had chosen an angle that would put him ahead of the stopped car and he slammed through the brush as if it were not even there.

When he got to the road he was only fifteen feet in front of the stopped station wagon. He could see Carol running toward the open front door and just before she got there he stepped into the middle of the road and pointed the Browning directly at her. When he screamed her name, she stopped dead in her tracks.

Linda couldn't believe what she was seeing. She had been sure that they were home free. Her first impulse was to hit the gas and take her chances, but just as she was considering this move she saw Bear swing the gun away from Carol and point it through the windshield, directly at her.

He yelled, "Shut it down!" To punctuate his point, he screamed, "If you think I'm fuckin' around here, I'm not!" and with that he shot off the driver's side-view mirror and re-aimed the gun at her face.

All three girls jumped at the sound of the gun. Linda quickly put the shifter in Park and turned off the ignition.

Bear motioned with the gun, for Carol to move away from the wagon and he told Linda and Gloria to get out and join her. Seeing the crazed look in Bear's eyes, they all knew that this was the end.

Chapter 87

Nothing could stop the bear now. His basic nature was in full control. He knew he was close to his prey. Then he heard another high-pitched crack come from just in front of him. He ran directly at the sound, determined to put an end to it the only way he knew how.

Chapter 88

The three girls did what they were told and moved away from the car. Bear smiled a gruesome smile, raised the 9mm and pointed it at Linda. He was going to tell the dumb bitch that she had brought this on herself, and then he would kill her.

Before he could put this thought into words, his senses became overwhelmed with a terrifying cacophony of sight and sound.

Simultaneously a blur of brown filled his vision and a horrific howling filled his ears.

William Robert Masterson was no longer the "Bear".

This was the bear and it was not, in the least, impressed by William.

Without slowing down, the bear slammed into him, pushing him off the road and into the trees. His reaction to the blow caused Bear to squeeze the trigger on the Browning. The now familiar cracking sound of this wild shot further infuriated the bear. It wrapped powerful jaws around the arm that held the gun. As it violently shook its massive head back and forth the arm was ripped free from the body.

Bear heard the gun go off but was not aware that he was still holding it in his hand, because the arm that the hand was part of was no longer attached to him. Then he felt the most excruciating pain he had ever felt. It was though a thousand red-hot needles had been plunged into his right shoulder. He knew that he no longer controlled his own body, as he felt it being tossed from side to side.

The blood flowed freely from the open wound in his shoulder. This severe loss of blood coupled with the overall shock to his body caused him to swoon.

Mercifully, he never really felt the bear's powerful jaws as its razor sharp teeth ripped out his throat.

Chapter 89

All three girls were screaming in horror as they watched the unthinkable happening in front of their eyes.

Carol was the first to come to her senses and she grabbed Gloria and pushed her through the open door into the back seat of the station wagon. At the same time, she called out, "Linda, Linda, Get back in the car!"

In what seemed to take forever, but was really only a few seconds, Carol saw Linda jump into the front passenger's seat and slide over behind the wheel. Carol slammed the back door shut and jumped into the front next to Linda.

Fortunately, the keys were still in the ignition and now Linda didn't hesitate. She switched on the ignition, slammed the gearshift into drive and floored it. The rear tires spit out two arcs of dirt as the car flew past the mayhem that was in process. The girls averted their eyes and their minds as best they could. They had already seen and heard enough and they knew, collectively, that they couldn't handle much more.

Chapter 90

Johnny knew they couldn't just sit here and do nothing. He saw that Beverly was doing her best to console Pete, but it wasn't enough. He looked at them both and said, "Let's get the hell out of here. We can go to the "Farm" store" and start putting the place back together."

Beverly asked Johnny if the store wasn't still a crime scene and suggested that Johnny call Detective Sullivan before they did something they shouldn't do.

Johnny nodded in agreement, grabbed his wallet, from his back pocket and pulled out Mike's home phone number. He dialed the number and waited while it rang. When a woman's voice answered, he told her who he was and asked if he could speak to Detective Sullivan.

Mike took the phone from Anne Marie and said, "This is Mike Sullivan." Johnny said, "Hi Detective, this is Johnny McCord and I need to ask you a question." As soon as Mike realized it was the McCord boy, he decided that he wasn't going to share any of the information that he had just gotten about the ABC Auto situation in Rome. He didn't want to mislead Johnny too badly, but he also didn't want to cause them more concern.

Johnny said, "Detective Mike, we are sorta going "stir-crazy" just sitting here and we need to do something to help keep our minds occupied."

When he understood why Johnny was calling, Mike breathed a little sigh of relief. Johnny wanted to know if they could go to his dad's store and begin to clean up the place.

Mike told them that the crime scene unit had finished gathering their evidence and that they could go ahead and put the place back in shape. He suggested they leave the police tape up to discourage any looting until they were able to get the front door fixed.

He asked Johnny for the phone number to the store, which Johnny got from Pete and gave to Mike. He also told Johnny that he was just leaving for his office and double-checked to be sure that Johnny had his office phone number. Johnny got a pad and pen from the kitchen counter and wrote "Detective Sullivan" along with both of Mike's numbers, marking "home" next to one and "office" next to the other. He then slid the pad into his shirt pocket.

Mike assured Johnny that he would call them at the store, when he had anything new to convey, and he asked Johnny to keep him posted on where they would be if they left the store.

Chapter 91

"Take it easy on the gas," Santino told Ramon. They were south of Atlanta, cruising down I-75 toward Macon. "We've already gotten too much exposure to the cops. It would really piss me off if you get pulled over for speeding."

Ramon nodded his head, eased back to 65mph and said, "Let's find a motel close to Macon and do the phone book thing again."

Santino replied, "Yeah, how many Mike Sullivans can there be in Macon? We'll give this thing until tomorrow night and whether we find the money or not, we get the fuck out of here and head back to Florida."

Ramon smacked the steering wheel with his hand and said, "I don't know man, 250 grand is a lot of lettuce to just leave behind. I'm not going back empty handed. I say we play this out to the end."

Santino knew that Ramon was a hardhead and sometimes took too many chances, but, he was right about the money plus he didn't need to get into it with Ramon right now. Santino thought to himself, "When the time comes, I'll make the final decision regardless of what Ramon says." So he turned toward Ramon and said, "Calm down! We'll take this one step at a time. I want that $ 250,000 just as much as you do. We're getting close to Macon. Keep your eyes peeled for some place to set up as our base of operations."

After traveling a few more miles, he saw a Holiday Inn sign on the side of the road. It indicated that the motel was just off exit 63, which was the Forsyth exit, coming up next.

He said, "Pull off on this next exit. We just passed a sign that said there is a Holiday Inn less than a half mile down this road. They probably have a restaurant and they must have a Macon phone directory. We can grab something to eat while we look up our new friend, Detective Mike Sullivan."

Chapter 92

Linda drove as quickly as she dared. She headed west on Foothills Parkway until she hit route 129 at Tallassee. She took a left on route 72 figuring that it had to get her back to I-75.

Still somewhat in hysterics, Carol screamed, "I can't believe we got away from them! That was the worst thing I have ever seen, but if anyone deserved it, that bastard did."

Linda glanced over at Carol and said, "Yeah, but now how do I get myself out of this mess?"

Then they heard Gloria crying from the back seat. She moaned, "Something is wrong, you have to get me to a hospital right away!"

As they crossed under route 411, Linda saw a sign for Sweetwater Tennessee. It indicated they should turn on route 322 and it was about five miles away. She said, "Hang on Gloria. We're only a few minutes from the town of Sweetwater. They must have a hospital there. I'll take you there, but you have to promise me you won't call the cops."

Carol said, "We promise Linda. If it weren't for you we'd probably both be dead. When we get to the hospital, just drop us off at the Emergency entrance, then park the car and wait for me. As soon as I get Gloria attended to, I'll come back and we can decide what to tell my family. Believe me, when I explain what you did for us, they'll do whatever it takes to help you."

Linda saw an Exxon station up ahead and pulled the

wagon in next to the pumps. She got out of the car and went over to the cashier's window.

She asked the girl, behind the window where the closest hospital was.

The cashier pointed down route 322 and told Linda that Sweetwater Hospital was 2 miles in that direction. Linda got back in the car and told Carol and Gloria what she had found out. Then she said to them, "OK, I guess we are all in this together and I know there isn't anyone else who can help me."

A few minutes later they arrived at the hospital and pulled up to the emergency room.

Linda said, "I'll wait in the parking lot. I'm gonna park way over there at the end of the lot, under those trees. Take care of Gloria, but please come back as soon as you can."

Chapter 93

Art Ravanaugh was extremely pleased with himself on this particular day. Selling advertising printing wasn't the easiest job in the world, but after twenty-two years he had gotten pretty good at it. Art had learned that, in sales, for every twenty "no's" you get; you can count on one "yes"." Well he had suffered through all the no's this week while he "Smokestacked" his way around Knoxville. He made "cold calls" on anything that looked even the slightest bit promising.

It really sucked that the 4th of July fell on a Wednesday. He didn't feel like driving back to his home in Atlanta on Tuesday, only to have to come back to Knoxville on Thursday. He made the decision to hang around and watch the local festivities on Wednesday, get up bright and early on Thursday and finish out the week.

When he awakened on this Friday morning he decided to call it quits for the week and take the scenic route home to Atlanta rather than the boring ride down I-75.

While driving through Pigeon Forge, he noticed a large, well-made, expensive sign for the "Pigeon-Forge Hotel and Lodges"

He thought to himself, "What the hell, Art, why not give it one more try?"

He pulled his 1972 Caprice Classic convertible into a visitor's parking space, pulled his samples and presentation kit out of the trunk and went in to find the lodge's Director of Advertising.

Some would call it luck, but Art knew that in sales you made your own luck, most often by just hanging in there. It just so happened that Pigeon-Forge Hotel & Lodges had just gotten that great looking new sign and needed to purchase printed brochures to match it.

After a full hour of "show and tell" about himself, his company their products, Art knew he had their full attention. They told him that they had heard good things about his company and were extremely impressed with his presentation.

When they asked him for pricing, Art immediately called his plant and was able to get a very competitive quote from his Sales Manager.

They handed him the artwork along with a purchase order for $ 26,000 worth of brochures and mailers.

At 10 percent commission, Art quickly calculated that he had already made his monthly quota, even though it was only the sixth of the month.

When Art returned to his car, he took out a blank yellow sticky-note and wrote a message to himself. He stuck the note to the top of the purchase order and placed it in his briefcase.

Two hours had passed since he left the lodge and Art was cruising along, with the top down, enjoying the beautiful sights along the Foothills Parkway.

Earlier, he had filled his thermos with fresh coffee and purchased a sandwich at a small restaurant on the outskirts of Pigeon Forge. He spotted a lake through the trees and decided to pull over and take a lunch break.

As he pulled off The Foothills Parkway, onto a dirt side road that led to the lake, he noticed something lying in the middle of the road.

He thought it might be a dead animal, a deer or something, and he slowed down to avoid running over it. As he got closer, it became obvious what kind of animal it was. It was the human kind!

He became apprehensive and really didn't want to stop, but maybe this person was injured and needed help. He couldn't just drive on without checking.

Art eased his ragtop to a stop and got out to see what the situation was. As he approached the body, he could see blood splattered everywhere. The full impact of the scene really hit him when he saw that one of the person's arms was missing.

"Pretty damn scary, isn't it?"

Art jumped when he heard the voice and spun around toward the sound.

Chapter 94

He wasn't sure how long he had been unconscious. All he knew was he was having trouble breathing and his shoulder hurt like hell!

Snake pulled himself off the ground and tried to catch his breath. Seeing the .38 lying next to the tree, he picked it up and stuck it into his belt.

Slowly, all the recent events leading up to his present situation came back to him. His last recollection was of the station wagon careening toward him.

He realized that he should be glad that he could get up at all.

Snake looked around the scattered campsite looking for Bear. Had he stopped the girls and then just left him lying here? He began to walk up the dirt road toward the Parkway. His breathing had pretty much returned to normal and he was relieved that he would only have a few bruises to show for his encounter with the wagon.

When he rounded the bend in the road, on the other side of the campsite, he saw the answer to his question.

Bear looked as though he had been caught in a thrashing machine. "No way the girls could have done this, even with the car", he thought. "It had to have been an animal, a big animal, probably a bear." Snake couldn't help smile at the irony of this.

It was eerily quiet and as Snake cocked his head to the side, listening for any sounds of the "beast" that had done this, off in the distance he could hear the unmistakable sound of a car approaching.

Until he knew who was coming, he wasn't going to expose himself. If this was a forest ranger, Snake didn't want to have to explain the situation, so he hid behind a large pine tree that still gave him a good vantage point from which he could see both the road and Bear's corpse.

He watched as a convertible slowed and stopped and he saw a man get out of the car and slowly advance to where Bear was lying.

Snake pulled the gun from his belt and stealthily crept up behind the man. He pointed the gun at the back of the man's head and said, "Pretty damn scary, isn't it?"

The man was obviously stunned and spun around to face Snake. What he saw was an arm with a snake tattoo pointing a gun directly at his face. Snake could see the fear in the man's eyes as he said, "too bad man" and pulled the trigger.

Both men were shocked when the revolver failed to fire, but Snake recovered first. He lifted the gun, said, "I'll be damned!" and struck the man hard on the head with the steel barrel.

Art went down like the proverbial "sack of potatoes". Snake bent over and took the man's wallet from his back pocket and checked quickly to see if he had any cash. He found one hundred and fourteen dollars in the wallet, which he stuck in his own pocket. He threw the wallet on the ground and went to the car.

When he got into the car he pitched the thermos out, but kept the sandwich. He swung the briefcase around and opened it. He rifled through the contents, finding nothing of value except a map. Then he saw the yellow sticky-note on top of a pile of papers and sneered to himself as he read it.

Before Snake drove away from the scene, he put up the convertible top and tossed the briefcase out of the car. It came to rest next to Art's unconscious frame.

Art would awaken several hours later, somewhat dizzy and with an extremely bad headache. After sitting up and looking around for a few minutes, the first thing he would focus on was the yellow sticky note he had written to himself earlier. On it was written, "Art Ravanaugh, this is your lucky day."

Chapter 95

Linda got out and helped Carol get Gloria out of the car, and when they had her safely inside the emergency room, Linda returned to the car and went to park where she had told Carol she would.

As soon as they got through the emergency room door, Carol grabbed a wheelchair that was sitting there and sat Gloria down in it. She wheeled her over to the admitting desk.

She told the admitting nurse that Gloria needed to be seen right away because she was eight months pregnant and had begun bleeding. The nurse immediately waved over a nursing assistant and told him to take Gloria to examination room number 3.

In an effort to protect Linda, she needed to explain why they had come to a hospital in Tennessee, rather than Marietta. Carol lied to the nurse. She told her that Gloria had been feeling great and wasn't due for four weeks, so they had decided to take a drive through the national park.

She explained that, on their way back, they had encountered a bumpy, dirt road and Gloria began to experience bad cramps and pain and then began to bleed.

They decided that they shouldn't risk trying to make it back to Marietta, and decided to find the nearest hospital. When the nurse asked her for Gloria's insurance information, Carol told her that they hadn't brought it with them, but she was going to call Gloria's husband in Marietta and have him bring it up right away.

The nurse was somewhat perturbed by this and told Carol that the doctor would begin his examination, but Carol needed to get the insurance company's name, address and phone number and bring it back to her as soon as possible. She gave Carol a small memo pad and a pen.

Carol said she would make the call right now. She realized that she didn't have any money, so she went out to the parking lot to borrow some change from Linda.

Carol wasn't sure that Linda would still be there, but there she was sitting in the wagon, smoking a cigarette. When she asked Linda if she had any money, Linda laughed and said, "Girl that is the least of our worries."

While she had been waiting for Carol to return, Linda had opened both of the money cases and put about $ 45,000 worth of assorted bills in her purse.

She reached into her purse and pulled out a twenty dollar bill, which she handed to Carol and said, "Here, use this. How is Gloria doing?" Carol answered, "I don't know, but the doctors are examining her now.

I need to call my brother, Pete, and get her insurance information. Why don't you come in with me and we'll find a phone. That way you can hear the conversation and maybe help me answer all the questions he's gonna ask?"

Chapter 96

Snake wheeled the stolen Chevy out of the park and headed West for I-75. He knew where he was going. There was no way he would give up all that money without a fight.

He kept to the back roads and looked for the first town he could find. He needed ammunition for the .38 and had to find a sporting goods store or a gun shop. Once he succeeded in this mission, he would return to the store in Marietta, where this had pretty much all begun. It was the only connection he had to find the girls and the money.

While his primary goal was to get the money back, he was determined to settle the score with Linda and this family who had screwed everything up for him and Bear.

He drove south on route 411 until he hit route 40. He swung west on 40 until he came to Cleveland Tennessee. He pulled the Chevy into a Texaco gas station and filled the tank. He had been impressed with the quickness of this car and he popped the hood to take a look. "Wow", he said, to nobody in particular, "402 cubic inches. If you're gonna steal one. It might as well be fast."

While the tank was being filled, he walked over to the outside phonebooth and let his fingers do the walking. He found what he was looking for. "Clyde's Sport Shop". After checking with the gas station attendant, he determined that the sport shop was only a few blocks away. Snake got a Coke and a couple of apple pies.

He paid for the gas, soda and food with some of the money he had stolen from Art. Then he drove the short distance to "Clyde's".

Snake smiled to himself when he saw the sign on the window, announcing, "Guns & Ammo".

He went into the gun shop and purchased a box of fifty .38 caliber shells for $ 8.00 including tax. "Damn", he thought, "nothin's cheap anymore."

When he returned to the parking lot, he looked up at the sky and saw the dark clouds slowly rolling in. There was no doubt in his mind that there was going to be some serious rain.

Sliding into the driver's seat he noticed a map that had slid onto the passenger's side floor mat. He reached over and picked it up and calculated just how far he was from his destination. According to the map, he could take route 411for most of the way. This would allow him to avoid I-75 until just before Marietta.

As soon as they found the guy he stole the car from, they would start looking for the Chevy. It was more likely that he would be noticed on I-75 than on the back roads. In any event, he planned to dump this car and get another one as soon as the opportunity presented itself.

Snake felt a rumble in his stomach and realized that it had been some time since he had a solid meal. The snacks he had bought just weren't going to cut it.

If all went the way he planned, he could find some

out-of-the-way spot to grab something to eat and then continue on.

It looked to be about 100 miles between here and Marietta. If he stayed under the speed limit and spent about forty-five minutes eating, he figured he could do it in about three hours. That would get him to Marietta sometime just after 7:00 p.m.

Chapter 97

The first thing Mike did, when he got to his office was to put on a fresh pot of coffee. He figured it could be a long one and he needed all the help he could get.

On one wall of his office four blackboards were hung side by side. Mike took a few minutes to erase all four boards and then he began to write notes on each board.

Board 1	Board 2	Board 3	Board 4
Citgo	Farm	Red	ABC
Station	Fresh	Top	Auto
Bikers	Bikers	Bikers	Bikers
Rob & Ass	ADW	Murder	Murder

Chevy Wagon

The obvious thing was that "bikers" showed up on every board and was the common denominator. What was not obvious, Mike thought out loud, was "what the hell happened at Red Top and at ABC Auto?"

Angela Sabatino was just coming to see Mike. As she approached the door to his office, she could hear him thinking out loud. She stuck her head through his open door and said, "Hey Mike, This one got you talking to yourself?"

Mike turned away from the blackboards and smiled at Angie. He said, "You betcha. Grab a cup of coffee and pull up a chair. I really need to bounce this stuff off somebody."

As Angie poured herself a coffee, she said, "Two heads are better than one, speaking of which, I've got some more information for you. The FBI identified the two strangers from the Red Top shooting for us. They were definitely brothers.

Their names were Max and Kurt Stremler, heavy hitters from Chicago. They are currently being investigated for drug trafficking. The FBI figures that at least forty percent of the cocaine being distributed in "Chicagoland" goes through the syndicate that these two guys belong to."

Mike had his elbow propped on the arm of his chair with his hand cupping his chin. He could feel the whiskers that had begun to grow. He got up from his chair and walked over to where Angie was holding the coffeepot. He picked up a clean cup and let her fill it to the brim. He carefully took a sip of the hot fluid and returned to face the notes he had neatly printed on the blackboards.

He cocked his head back over his shoulder, in Angie's direction, and remarked; "Now that's interesting! The question is, were they on their way south to make a buy or had they already made the buy and were heading back to Chicago? In either case, there's probably a whole lot of cash or cocaine, probably both, involved in this thing. Apparently there's enough that they're willing to kill to get it back."

Angie nodded in agreement and with a quizzical

expression said, "But how do the ABC killings fit in to all of this?"

Mike pointed to the last board and said, "There it is, that little entry dangling off the end. The *Chevy Wagon* is what connects our bikers to ABC and probably to the ones who did the killings there. The only possible lead we have on them is a black Camaro that was seen by one of Rome's patrol cars, fleeing from the area at about the time of the murders."

Chapter 98

The "Farm" store was really a mess. Johnny lifted the yellow and black "POLICE LINE DO NOT CROSS" tape and entered through the broken front door. The glass, from the door, was everywhere.

During the battle that had taken place here, a lot of shelves had been knocked down, and the ones that were still upright had most of their contents strewn around on the floor.

Pete checked the back door and found that the lock had been broken when the bikers kicked it in. They were going to need a carpenter to fix both doors and Pete grabbed the local yellow pages to see how soon they could get them repaired.

Beverly swept up the broken glass while Johnny put the shelves back into their proper positions. Pete concluded his phone conversation with a local, Marietta contractor.

He explained to Johnny that he could handle both the doors and the replacement glass. The soonest they could be here was 7:00 am tomorrow, but since it was a Saturday there would be an overtime charge. Pete had told them to come ahead and we will pay the overtime because the sooner they fixed the doors the less time for potential looters to "rob-them-blind".

As Beverly watched Pete on the phone, she found herself thinking about her brother. She knew that he would be worried about her and she didn't want to leave him hanging. She asked Johnny if it would be all right to use the phone to call him.

Johnny had been concerned about Beverly's situation as well. He knew how he felt about Gloria and Carol being missing and could easily imagine how Beverly's brother, Mike, must be feeling. He said, "Sure."

She was pretty certain that Mike would be home and as she listened to the phone ring, she prayed that he would answer. She let the phone ring about seven or eight times and was just about to hang up when she heard her brother's voice say, "Hello."

Beverly sucked in a deep breath of relief and responded, "Mike, it's me Bev."

Mike said, "Bev, where are you? Are you ok? I've been worried sick about you!"

"I'm good Mike. I just had to get out of there. Dad freaked out on me and I didn't know what else to do."

She glanced over at Johnny and Pete, who had been listening but trying not to be too obvious about it. They smiled as they heard her say, "I'm with some friends up in Marietta, it's a real nice family and they've kinda been watching over me. It's a long story and I want to tell it all to you, but I can't right now. Just know that I'm fine. What about you, are you ok?"

"Yeah, when I got home Wednesday night, I found dad sitting at the kitchen table. He was sobbing like a baby. We talked for a while and he explained what had happened. He said that he was really sorry and realized that he needed help, so yesterday morning I took him to Macon. He admitted himself into a rehab center there.

He can't have any visitors for seven days. Speaking of time, when are you coming home?"

"I'm not sure, but I'll call you on Sunday. Hopefully, by then I'll have an idea of what I'm going to do next. In the meantime, take care of yourself and don't worry about me."

Mike replied, "I am worried about you Sis, where can I reach you? Give me a phone number just in case."

"It's pretty complicated, Mike. You really can't get hold of me now. It's nothing for you to be concerned about. I love you, Mike. Just hang in there 'til Sunday and then I'll be able to tell you everything. By the way, I have your jacket. I grabbed it when I left. I'll bring it back."

Beverly hung up the phone and rejoined the boys in the cleanup.

They had been at it for about another hour when the phone rang.

Johnny, being the closest to the phone, grabbed it from the wall and spoke into the mouthpiece. "McCord's Farm Fresh store", Johnny McCord speaking."

When Carol heard Johnny's voice on the other end of the phone, she began to sob. By now Johnny's nerves were pretty frayed and when he heard crying on the other end, he shouted, "Who is this?"

Carol managed to regain some of her composure and replied, "It's me, Johnny, Carol!"

Johnny's heart was racing as he said, "Carol! Where are you? Where's Gloria? Are you girls ok?"

Only able to hear one side of the conversation,

Pete rushed to the back of the store and grabbed the extension. He screamed, "Carol, it's me, Pete, how is Gloria and the baby?"

"We're alright so far, considering what we've been through."

Johnny jumped in, "Everyone's been looking for you; me & Pete, the local cops and the state police in three states! Where are you?"

Carol stuttered out a pleading reply, "No police Johnny! You have to promise me, no police! I'll tell you where we are and you and Pete can come to us, but please don't get the cops involved yet! I'll explain it all to you when you get here"

Johnny and Pete were both confused, but hearing the pained demand she was making, Pete quickly interjected, "Ok, Carol, no cops, we promise. Now tell us where you are?"

Carol told them that they were at Sweetwater Hospital in Sweetwater Tennessee and the doctors were taking care of Gloria as they spoke. She asked Pete to give her Gloria's insurance information, so they could complete Gloria's admission into the hospital.

She explained that the hospital was approximately 150 miles from Marietta, just above Athens Tennessee just off interstate 75.

"It should take you about two and a half hours to get here. We'll expect you between five thirty and six o'clock. Meet me in the emergency room waiting area"

Johnny reached into his shirt pocket and pulled out the notepad that he had used to write Detective

Sullivan's phone numbers on. He tore that sheet off the top and used the next sheet to record the directions that Carol had just given him. He replaced the pad in his shirt pocket, forgetting to retrieve the top sheet which was still lying on the counter next to the phone.

Pete had pulled their insurance card from his wallet and as he relayed the information to Carol, she wrote it down on the pad that the nurse had provided to her. Then she read off the hospital's phone number and address, which was preprinted at the top of the pad and waited until Pete assured her that he had it all.

Pete asked Carol if he could speak to Gloria. She said, "No, she's in the emergency room, but she's ok. Just get here as soon as you can. I love you both."

They all said their good-byes and broke the connection. Pete ran to the front of the store and gave Johnny a bear hug.

Beverly was standing off to the side, feeling a little bit like a fifth wheel. Seeing this, Pete let go of Johnny and went over and hugged her as well. He grinned at her and said, "Hey we're all family. Let's head north."

Johnny said, "I don't know what's going on here and I'm really not comfortable with it. We really ought to call Detective Mike." He was torn between the two choices, but all he could think of was how insistent Carol had been. "Maybe this isn't over yet," he thought.

"Just to be on the safe side, we're taking the guns with us," he said.

He gave Beverly a concerned look and said, "Are you sure you want in on this?" Beverly smiled at both of them and then her smile turned into a look of defiance. She replied, "Just try to stop me!"

Pete grabbed some drinks from the large store cooler and placed them in a smaller portable one while Beverly filled a small shopping bag with chips and cupcakes.

Johnny picked up their weapons and they left the store. They departed by the back door. When they got outside, Johnny pulled the door closed as tight as he could, but it continued to swing slightly open.

With the lock still broken he knew that it wouldn't really stop anyone from gaining entrance, but he grabbed a cinder-block that was lying under the car port and leaned it against the door to hold it shut. "Well," he thought to himself, "this is still the *Good old South*. Everyone trusts everyone here. Maybe nobody will break in."

With that they jumped in their mom's Buick. Johnny placed the two pistols in the glove box, cranked up the engine and they headed for Sweetwater.

Chapter 99

Anne Marie had spent most of the day doing her weekly dusting and cleaning. Friday was the day she always performed these tasks to allow her the freedom to relax with Mike on the weekend. She had even taken all of the plaques down from the kitchen wall and cleaned and dusted them front and back. They were sitting in three piles on the kitchen counter, four to a pile. Once she had wiped off the wall, she would re-hang them in their proper places.

Out of nowhere, Anne Marie found herself feeling a little blue. She knew that this was the life she had chosen when she married Mike. He was a cop and police work was a demanding mistress, but that still didn't stop her from being a little bit irritated this afternoon and jealous of that mistress.

After all it was Friday and she had been looking forward to their weekly Friday night out for dinner.

When Mike left for the office earlier, he told her he might be working late. What that meant was that she could forget about a nice romantic dinner with him tonight. Once he got involved in one of these violent, complex cases, he went into another world, a world that didn't include her. She knew she would be lucky if she saw him at all this weekend. She put down her dust rag and decided to finish this job tomorrow.

Anne Marie realized that she was just feeling sorry for herself. Well she wasn't the kind to sit around and mope. She had friends of her own and she decided to call one of them.

Adele lived just two blocks down the street from the Sullivans and she was happy to hear from Anne Marie. Adele had also been married to a policeman, but while her husband was writing out a speeding ticket for a motorist, a drunk driver had lost control of his car and plowed into him. He was killed instantaneously.

That had happened over three years ago and Anne Marie had offered Adele her support and friendship ever since.

Adele told Anne Marie that her call was timely in that she was inviting two other friends over and they could play Bridge. She said, "Just come on over and don't worry about bringing anything to eat because we're going to splurge and have sandwiches delivered from the Deli."

Anne Marie took a moment to write a note for Mike. She explained where she was going and when she expected to return. She also reminded him that Adele's phone number was on the neatly typed list that she kept attached to the refrigerator with a magnet.

As she was placing the note on the kitchen table, she recalled that the TV weatherman had predicted rain today. It was still so nice out that she elected to forego her car which was parked right in front of the house, and walk the two blocks to Adele's.

She did, however, have the foresight to take her umbrella with her.

Chapter 100

While Ramone ordered coffee for them both, Santino leafed through the pages of the Macon phone directory. The good news was that there were only two Michael Sullivans listed. The problem would be to determine which of the two, if either, was the one they were looking for.

There was a framed map of the local area hanging on the wall outside of the restrooms, next to the pay phone. Santino saw that one address was located slightly north and west of Macon in a suburb called "Ingleside". The other was southwest in another suburb called "Unionville". Santino ripped the page out of the phone book and made some notes in the margin from what he saw on the map.

Since Ingleside was closer, they decided to go there first. It was located in a housing development near a small lake, in an area called "Freedom Park".

After driving slowly past the first address shown in the phone book, they pulled over and parked about a block away at the corner of Davis Street and Short Street. It was now about 5:00pm and they couldn't be sure if Detective Sullivan would be home, but should they take that risk? They decided that if he was home, great! If he wasn't, they would just have to wait for him.

Santino recalled passing a shopping center on the way and decided to go back and find a public phone. *"Better to be safe than sorry",* he thought.

When they got to the shopping center, they found

a phone kiosk. Santino got out of the car and dropped a dime in the slot. He dialed the first phone number and waited for an answer. When a soft female voice answered, he said, "Hello ma'am, my name is Detective Cruz. Sorry to bother you at suppertime, but, I'm trying to locate Detective Mike Sullivan. Is he at home or can you tell me where I might be able to reach him?"

The woman on the other end of the phone said, "I'm sorry young man, but you have the wrong number. My husband, Michael, is a retired insurance salesman, not a detective."

Santino thanked the woman, hung up, turned to Ramone and said, "I guess we're going to Unionville."

Just as they had done at the first address, they had agreed to do a slow run past the second house. As they drove the few short miles from Ingleside to Unionville, the sky had become overcast and a few drops of rain began to bounce off the windshield of the black Camaro.

Ramone, who was sitting in the passenger's seat, laughed and said, "It's a good thing we brought our rain gear, we stay dry and I get to hide this baby. He had his hand on a menacing looking 12 gauge, sawed-off shotgun."

When they reached the street they were looking for, Santino said, "What was that house number?" Ramone picked up the torn-out page from the phonebook, placed his index finger under the second underlined listing and replied, "211."

Santino did a quick calculation in his head and

stated, "That should be the sixth house up here on the left."

As they slowly cruised past the house, something caught his eye and he told Ramone that he was going to circle the block and check that something out.

He drove even more slowly this time and when they pulled past the car parked in front of "211", he exclaimed, "Well whatta you know, advertising helps!"

There on the back bumper of the parked car was a rectangular, blue & red decal. The center of the decal had "FOP" in large gold lettering and printed around the edges were the words, "Fraternal Order of Police."

"This is definitely the right place", he remarked out loud. He sped up so as not to look suspicious to anyone who might have observed their passing. He pulled up to the next corner and turned left. At the following corner he turned left once again. In his mind he was calculating how far down the street he needed go to park in front of the house that backed up to the Sullivan's back yard. When he reached that point, he pulled the Camaro into the nearest parking spot.

The rain was now coming down much harder and the sky had gotten seriously darker. Both men reached into the back seat and withdrew black rain slickers. With great effort, in the confined space of the car, they shrugged into their rain gear. They exited the car and made their way through the downpour.

Santino told Ramone to work his way to the back door of the Sullivan house and he would approach from the front. The good news about the car with the "FOP" decal was that it identified their target.

The bad news was that since the car was there, somebody was probably in the house and there was no way to know who or how many.

They both worked their way alongside the house in front of them, through the backyard and into the backyard of the Sullivan home.

Ramone took a position on the small patio next to the back door and Santino worked his way around to the front door.

Santino rang the doorbell. There was no turning back now and he pulled out his .38 and held it behind his back. In an effort to take advantage of any time it might buy him, he took the "fake" detective badge out and held it in front of him with his left hand.

He could hear the doorbell ring as it echoed through the house, but there was no response. He tried again with the same result. Just to be sure, Santino put the badge back in his pocket and banged on the door hard, with his left fist.

When no one answered, he left the porch and went around to where Ramone was waiting. He said, "No answer. Let me see you do your magic."

Ramone smiled and handed the shotgun to Santino. He produced a small leather case from his back pocket. In it he kept a set of tools for picking locks. In less than a minute, he had skillfully unlocked both the screen door and the back door. Ramone's talent always amazed Santino, but what would you expect, Ramone had spent his teens working for his father, who just happened to be a professional locksmith by trade.

Ramone put his tools away and retrieved his gun from Santino. Then they both entered into the kitchen of the Sullivan house.

Since the bungalow had only one floor, it didn't take them long for a quick room by room search. They determined that the house was empty.

After meeting up back in the kitchen, Santino noted the time on the Sullivan's rooster clock. It was five minutes after six. As he looked around the kitchen, he spotted the message that Anne Marie had left for her husband. It said that she would be returning home from her friend's house around eight o'clock.

They compared notes on what they had seen in their search of the house. Ramone told Santino that there was a phone in the master bedroom, but, to his surprise he didn't find any weapons. "I thought all these cops were fanatics about guns." Santino replied, "Yeah, I didn't find any either. Maybe his old lady don't like guns in the house."

As Santino was speaking, he was opening and closing all the cabinets and drawers in the kitchen. When he opened the cabinet under the double sink he found a large roll of duct tape and in one of the drawers he found a big-ass first-aid kit and a large pair of scissors. He grabbed the duct tape and the scissors and turned his gaze back to Ramone, he continued, "These just might come in handy. All we can do now is wait, but there ain't no reason we can't check out their fridge while we do."

He commenced to place the two items in one of the sinks and then made his way to the Sullivan's refrigerator.

Chapter 101

Art's eyes slowly opened as he felt the droplets of rain on his face. He was aware of a dull throbbing in his head and instinctively placed his hand on the spot that hurt. When he put his hand in front of his face he saw the wet, red stain. He blurted out, "What the hell!"

Then he remembered. He had been pistol-whipped by some tall, skinny, mean-looking bastard. As he carefully pulled himself to his knees, he saw his briefcase and papers strewn around him.

Art wanted to laugh when he saw the note he had written to himself earlier, but he found that his head hurt too much and it was really more ironic than funny. He grabbed all of his papers and put them back in the briefcase. About fifteen feet away he saw his wallet lying by the dirt road, where his car had been parked.

He recovered his wallet and to no surprise found that his cash was gone. Gingerly touching his head once more and deciding that it was no longer bleeding, he began to walk up the dirt road toward the Foothills Parkway.

As he reached the parkway, the sky darkened and the rain began to pelt him with conviction. It was refreshing on the one hand and aggravating on the other. Looking down the road, Art saw two headlights approaching. He staggered to the middle of the parkway and waved his hands at the oncoming car.

As it got closer, he could make out the words, "Park Police", painted on the hood.

"Well," Art thought, "Maybe this was his lucky day after all."

The green and white Jeep pulled over and stopped. The flashing red lights were turned on, but no siren was blaring.

The park ranger exited his vehicle and walked toward Art, keeping his hand on his sidearm. He observed Art holding a briefcase in one hand and waving to him with the other. He also noticed the blood covering Art's forehead.

Realizing that this man was no danger to him, he released his hand from his sidearm and hurried to assist him.

"What the hell happened to you?" he said. Art stumbled into the ranger's arms and started to explain. The ranger said, "Let's get you out of the rain and into the car and then you can tell me what happened."

Once Art was safely seated in the back seat, the ranger opened his first-aid kit and handed Art a large gauze pad to hold on his wound. He pulled out a canteen and a paper cup and offered Art a drink of water.

Art told him that he had been car-jacked and would probably have been killed if the attacker's gun hadn't failed to fire. When Art got to the part about seeing the body on the ground, the ranger asked him if he felt well enough to show him where it was. Art told him he felt ok and he pointed back down the dirt road towards where Bear's body lay.

The ranger pulled alongside the dismembered body

of William Masterson and told Art to remain in the Jeep while he checked out the situation.

As he walked around the body, something caught his eye. In the woods about fifteen yards beyond the body he saw what appeared to be a human arm.

When he approached the arm, he could see that there was a handgun clutched tightly in the fingers. It was a 9mm semi-automatic. He decided that he needed help on this one and quickly returned to the Jeep.

Once inside, he plucked the radio's handset from the dashboard and called the Park Police home base. He described the situation and asked them to request backup from the Tennessee State Police. After approximately five minutes, the call came back that a car was on the way and should be there in fifteen or twenty minutes. Art looked at his watch and noted that it was 4:45 p.m.

Chapter 102

Considering the fact that the rain was coming down pretty heavily, Johnny made good time getting to Sweetwater Hospital. They arrived shortly after 5:15 p.m.

He pulled up to the emergency room door and let Pete and Beverly out under the protection of a large awning. Then he parked in the nearest open spot and ran through the rain to the entrance.

When the automatic sliding doors parted, he could see Pete and Beverly huddled in a corner at the back of the waiting room. They were talking to his sister and another taller girl with blonde hair. He took his hand, wiped the rainwater from his face, shook it from his head and hurried over to find out what was going on.

Pete was hugging Carol and she was in tears. As Johnny joined the group, Carol was pointing to the front desk and telling Pete to see the nurse who was sitting there.

Pete released Carol from his grasp and told Johnny that he was going to see Gloria. Carol reached out and grabbed Johnny and started to sob once more. Johnny said, "We're here now, Hon, you're safe."

He motioned for them all to sit down in the waiting room chairs and sofas. As soon as they did, Carol fought back her tears and began to fill them in on all that had occurred since they were kidnapped from dad's store."

The first thing she did was to assure Johnny that Gloria was going to be all right. She told him that the doctors had decided to do a caesarian section and get the baby now. They told her that considering the trauma, both physical and mental, that Gloria had experienced, they didn't want to take any chances.

Carol began to chronicle the events that led up to this moment. As she did, the expression on Johnny's face became hard and he glared over at Linda, but by the time Carol had completed her story, his expression had softened. He reached out and took Linda's hand. While gently squeezing her hand, he thanked her vigorously for helping Carol and Gloria.

He looked into her eyes and said, "The most important thing is that the girls are safe, that all three of you are safe, but I'm not sure where we go from here. A lot of crimes have been committed and a lot of people have been hurt. On the other hand, there is no doubt that we owe you big time."

After a few moments of thought, Johnny continued, "Linda, We need to get you back to Georgia. There are friends there who can help us make the best decisions. Pete will stay here with Gloria. We'll leave the Buick for him. The rest of us will take the station wagon back to Marietta and try to get you whatever help we can."

Linda realized that her options were limited and if she ever hoped to have any kind of a normal life, she would have to "Face the Music" sooner or later. If she took off by herself, there was no telling what would happen to her. She knew that all that money, and it was a lot, would only get her so far and that assumed she didn't get caught.

She decided that these were good people and she would go along until she found out what they could do to help her. She reasoned that she could trust them, because if she couldn't they would have already called the cops.

Johnny told the others that he was going back to see Gloria and Pete and explain to them what they intended to do. Johnny found the emergency room. He went over to Gloria's bed and gently hugged her. He asked Pete to follow him out to the parking lot, explaining that he needed to shift one of the guns to the station wagon. He told Pete that he was leaving mom's Buick for him and would leave one of the pistols in it. After making the exchange in the parking lot, he gave Pete the Buick's keys, said his goodbyes and watched as Pete returned to Gloria's bedside.

He told the three girls to follow him to the car. As he pulled the wagon out of the hospital's parking lot, Johnny explained to Carol, Beverly and Linda that he was going to drive to the "Farm" store, in Marietta and use their phone in an attempt to reach Detective Sullivan.

He turned his head toward Linda, who was sitting in the front passenger's seat and said, "Detective Mike is a good man. Whatever he tells us to do, we'll do. Ok?" Linda hesitated for a moment and then responded, "Ok."

Chapter 103

Snake made good time getting to Marietta, even with the rain and the dinner break. Things were going his way. The rain had certainly helped him avoid being noticed on the way down 411. "Maybe", he mused, "nobody was even looking for him yet."

As he swung the convertible onto the Four Lane and cruised slowly past the "Farm Fresh" store, he could see the yellow police line tape across the front of the building. Other than that, there didn't seem to be any activity in or around the store.

Even though it was still raining quite hard, he decided it would be better to get wet than to expose the stolen car to the traffic on the Four Lane, so he parked around the corner. He would work his way back to the store on foot.

After finding a suitable parking place, on a side street next to an office building, he opened the new box of shells and loaded the .38. He took two more handfuls of bullets and slid them into his pocket. "I'm not gonna get caught short again!" he thought to himself.

The one-story office building was only about a half-block from the McCord's store.

Between the office building and the store was an empty field with a "For Rent" sign stuck in the ground, at the front of the property, close to the Four Lane. There were a lot of high shrubs and a few trees toward the back of the field and Snake wended his way through these until he arrived at the back of the store.

It had only been two days since Snake and the others had left this place, but it seemed like a month. He picked up the cinder block that was holding the screen door closed and set it to the side and opened the screen door. Obviously, they hadn't had time to fix the inner door and other than a muffled squeak, it offered no resistance when he pushed it open.

He went into the store and closed the door after him.

Chapter 104

Art was still sitting in the Park Police jeep, when the Tennessee State trooper arrived. It was actually a two vehicle caravan. A large, black van pulled in right behind the trooper's patrol car. The writing on the side of the van identified it as a "Tennessee Crime Scene Investigation" vehicle. When the woman who was driving the van got out, Art could see the "CSI" written on the back of her rain slicker. She carried a large black case embossed with the same initials.

Because of the downpour, Art's window was closed, but as he peered between the rivulets of rain running down the window, he could see the trooper, the Crime Scene Investigator and the park policeman. They were obviously discussing the crime scene.

The Park policeman handed something to the investigator, turned his head toward Art and pointed toward him. After a few minutes, the trooper took the object from the investigator, turned away from the two of them and walked over to Art.

He pulled open Art's door and asked, "How are you holding up, Mr. Ravanaugh?" Art responded that he was pretty sure that the bleeding had stopped, but he was still feeling a little woozy.

"Well we're gonna take care of that right now." said the trooper. "I'm going to take you to Sweetwater Hospital. It's the closest hospital to here. It'll only take me about thirty minutes to get you there.

Sweetwater is one of Tennessee's best hospitals and they'll give you the complete once over."

He handed Art's wallet to him and said, "You'll probably need this." He watched as Art gathered his belongings then helped him over to his patrol car. Once Art was safely in the car, the trooper pulled his car up to the other two and assured them that he would take a full report from Art once they arrived at the hospital and he was fully checked out.

The trooper made sure that Art was buckled in, turned on the flashers and siren and said, "In this rain, it'll be a lot safer for everyone if they can see and hear us coming."

They managed to cover the distance to the hospital in just twenty-eight minutes.

Chapter 105

The cubicle was stark white with just a curtain separating them from the emergency room hallway. Pete had pulled a chair up close to Gloria and was gingerly holding her hand between both of his. He never liked being stuck with a needle, but who did? He couldn't help wondering if it had hurt when the nurse put the IV needle into the back of Gloria's other hand.

The lights had been dimmed and she had finally nodded off. He found himself staring at the monitors that were keeping a close watch on her blood pressure and heart rate. His mind wandered as he tried to remember what systolic and diastolic meant.

Just when he caught himself closing his own eyes, he heard the sound of the curtain sliding open. A doctor entered their cubicle and plucked Gloria's chart from the holder attached to the foot of her bed. He walked over and shook Pete's hand and quietly introduced himself.

He smiled as he observed Gloria sleeping. Looking back to Pete, he said, "It seems as though this young lady has had a rough day." Pete thought, "Doc, You don't know the half of it."

The doctor went on to explain to Pete that they were preparing to move Gloria out of emergency and into the operating room staging area. They were waiting for some final test results and were going to prepare her for the C-section.

He told Pete that he would have someone meet Pete back here in the emergency waiting room and take him to the staging area so that he could have a short visit with Gloria before they actually took her into the operating room. He said, "It'll probably take about ninety minutes to get her ready, so why don't you grab something from the cafeteria while you're waiting."

Pete realized that he hadn't eaten in quite a while and said, "That sounds like a good idea. Where is the cafeteria?" The doctor pointed toward the emergency waiting room and said, "Just go to the end of the waiting room and take a right turn at the restrooms. It's down the hall on your left. As long as you're in the cafeteria or the waiting room, we'll find you."

Chapter 106

Mike and Angie had spent the better part of three hours going over all of the information they had gathered.

Mike was looking at the blackboards when it occurred to him that he had forgotten to list something. He got up from the chair he had been sitting in and walked over to Board # 3. He picked up a piece of chalk and added to the list.

Board 3
Red Top
Bikers
Murder

Camper

"It's the damn camper!" he shouted. "The Stremler brothers were on the way south to meet up for a buy. They must have had the money in the camper and when they came out on the losing end of the shootout with our motorcycle friends, the money didn't get to where it was supposed to go.

After this all happened, the bikers must have gone to ABC Auto to get a different set of wheels, the station wagon. Then some strangers in a Camaro show up at ABC and kill two people. They must have found out about the station wagon and are probably looking for it now."

Angie just listened until Mike had finished and said, "It all makes sense, but it still leaves me with three questions. Number one is how did they get onto ABC Auto?

Number two is where is the camper now? And number three is did the bikers find the money?"

Mike replied, "My guess is that they must have found the money or they couldn't have bought the wagon. They probably hid the camper somewhere outside of Rome. The Camaro crew knew that the Stremlers had a camper and they probably heard it being described on the news. Figuring the bikers would dump the camper, they could have just gone down the list of used car lots until they found the right one.

Considering the name "ABC", it wouldn't have taken too long to hit the right one. So now we have two kidnapped girls riding around in a station wagon with what remains of a biker gang. We have person or persons unknown driving a black Camaro who are looking for the station wagon and ready to kill all the occupants to get the money they believe them to have."

Angie said, "Unless we can locate the station wagon or the Camaro, we aren't going to be able to do anything until more "bad shit" happens!"

Mike said, "I'm going to get hold of the McCord boys and get them up to speed on this."

He picked up the phone and called the "Farm" store. After letting the phone ring close to ten times, he concluded that they had left the store. He looked up the phone number for Emory-Adventist hospital. When he was connected to their switchboard, he identified himself and asked to be transferred to Mr. McCord's room.

Martha was sitting at Roger's bedside, holding his hand and talking about their kids. When the phone rang, she answered it with crossed fingers and a prayer on her lips, wishing and praying that it was good news.

When he heard the voice on the other end say, "Hello", Mike asked if this was Mrs. McCord and told her it was Detective Sullivan. He said, "The reason for my call is twofold, first of all, how is Mr. McCord doing?"

Martha told him that Roger was coming along fine and would probably be released, from the hospital, in the next day or two. Then she added, "You said there were two reasons for your call. Do you have any word on the girls?" Mike responded that he had not gotten any new information. Martha's heart fell. Mike then asked her if she had heard from Johnny and Pete.

Martha told him that the last time she talked to them was a little before 1:00pm. She said that they were going to go back to the store and try to clean it up, once they cleared it with the police. Mike confirmed that they had spoken to him a few minutes later and he had told them that they could go ahead.

Then, trying not to get Martha overly concerned, he said, "They told me they would keep in touch, but, I haven't heard from them. I thought maybe they were with you at the hospital." He added, "I tried calling them at the store and no one answered. They probably went to get something to eat, or were on their way to the house. Well, just keep your hopes up and if you hear from them remind them to check in with me.

I'll call you just as soon as I get any new information." Martha thanked him and they hung up.

Considering his and Angie's new findings and their conclusions, Mike had become more concerned about the black Camaro and its occupants. He didn't see any way that they could know about the McCord family, but, they had found out about the wagon that the biker's had purchased.

Mike decided that rather than take any chances, he would drive to Marietta and personally locate Johnny, Pete and Beverly.

Looking at his watch, he calculated that he could get to Marietta by 8:00pm.

Chapter 107

After giving Art the once over, the emergency room doctor told him that he didn't see any signs of serious injury. Just to be on the safe side, he sent Art to x-ray to check the area of his head where he had been pistol-whipped.

After completing the x-rays, they bandaged his head and sent him out into the reception area to await the results.

The trooper was waiting for Art and suggested they go to the cafeteria, where they could grab a snack and go over the details of the incident for the trooper's report.

The cafeteria was fairly crowded, not so much with patients or family members of patients, but with nurses and doctors eating their Friday evening meal.

They walked through the food line and selected sandwiches and coffee. The trooper scanned the room and pointed to a table in the corner, where the fewest number of people were seated.

As they sat down to eat and discuss the assault, the trooper took casual notice of a young man sitting at the nearest occupied table to them. The young man looked up from his meal, gave the trooper a slight nod and returned his attention to his own meal. The trooper returned the nod with a slight smile then, cleared a space in front of him and pulled out his incident report pad.

Pete wondered what had happened to the man two tables over. The bandage around his head and the fact that he was sitting with a State Trooper led Pete to conclude that he had probably been in a traffic accident.

Now that he was alone, Pete's mind began to wander back over the horrific story that the girls had related to them. Every now and then he couldn't help but overhear some of the conversation between the trooper and the injured man.

When Pete heard the words, "snake tattoos", he felt his heart skip a few beats. Now his full attention became focused on their conversation. He heard Art say, "My car is a 1972, dark blue, Caprice Classic convertible with a white top."

The trooper held up his hand to stop Art and explain, "Mr. Ravanaugh, you may not recall, but, you gave that information to the Park policeman. We used your driver's license to double check with MVA back in the woods. An APB has already been put out for your car.

Other than the tattoos and the gun, can you recall anything else, like what type of gun it was?"

"Not really," Art replied. "I just thank God that the gun didn't go off." With a forced laugh, he added, "Maybe you can determine what kind of a gun it was from the impression it left in my head."

At that moment a nurse walked over to the table and told the trooper that Mr. Ravanaugh's results were back and the doctor wanted to see him.

Art and the trooper picked up their food trays and followed the nurse out of the cafeteria, stopping to dump the trays on their way out.

Pete let out a deep sigh and sat back in his chair. He

was convinced that there was no way that this could be a coincidence. This Snake character was obviously still alive, mean and armed.

He knew he had to let Johnny and the girls know what he had just learned, the only problem was how to get in touch with them.

His contemplation was interrupted as one of the nurses came over to Pete and told him that they were ready to take Gloria into surgery. Since it would be about twenty minutes before the surgeon arrived he could spend a little time with her before they began.

Chapter 108

Even though it was barely 7:45pm, the overcast from the rainclouds outside made it dark inside the store, especially back here where there were no windows. As he eased his way through the back room, he vividly recalled the last time he was in this place. Basically, all hell had broken loose.

When he banged his knee against some unseen obstruction, Snake grabbed his lighter and flipped it on. He was now able to carefully wend his way toward the front of the store without encountering any other obstacles.

He figured that there had to be something in the store that would give him a clue as to where these people lived. Once he figured that out, he was going to exact his revenge.

As he got closer to the front part of the store, there was sufficient light from the large storefront windows to enable him to see without the assistance of the lighter. He extinguished it and carefully avoided the area close to those windows, to insure that he would not be seen from the outside.

He worked his way over to the store's main counter. There he saw a telephone sitting on the counter next to the cash register. Unable to restrain his natural instincts, he attempted to open the cash drawer. To his surprise it offered no resistance to his attempt and opened with a "ka-ching".

He was disappointed to find it void of any folding money, but he gleefully scooped up the change that had been left and stuffed it in his pocket like a little kid shoplifting candy.

In one of the cash drawer's slots, he found a stack of business cards. Printed on the cards was:

McCord's "Farm Fresh" store
Groceries & Home Goods
6351 N. Cobb Parkway
NE (The Four Lane)
Marietta, GA 30008

Roger McCord — Owner

Business Phone: (770) 555-1234
Home Phone: (770) 555- 8749

He took one of the business cards and placed it on the counter next to the register.

On top of the counter there was a clean coffee cup whose sole purpose seemed to be holding the pencils and pens that extended above its rim. Next to the cup were several pieces of paper with notes on them. Snake reviewed the notes one by one. The only one that caught his attention was the one on the top that had "Detective Mike" written on it. Below the name was a home and office phone number. He stuffed this note into his shirt pocket for possible future reference.

He thought to himself, "What I need is a phone book." As he scanned the area he saw that directly under the phone and beneath the counter top, there was a shelf. On the shelf was a phone book.

Chapter 109

The drive from the hospital was filled with mixed feelings by all four of the wagon's occupants.

Carol sat up front with Johnny. He kept reaching over and patting her on the knee, telling her she was safe now and the nightmare was finally over.

Beverly and Linda sat in the back seat and had trouble finding anything to say to each other. Carol sensed the tension and turned sideways so she could see all three of the others. After a short pause, she said, "I know you are both upset with Linda, but please try to remember that she saved our lives." Johnny replied, "I know that Carol, and I'll do everything I can to try and get her off the hook."

They were on the Four Lane just a few blocks from the "Farm" store. Johnny turned to Linda and said, "Linda, trust me. We need to get hold of Detective Sullivan and let him tell us what to do. He is your best chance for working your way out of this mess. What do you think?"

Linda had been thinking about this ever since they left the hospital in Sweetwater. She never thought, in her wildest dreams, that things would go this badly. Riding with Bear and his bunch had ceased to be fun after the melee in the store and it had just gone downhill from there. She reflected on hearing Bear telling Snake how they were going to get rid of her and she wondered if there was any possible chance for her to start over again.

She said, "I can't spend the rest of my life running and looking over my shoulder. If you really think your detective friend can help me, I'm willing to take the chance."

Johnny replied, "Good for you. I'm gonna stop at the store and call Detective Mike. He needs to tell us what to do next."

The rain had begun to subside and as Johnny pulled into a parking spot, right in front of the entrance to the store, he rolled down his window and held his hand out. He said, "Let's give it a couple of minutes. No sense in getting any wetter than we have to."

He put the gear shift into park and shut off the engine. After a few minutes, the rain had stopped altogether and Johnny said, "Let's go." Linda and Beverly got out of the car and walked around to where Johnny was standing. Carol was much more tentative as she closed her door and followed the rest.

Chapter 110

Snake saw the glare of headlights as a car pulled into the parking lot of the store. At first he thought it might just be someone turning around, and then he heard the motor shut off and saw the lights go out.

He had ducked down behind the counter as quickly as he could and now that the glare was gone, he slowly eased his way into a position where he could look out the window and still not be seen.

As he watched from his hiding place he immediately recognized the station wagon. He couldn't believe his eyes. He exhaled deeply and murmured, "This is gonna be easier than I thought, they brought the money back to me."

He observed a tall man, probably in his thirties; climb out from the driver's side. He had no idea who this man was.

Then he saw Linda, Beverly and Carol get out of the car and join the man. When he saw Linda, he growled to himself, "That bitch is gonna be sorry she ever crossed me." Then he saw Beverly and thought, "Whaddaya know the hitchhiker's with them." and finally, looking at Carol he thought "The young one, I may get a piece of that yet."

Snake knew that the only way they could enter the store was through the back entrance which he himself had used. He wouldn't be able to watch both the car and the back door.

He knew he had to get the drop on the guy; the girls

would be no problem. Once he found the money, he would kill them all. No witnesses!

The noise from the rain had ceased and only the thin piece of cardboard that covered the broken front door separated him from them. Snake could hear their conversation as if he had been invited into their midst.

Carol grabbed Johnny's arm and when he turned to face her she said, "I don't know if I can go back in there, especially in this gloom. Maybe it'll be ok tomorrow when the suns out, but, right now I don't think I can handle it."

Johnny was concerned for Carol and didn't want to cause her any more grief so he suggested that they wait here by the car while he went in and called Mike Sullivan. Carol looked relieved and the girls watched as Johnny walked to the end of the store and turned the corner. Johnny walked to the back and headed for the rear entrance.

As he approached the door he noticed that the cinder block had been moved away from the door. He knew that somebody would have had to purposely move the block and he wondered if some asshole had robbed the store.

The screen door had partially opened when the cinder block had been moved and Johnny reached out to grab the door. Just as his hand touched the door, he heard the wailing of a siren coming from the front of the store. He immediately forgot the door and turned and ran back around to the front. He could see the girls staring at the flashing blue light as it closed in on them.

Snake had watched the man leave the three girls and start for the back of the store. He figured that if he could subdue the man the girls shouldn't be much of a problem.

He quickly began to work his way toward the back door so he could surprise this stranger.

The noise from the siren startled Snake. The good news was that it also masked the banging and thumping he made as he knocked over boxes and shelves in his rush to get to the back door. All he knew was that he had to get out of here quickly. It was time to go to Plan "B", whatever the hell that was.

He didn't know why, but, he actually took the time to replace the cinder block against the door. This task accomplished, he stooped over keeping a low profile, and ran as fast as he could back toward the car he had parked two blocks away.

Chapter 111

Mike Sullivan had only been a block away from the Farm Store when he saw the vehicle parked in front. As he got closer he recognized it as the station wagon that was the focal point of the carnage at ABC Auto.

"What the hell is it doing here?" he thought as he automatically turned on his siren and flashers.

He careened into the parking lot and slid to a stop, keeping the passenger side of his car facing the station wagon. He jumped out of the car, pulled out his service revolver and using the open car door as a shield, pointed his weapon at the group of three standing in front of the store.

Johnny recognized Detective Sullivan immediately. As he arrived where the others were standing, he slowly approached Mike with both hands in the air and hollered, "It's me, Johnny, and the girls. We found them and I was just going into the store to call you."

Seeing who it was, Mike let out a deep breath and lowered his revolver. "You had me goin' there for a minute." and a big smile broke out on his face.

Holstering his gun he walked around the car to greet them. He knew Johnny and Beverly but he didn't recognize the other two girls.

When Johnny saw Mike looking quizzically at Linda and Carol he gently pulled Carol in front of him. "This is my sister, Carol. She has been through a lot. My sister-in-law, Gloria is in the hospital back in Sweetwater, Tennessee.

a baby very soon."

Mike walked over to Carol and gently took her hand in both of his. "I'm very happy to see you safe and sound, young lady. We've been doing all we can to find you and Gloria."

Still holding Carol's hand, he shifted his gaze to Linda and said, "And who might this be?"

Linda had been fearfully anticipating this moment. Ever since she had agreed to talk to this man, she had been rehearsing what she would say, but now that the moment had arrived, she didn't know where to begin.

Johnny could see how nervous Linda was and remembering what she had done for his family, he figured that this was the moment that he owed her his best shot at getting her off the hook.

"Detective, this is Linda. She is the reason we didn't contact the police before now. I know we should have, but we owe her a lot and I figured if anyone would give her a square deal, it would be you. Believe me when I tell you that if it wasn't for Linda, Carol and Gloria would be dead by now."

Chapter 112

Snake wasn't going to give the money up without a fight, but his plan didn't include fighting the cops. He got back into Art's convertible and wheeled it around to the Four Lane. Now that the rain had ceased, the sky was beginning to brighten. He eased his way slowly along the shoulder of the road until he got as close to the front of the store as he could, without being noticed.

He was relieved to see that that both the wagon and the cop car were still in front of the store. Now he would sit and wait. He wasn't about to let the wagon out of his sight unless he had no other choice.

If more cops showed up he was out of here. He would switch cars and get as far away from Georgia as he could, but while there was still a chance to get the money back he would wait for that chance.

He very seldom smoked, but for some reason he had held on to Rachel's Marlboros. He took one out of the box and lit it up with the car's lighter. As he took a deep drag on the cigarette, he thought about Rachel. The more he thought about her being gone, the more pissed off he became. Not that he had any special feelings for her, but she was a nice easy piece of ass. Snake was still mad that he hadn't gotten a chance at that young one. "Maybe yet", he thought.

Just then he noticed the cop car pull out of the parking lot. It turned right and headed away from where he was parked.

The station wagon pulled out right behind the cop and turned left, heading right at Snake.

He quickly cupped the cigarette in his hand to hide its glow from sight. He crouched down on the seat and waited for the wagon to pass him.

As soon as he was sure the wagon had passed by, Snake straightened up, started the engine and hit the gas. He found an opening in the busy, Friday night traffic. He made a quick, illegal U-turn and followed after the station wagon.

More people had decided to come out now that the rain had ceased. This provided more cars for him to keep between him and his prey. He still didn't know what Plan "B" was, but he knew that he would be ready when he got his chance.

Chapter 113

Johnny looked over at Linda and said, "Well so far, so good. I knew that Detective Mike would try to help you as much as possible." Linda, Beverly and Johnny were on their way to Mike Sullivan's home in Macon.

While they were talking, outside the Farm Store, Mike had asked Johnny if he still had his home phone number. Johnny searched for it and then remembered that he had torn it off the pad and left it on the counter here at the Farm Store when writing down the directions to Sweetwater hospital earlier.

Rather than have Johnny go back inside, since he needed to give them directions to his home as well, he dictated the phone number and directions to Johnny and Johnny wrote them down on the same pad.

He told them that he would join them at his home, after he took Carol to the Hospital to reunite her with her mom and dad.

Mike said that he would call his wife, from the hospital, and let her know they were coming. He advised them not to stop for anything and go directly to his home. He explained that he would have a lot more control over Linda's ultimate situation if he handled it from his home turf in Macon as opposed to doing anything in Marietta.

Mike calculated that he would only be about a half hour behind them and they should all be at his home by 10:30pm.

Beverly, who was seated in the back seat, reached

up and placed her hand on Linda's shoulder. She said, "Johnny's right about Detective Mike. He's a great guy and he wouldn't be sending us to his home if he didn't think he could find a way to help you."

Chapter 114

As Mike drove toward the hospital, he made small talk with Carol. He could almost feel a sense of relief coming from her as she seemed to relax. She had gone through more terror than anyone should have to suffer, especially a twelve year old girl.

Mike was trying to decide what to do about this girl, Linda. She had shown good faith by showing him the two cases of cash at the Farm Store. Mike had transferred the money from the wagon to the trunk of his own car. The connection between the kidnappings and the killings at ABC Auto had now become crystal clear.

He would have to share this information with the rest of law enforcement pretty quickly, but, he had promised Linda he would listen to her story first.

As soon as he got home, he would call Macon & Marietta PD, as well as the state police in Georgia and Tennessee and brief them all on the new details to which he was now privy.

When he and Carol approached Mr. McCord's room, Mike gently guided Carol ahead of him so she could enter the room first.

Roger was out of bed and fully dressed. He was being released from the hospital, a day early, and he and Martha were trying to decide where to go.

There was no way they were going back to the store, so they agreed that they would return to their home and make the best of it there.

When they saw Carol come into the room they immediately forgot about their housing dilemma. There ensued lots of hugs, kisses and tears along with an equal number of large smiles. This was the part of Mike's job that made him keep coming back for more.

Mike remembered that he had to call Anne Marie. He told them to meet him in the lobby and he would drive them home on his way back to Macon. Since it was a long distance call, he excused himself and went down to the lobby to use a pay phone. As he was leaving, a nurse arrived with a wheelchair to transport Roger to the front door.

Mike deposited the correct amount of change in the phone and dialed his home. After a few rings it switched over to their cassette answering machine. After listening to the standard *Leave a message at the tone*, Mike began to speak. "Annie, I just wanted to give you a heads-up. I will be home by 10:30, but, you are going to have some visitors around 10:00."

He told her that Johnny McCord and Beverly, who he had told her about, plus one other girl called "Linda" would be showing up in a blue Chevrolet station wagon. He said that this Linda was in possession of a lot of money and a big bag of trouble and needed Mike's help. He told Anne Marie to let them in to wait for him.

Mike wasn't keen on leaving a message. He had hoped that she would be there so he could give her chapter and verse.

With the limited time available for the taped message, he just barely finished the basic details before the machine shut off. Well, it would be worse if strangers showed up and Anne Marie didn't at least have some warning.

Mike exited the phone booth and saw that the McCords had all gathered outside the hospital's front doors. He waved and headed toward them.

Chapter 115

Ramone and Santino were getting antsy. They had been waiting for close to three hours and were beginning to wonder if it was time to "pull the plug". Her note said that she would be home about 8:00. It was now almost 8:45. Was this a wild goose chase or should they wait? They were discussing their alternatives when the phone rang. After four rings it switched over to the answering machine. They heard Mike Sullivan's message.

When the recording was finished, they looked at each other and smiled. They had no idea who Johnny McCord and Beverly were, but ABC Auto was back in play. The bag of money, the girl called Linda and the blue Chevrolet station wagon would be worth the wait.

Chapter 116

Anne Marie looked out the window of Adele's living room and saw that the rain had stopped. She decided that this was a good time to go home and wait for Mike.

She said her goodbyes to the girls. She told them that she had really enjoyed the card game and that they should get together again soon.

As she walked the few blocks back to her house, she inhaled the sweet smell of the ozone left behind by the summer rain. Somehow that smell always reminded her of when she was a little girl. Swinging her closed umbrella back and forth, she envisioned herself dancing through the rain with Gene Kelly in one of her favorite musicals.

Anne Marie entered her home and shut the door behind her. Standing in the living room facing the kitchen, she was overcome by a sense that something wasn't right.

Suddenly, from her left a man arose from her living room sofa. At the same time a second man appeared to her right, in the hallway that led to the bedrooms. He was holding an extremely lethal looking shotgun pointed down at the floor. It seemed like a casual way to hold a gun on someone, but, there was no doubt in Anne Marie's mind that he knew how to use it.

The first sound came from the man who had been on the sofa. He spoke in a low voice, with a definite Latino accent. "Don't do anything stupid Mrs. Sullivan and you won't get hurt."

Santino told Anne Marie to put down the umbrella and go in and sit at the kitchen table.

Anne Marie was terrified but she tried not to show it. "How do they know my name?" she thought. Mike had always told her that if she ever found herself in a dangerous situation she should try and keep her calm unless there was no choice but to fight.

In this case, she decided to let them do all the talking until she found out what was going on. She slowly moved to the kitchen and did as she was told.

Chapter 117

Johnny and the girls were driving south on I-75 toward Macon. They had passed Forsyth about ten miles ago, but still had another twenty miles to go. Beverly asked Johnny to find a rest stop so she could use the ladies room.

Even though Detective Sullivan had told them not to stop, Johnny knew that when nature calls it calls. They really needed gas anyway and he wanted to call Pete and check on Gloria.

They saw a sign for a 76 Truck Stop at the next exit so they pulled off and drove about a quarter of a mile until they reached the truck stop. There were several rows of gasoline and diesel oil pumps. Most of them were occupied. It looked to be a very popular place.

Johnny noted that there was a phone booth out front. He pulled up to one of the few available pumps and as he began to fill up the girls took off for the ladies room. None of them had noticed the dark blue convertible that had pulled onto the shoulder on the opposite side of the road.

He pulled the pad out of his pocket and found the phone number for Sweetwater hospital. He replaced the nozzle of the hose into the pump and walked over to pay for the gas through the little plexiglass window out front. He saw Beverly and Linda heading back to the car.

Johnny moved the wagon away from the pumps and pulled alongside the phone booth.

The girls had watched him move the car and they redirected themselves to meet him at the phone booth. He told the girls he wouldn't be long and got out of the car and entered the phone booth.

He called the number for the hospital and when the front desk answered he asked if they could locate his brother who was waiting with his wife in maternity. The girl who answered told Johnny to hold while she called the waiting room.

Snake saw the man he didn't know in the phone booth. He was puffing on another one of Rachael's cigarettes while watching the action across the street. He noticed that the young girl he had the hots for, was no longer with them. "Well, she would have been more trouble than she was worth", he thought. "Anyhow, now I got one less to worry about. Once I get the money, I won't have any problem getting all the young ass I want."

Snake knew they were going in the general direction of Macon, but, had no clue as to exactly where they were headed. He couldn't wait forever to make his move. A nice secluded spot was needed and this place didn't fill the bill.

Johnny listened as the voice came back on the line and said, "I've located Mr. McCord. Let me transfer you to that phone."

Johnny said, "Hello, Pete?" When Pete heard Johnny's voice he answered "Johnny, I'm a dad! It was touch and go but Gloria is fine. Where are you guys?"

Johnny was happy and relieved. He said, "That's

great, Pete. We just pulled over to get gas near Forsyth. I need to get rolling, but, I wanted to check on Gloria first. I'll call you once we get to detective Mike's house."

Pete's voice suddenly got serious and he told Johnny about the conversation he overheard in the hospital cafeteria. He said, "It's got to be that asshole Snake that the girls told us about."

Johnny told Pete that he would let Mike Sullivan know about Snake, as soon as he saw him. He said, "We have to let him know that this guy is still floating around somewhere. Tell Gloria we love her. I'll touch base with you later."

Johnny hung up the phone and climbed back into the wagon. The girls had just sat in the car, without much conversation between them, waiting for Johnny to finish his phone call.

Johnny pulled out to the street and waited for an opening in the traffic. He found one as he pulled out in front of a slow moving eighteen-wheeler.

Beverly was casually looking out of the window and listening to Johnny as he related what Pete had just told him. She noticed the dark convertible with the white top almost at the same time Johnny was describing the car that Snake had stolen.

Linda and Johnny heard the loud groaning, "Oh no", uttered by Beverly. Linda turned around to see what was wrong and Beverly pointed behind and to the right side of the wagon. She stuttered, "I- I- I think it's him!"

"You think it's who?"

"It's Snake. He just pulled out about three cars behind us in a dark blue convertible with a white top."

Now Linda began to lose it. "Johnny, I'm telling you, he's crazy. You have to get as far away from him as possible!"

Johnny checked the rear view mirror. It was close to full darkness now and all he could see was the eighteen-wheeler hulking behind them, blocking out the line of cars behind it. He put his hand on Linda's arm and gently aimed it toward the glove box.

"There's a pistol in there and an extra clip of bullets, hand them to me." Linda reached in the glove compartment and pulled out the Colt 45 and the extra clip. She handed them to Johnny and he slid the extra clip into his pocket and, after checking the safety, he slid the gun between his legs.

Chapter 118

Mike Sullivan was happy to go a little out of his way to drop the McCords off at their home. When he saw the damage to their house, he couldn't help wondering how this much bad luck could come to one family all at once. They thanked him for the ride and assured Mike that they were not stranded. They had Pete's Jeep and Martha had driven it many times.

The rain had finally let up and Mike wanted to get on his way. He told them that he would have Johnny call them as soon as he got to Macon. Normally, Mike didn't speed, but, given the circumstances he let his foot get a little heavy on the gas. The roads had dried out and as long as he didn't drive like a maniac, he was good-to-go even if by chance he were to be pulled over by a trooper.

It was just after nine-thirty as he passed by Locust Grove. He was still feeling a little uncomfortable about not actually talking to Anne Marie about the visitors he had sent her way. He wasn't overly concerned that she hadn't answered the phone; she had probably gone to visit with Adele. He just knew that Anne Marie wasn't big on surprises.

Mike decided to drive for another twenty minutes. Then he would pull off the road and call Anne Marie again.

Chapter 119

The silent treatment didn't seem to be working after all. Anne Marie had managed to keep quiet for a good ten minutes, but, the two men said nothing. She reckoned that if they were going to hurt her, they would have done it by now, so with her hands folded in front of her on the kitchen table, she looked up at them and slowly asked, "What do you want?"

Ramone looked at Santino, with a big toothy grin, and said, "Well I guess we won that contest." "Yeah", replied Santino, "Sooner or later they just got to know."

Santino laughed and turned to Anne Marie. He said, "We got some business with your husband. He is Mike Sullivan the cop ain't he?" Anne Marie thought about denying it, but, she figured that they obviously already knew and lying would probably cause her pain without having gained anything for it.

She replied, "Yes, my husband is Detective Michael Sullivan. What business do you have with him?" Ramone feigned an impressed look and said, "My, ain't we formal, Detective Michael not Mike the cop, he must be a big deal or something." He reverted quickly to a more sinister look and continued, "But, enough of the small talk, I want you to get up slowly and go over and listen to your phone messages." Anne Marie pressed the "play messages" button and listened to Mike's voice.

When the message ended, Santino said, "That's the business we have with your husband. Sit back down and tell us all you know about these people who are going to visit you."

Anne Marie began by saying, "I've never met or talked to any of these people. I only know that this Johnny McCord's family was attacked by some bikers up in Marietta and this girl, Beverly was somehow dragged into the situation. I have no idea who this girl, Linda is and why they are coming here. Honestly, that's all I know."

Santino looked at Ramone and pointed to Anne Marie. He said, "I think the little lady is telling the truth, so I guess we'll just all wait and find out who's who, when they get here. You go back and wait in the living room and I'll stay here and keep her company." The rooster clock, on the kitchen wall, showed 9:50pm.

Chapter 120

His engine was still running, so all that Snake needed to do was to flick on the lights, put it in gear and go. Before he could claw his way back into the flow of traffic, the big rig had passed him along with two other cars. He wasn't real happy about the eighteen-wheeler, since it blocked his ability to see the station wagon. Losing them now would end any hope he had of getting that money, so he decided to make his move.

This was the time and this was the place. Once they drove around the first curve, beyond the lights of the truck stop, they entered a very lonely and dark stretch of road. All he had to do was get behind them and find a stretch of road that would allow him to force them into the trees that lined both sides of the highway. He checked to see that his .38 was sitting on the front seat, within easy reach, and then he accelerated and began to close in on the car in front of him.

Johnny told the girls that he was going to try to lose Snake. He slowed down to keep just in front of the slower moving truck and let the cars in front of them pull away. They passed the entrance to I-75 and continued down this back road. Now there was very little traffic in front of them. Fortunately, the big rig didn't get on the interstate, but, stayed behind them. There was about a quarter mile of open space between the wagon and the car in front of them.

Johnny pushed the accelerator to the floor and looked for somewhere to turn off the road.

There it was. The sign said "Private Road – Keep Out".

Johnny killed his lights and slid through the right turn onto the dirt road. To avoid having his brake lights come on, he let the wagon slow of its own accord. Johnny eased the wagon forward as carefully as he could to insure that they stayed on the road and didn't veer off in the trees.

Snake pulled out to the left of the first car in front of him and hit the gas. He could see that most of the cars were turning back on the interstate ramp, but, not the wagon and not the eighteen-wheeler. As he pulled alongside the next car, he saw that the wagon had speeded up and was turning up ahead.

Snake was already flying pretty low, but, it seemed as though the truck and the car behind it had speeded up just to make it difficult for him to pass them. "Those assholes", he thought to himself, although being the dick that he was, he had done the very same thing to cars that had tried to pass him on occasion.

He knew that the Caprice had plenty of extra power and he had to make a decision fast. He had to choose between slowing down and hoping the cars would let him back in or going "balls-out" to pass them. The bottom line was that he had outfoxed himself. In either case, he was going to overshoot the road onto which the wagon had turned. He slammed the pedal down and flew past the truck.

As soon as he got clear of the truck, he slid back into the right hand lane and looked for a turn-off.

Snake knew that, on these back roads, it might take forever to find another place to turn, so when he had gotten a few car lengths ahead of the big rig, he careened off onto the shoulder. It took all of his strength to keep the car from getting away from him. "Screw it", he thought, "it ain't my fuckin' car."

There was a lot of banging and scraping as stones and fallen tree branches bounced into and off of the undercarriage. Finally, the convertible came to stop just as the eighteen-wheeler passed him with its horn blaring and the driver pumping his fist at Snake. Snake laughed and gave the driver the finger.

When the few cars that were behind the big rig had passed, Snake did a quick U-turn and headed back until he found the dirt road. When he saw the sign, he laughed at the stupidity of the wagons driver. He thought, "You dumb shit, you put yourself in a dead end situation, now you're going to find out what "dead-end" really means."

Chapter 121

Just as Ramone got ready to plunk himself back down on the living room sofa, the phone rang. Santino hollered at him, "Quick, get on the other phone." He reminded Anne Marie that any wrong words would cause her great pain. "I don't like to hurt helpless little ladies, but, Ramone won't hesitate to cut you up, if I tell him to."

After the second ring, Mike started to get concerned, but then he heard Anne Marie's voice say, "hello" and he immediately felt better. "Hi babe, did I catch you on the john?" Trying to play her part, Anne Marie responded with a little laugh and answered, "No, smarty-pants, I just finished listening to your message and I was watching out the front window for a blue station wagon." Santino was standing right next to Anne Marie with his ear close to the receiver.

For some reason, Mike thought that the phone connection sounded a little strange. He couldn't put his finger on anything specific so he continued, "I'm a bit surprised that they aren't there yet. I just wanted to be sure you were home, when they show up." Maybe he was imagining things, but, Mike thought he heard someone breathing, in the background. Rather than take a chance, he rolled into the scenario that he and Annie had discussed a thousand times.

"Have you gotten your results from Doctor Warren?" Santino looked quizzically at Anne Marie, but, she didn't skip a beat, as she responded, "No hon, but no news is good news, right?"

Now Mike knew something was wrong. Somebody was in the house with his wife and she would not have uttered that response unless it was a serious and dangerous situation.

He knew that if he used all the bells and whistles available to him; he could make it home in twenty minutes, but he wanted to gain some advantage on whoever was threatening Anne Marie.

In order to get the element of surprise back on his side he replied, "Right Annie, if it was anything serious, he would have called you right away. Now, before I forget, the main reason I called was to let you know that I got delayed because I drove the McCords home from the hospital. I'll do the best I can, but I probably won't get home before 11:00."

Chapter 122

Johnny was steering the wagon, as carefully as he could, down what was now a very dark and narrow dirt road. He hoped that the girls were mistaken and that the car that Beverly saw was not this Snake character. In any case, this was not the time for reminiscing, but, the mind is a funny thing and his was bringing back a memory from years before.

Johnny and his buddy Will were just seventeen years old. The event took place at night back in a suburb of Baltimore, Maryland. They had back-porched a couple of six packs of Budweiser and weren't feeling any pain. Johnny's old girl friend had dumped him and he decided to go past her house and squeal wheels, just to aggravate her. As they left her neighborhood, they made an illegal turn at a high rate of speed. That was when they saw the lights from a cop car flashing behind them.

Johnny figured he knew the area pretty well so, being a dumb teenager, he decided to turn off his lights and elude the cops. He made a fast turn up a dirt road, just as he was doing now. Unfortunately, the cops saw his brake lights go on as he tried to avoid a telephone pole. That situation did not go well and he ended up losing his driver's license for a year.

Well this was different. Back then the good guys were chasing a couple of stupid teens. Now, if it was Snake, a bad guy was chasing three good people, one of which was armed.

Johnny pulled himself out of his reverie as he notice the change in his surroundings.

The dirt road was opening up to a large circular driveway that fronted a small replica of an old, Georgia mansion, fully equipped with a stairway leading up to a decent sized enclosed porch supported by large, white columns. The area was illuminated by ornate porch lights on both sides of the front door.

This was the end of the line; there was nowhere else to go.

Johnny told Linda and Beverly to get out of the car and go up to the house. He told them to explain the situation to the homeowner and ask them to call the local police.

"What are you going to do?" Beverly asked him. "I'm going to try to keep these people out of it. Just do what I asked and stay here 'til I come back for you."

Johnny pulled up in front of the steps, let the girls out and circled the driveway. He carefully eased the wagon about two hundred yards down the dirt road, back the way he had come. He found a place where two sizeable trees were very close to the road, one on each side. There was barely enough room for two cars to pass each other.

He slid the wagon sideways, between these two trees. Now there was no way a car could get past the station wagon. Looking back toward the highway, he could just make out two small dots of light coming toward him. "Well it looks like Beverly was right," he thought.

He turned off the ignition and slid the keys into his pocket. To insure as much darkness as possible, he reached overhead and broke the plastic cover on the dome light with the butt of his Colt.

Unscrewing the bulb and tossing it on the floor he exited the darkened car. Leaving the door wide open, Johnny walked around the car and opened each of other doors as he went.

Chapter 123

Anne Marie said goodbye to Mike and hung up the phone. Santino looked at her, squeezed her arm tightly and said, "What's this Doctor Warren shit about?" She quickly responded, "I had a couple of fainting spells and my doctor wanted to check my blood sugar. It's probably nothing. If it was, I'm sure he would have gotten back to me today."

Ramone walked back into the kitchen and looked at Santino for some comment. Santino seemed satisfied with Anne Marie's explanation and he told Ramone to go back in the living room and keep an eye out for the visitors.

Mike left the phone booth, jumped into his car, turned on the lights and siren and floored it. He wanted back up, but, he didn't want anyone doing anything before he got home. This was his wife and he wasn't going to trust anyone else with making any decisions that might further endanger her. It would take at least five minutes for the Macon police to respond, assuming that this wasn't one of those rare times when a patrol car just happened to be in the neighborhood.

Mike knew that Bill Rowan was on duty tonight and if there was anyone he could trust it was Sergeant Rowan.

He was now doing ninety miles-per-hour and made the decision to wait until he was within eyesight of his home, before calling Bill.

Chapter 124

Linda and Beverly climbed the steps to the "mini-mansion" and depressed the doorbell button. They could hear the bell ringing inside the house. After waiting for a few seconds, without any answer, they rang the bell a second time.

Either no one was home or they just weren't answering. Linda looked at Beverly and said, "We can't just stand here in the light waiting. If Snake gets past Johnny, were both sitting ducks." Beverly agreed wholeheartedly. She suggested, "Let's get off this porch and head back into the trees where it's dark."

They nodded in agreement, went back down the steps and headed off into the woods, keeping as far away from the road as they could without losing their bearings. When they reached a point that they felt was sufficiently wooded to hide, they stopped.

They were looking in the direction of the road and they could just make out the light getting brighter and brighter, which they were sure was coming from Snake's approaching headlights.

Linda asked Beverly, "You've spent more time with Johnny, do you think he's a match for Snake?" Beverly replied, "I don't know. He looks like he can handle himself, but, Snake is obviously crazy and has already killed people. I wish somebody was home back there. At least we would know that the cops were on their way."

Chapter 125

Mike Sullivan decided to survey the situation by driving down the street that was behind his house. As he passed the opening between the two houses behind his, he could see that the light was on in his kitchen. He thought he saw some movement, but, he was too far away to learn anything that might help him

Mike knew that he shouldn't temp fate any longer and he grabbed the mike from his police radio. Just as he was about to depress the talk button, something caught his eye. There it was, parked near the intersection, a black Camaro, complete with Florida tags. Now Mike was really afraid for Anne Marie. He didn't believe in coincidence. This had to be the car that had been spotted leaving the area of the two murders in Rome at ABC Auto where the station wagon that Johnny was driving right now, had been purchased.

He pressed the talk button and identified himself. Bill Rowan answered immediately, "What's up Mike?" Mike took a deep breath and began to explain what was happening. When he had finished, Sergeant Rowan asked, "What do you need?"

Mike told him to send at least five men with body armor, shotguns and sniper rifles. He told Bill to have them park at the both ends of his block and to come in silently, on foot, no sirens & no flashing lights.

"Tell them that Anne Marie's life is in jeopardy and they shouldn't make any kind of a move until they talk to me."

Bill Rowan said, "Don't worry Mike, I'm not going to send them, I'm gonna bring them myself."

Chapter 126

Johnny had taken up a position behind a tree with a large trunk. It was located on the right side of the dirt road as you were driving toward the Georgian house. He decided to pick a spot that was even with the wagon's passenger side door and about twenty feet into the woods. If Snake wanted to check out the wagon, he would have to come into Johnny's field of fire.

From his hiding place, Johnny watched as the car came closer and closer. He checked the Colt 45, switched off the safety and made sure that there was a shell in the pipe.

Snake kept his headlights on and slowly drove down the dirt road. He didn't see any movement in front of him, and then just like that he saw the station wagon. It was about one hundred yards in front of him and there were no lights on inside of it. It just sat there sideways, with all of the doors open.

He decided that two could play this game and he turned off his headlights. He inched the convertible forward until he came within ten feet of the wagon. There was no activity around the car. He guessed that once they realized there was nowhere else to go they decided to abandon the car and take off on foot.

It was obvious that they had parked sideways to stop him from going any farther. There were large trees, on either side of the dirt road that blocked his way. "Where did they go and why did they leave the doors open?" He thought. "Well there's only one way to find out."

Snake turned off the ignition, grabbed the .38 from the passenger's seat and slid out of the driver's side door.

Even though the rain had stopped several hours ago, heavy clouds still hung in the air and blocked out any help from the moon, but Johnny had gotten a good look at the guy when the interior lights came on as he slid out of the convertible. He was convinced that this was the guy they called "Snake". He got a real good look at his face and damned if the son-of-a-bitch didn't look like a Snake.

Johnny also saw the gun in Snake's hand, which he immediately recognized as a Smith & Wesson .38. "Well," he thought, "the good news is that he's only got six shots and I've got fourteen."

He could have taken Snake out right there, but, he couldn't bring himself to back shoot someone, in fact, he wasn't going to shoot at all unless he actually feared for his own life or that of the girls. He decided to wait and see what Snake would do next. When the door closed on the Chevy, Johnny began to question whether waiting had been the right decision because it instantly became dark again and Snake disappeared from sight.

Chapter 127

There were no side windows on one side of Mike's house. After parking his car on the same side of the street as his home, two houses down, he had worked his way past the house adjacent to his own and was now pressed up against the side of the house that had no windows.

He eased his way to the front corner of his home and carefully slid around to just a few feet from the front window. He had his left hand pressed against the brick front and his service revolver in his right hand. He could feel the wetness from the earlier rain and it felt cool.

Ramone was sitting on the sofa, directly on the other side of the wall from where Mike was now crouched down. If the wall had disappeared they would have been able to touch each other.

Santino hollered into the living room, "Do you see anything?" Ramone carefully lifted one of the slats on the venetian blind and took another look out the window. He shook his head and replied, "Not yet."

When Mike heard the voices from inside, he knew that one of them was just on the other side of the wall. He dared not look in the window. What he needed was some kind of distraction to get whoever was on the other side to move.

Chapter 128

"Linda... Linda where are you hiding girl? You know I'm gonna find you. I see you got a new boyfriend and that little hitchhiker girl. She really did a number on Bear's leg, but, I guess you know that you don't have to worry about him anymore. What you do have to worry about is me. Why don't you just give me the money you stole from me and I'll let you all go. Come on now, you don't think your boyfriends gonna protect you from me. Do ya?"

Snake was getting impatient. He decided to try another approach, after all fear was a good motivator. He shouted, "By the way, what happened to my little girlfriend? I was looking forward to getting in her pants, but I never got the chance to finish up with her. Maybe your little hitchhiker girl would like to take her place!"

The girls looked at each other, with fear in their eyes. Linda put her finger to her lips and whispered, "Don't let him get to you, just keep quiet." Beverly nodded and they both crouched down behind the foliage.

Johnny had heard enough. This piece of shit had put his dad in the hospital and terrorized Carol and Gloria. He knew that Snake was talking about his little sister and it was time for payback.

He could tell approximately where Snake was from his voice, but, he needed something more. He might only get one chance at this bastard and he had to make it count.

The utter darkness was both a good and a bad

thing. Johnny couldn't see Snake, but then again, Snake couldn't see Johnny. Johnny decided that he would not shoot first. There were two reasons for this decision.

First, he still hoped that he could take this guy out without killing him. Secondly it was pitch-black and Johnny needed some kind of real target.

Johnny and his friends had spent a lot of time doing target practice back in Virginia. Johnny's best friend, Danny, used to come down from Baltimore for the weekend and shoot with them. Danny had been a policeman for a brief period of time and was an excellent shot. He favored his Browning 9mm which was similar to, but, not as powerful as the .45 Johnny held in his hand.

Danny had shared a few pearls of wisdom, about shooting semi-automatics. He told them to fire three quick shots in succession. Then he showed them how to rapid fire in the most effective manner.

To offset the kick of the gun, he told them to aim low and let the gun take over. It would naturally move upward after each shot and unless your target was over seven feet tall, a fourth shot would be a total waste.

While all of this was important, the advice that would come in most handy, in Johnny's present situation, concerned shooting in the dark.

Danny explained that since close to ninety percent of all people are right-handed, you should aim six inches to the right of the muzzle flash from their weapon and then hope they were not part of the other ten percent.

Johnny began to think about what Snake had just said

about his sister. In that moment he came to the conclusion that, not only his sister, but the whole world would be better off without this asshole. The second reason for his not shooting first had just jumped right up into first place. Now all Johnny had to do was to get Snake to shoot first.

Johnny felt around quietly with his toe until he found what he was looking for. He reached down and picked up a rock about the size of a golf ball. He flipped the rock like a hand grenade, high and to his left. When the rock hit the ground with a thump, he got what he wanted. Two shots rang out and Johnny saw the flash of Snake's gun. He was off to Johnny's left almost directly across from where the rock had landed.

Johnny faced into the woods and hollered, "That's two!"

Snake was a little startled by this. He swung around, trying to pinpoint the direction of the voice. Then he sneered and screamed back, "You think I only have six shots, asshole?" With that, he blindly fired off two more rounds into the woods. He fished four shells out of his pocket and replaced the spent shells. Then he continued, "Who the fuck do you think you are, Dirty Harry? I've got a whole pocketful of bullets and Dirty Harry had a big gun!"

Then he fired again.

Johnny quickly pulled the trigger three times. As he did, he couldn't stop himself from saying, "Well so do I, Punk!"

Unfortunately for Snake, he was right handed and now he was dead.

Chapter 129

Mike knew that he couldn't leave Anne Marie to face these two killers alone inside the house. Backup was on the way, but he had to try to get Anne Marie out of harm's way before all hell broke loose. He decided to enter the house and see if he could deflect their attention away from his wife.

Mike knew they were expecting him to come home, but, he was sure that they didn't know that he was aware that they were waiting for him. He carefully backed away to the side of the house and retraced his path across his next-door neighbor's front yard. He knew that he could not be seen from the front window of his own house.

As he crossed the sidewalk leading to his neighbor's front door, he saw a newspaper lying on the sidewalk. "They must have gone away for a long weekend" he thought. He picked up the paper and folded it over his service revolver. Mike made his way out to the main sidewalk, far beyond the view of his own front window. He pulled the .38's hammer back two clicks and took a deep breath.

He walked casually back up the sidewalk and turned up the walkway that led to his own front door.

Ramone watched a man walk casually up the sidewalk and turn in towards the front door. He looked in the kitchen and snapped his fingers to get Santino's attention. He motioned toward the door and jumped off the sofa, moving to where he would be hidden behind the door when it opened.

Chapter 130

Sergeant Rowan had his S.W.A.T. team split up and park at either end of the block. As they made their way toward the Sullivan house, Rowan tried to locate Mike. Then, out of the blue, he saw Mike walk up to his front door and put his key in the lock.

"This wasn't the plan", he thought as he watched the door open and Mike go inside. After splitting up, there were two four man teams plus Rowan. He instructed three of the team that was with him to go around and cover the back of the house. He used his walkie-talkie to instruct the second team to move across the street and cover the front of the house.

Knowing Mike, he figured he must have changed the plan because of Anne Marie's situation. It might not be following protocol, but, this was Mike's wife and it was personal.

For the time being, Bill Rowan decided that he would wait for some signal from Mike or for any serious commotion that would cause him to tell his men to immediately assault the house.

Chapter 131

Mike opened the front door and spun to his left. The newspaper fell to the floor as he pointed his gun at the sofa. The sofa was empty. With his peripheral vision he could see Anne Marie sitting in a chair at the kitchen table. She was facing Mike and he could see the fear on her face. There were no intruders in sight.

"Drop the gun, asshole!" Mike felt the cold barrels of a shotgun pressed into the back of his neck. He had no choice except to do as he was told. He let the .38 drop onto the sofa and raised his hands in the air.

All he could think of was Anne Marie. "He could tell that she was scared as hell, but, at least she seemed to be unhurt." As Mike began to say something, Ramone brought the barrels of the shotgun down on the back of Mike's head.

It wasn't hard enough to do any permanent damage, but it brought Mike to his knees and he saw a burst of light as he fell to the floor.

"You think you're pretty smart doncha cop? It looks like you knew we were here. I guess you and the little lady have some kinda signals. Am I right?" Mike didn't see any point in answering the question, so he just kept quiet and tried to regain his senses. He reached back and grabbed his head and he could feel what he knew was warm blood flowing down the back of his neck.

"Hurts, don't it?" Ramone said. "Well, now that you know whose boss, we can get on with it."

Anne Marie jumped up from her chair and screamed, "Don't hurt him you bastard!"

Santino had been standing out of Mike's sight behind the half-wall that separated the kitchen from the living room. He walked over to Anne Marie and slammed her back down in the chair. "We ain't gonna hurt him any more than we have to. If we get what we came for, you can both go on about your lives like we wasn't even here."

Mike knew that this wasn't true. He was well aware of what these two animals did to Manny and Sandy at ABC Auto and he knew that they had no intention of leaving anyone alive.

Santino walked away from Anne Marie and went into the living room. He told Ramone to keep his eye on the woman. Ramone drifted into the kitchen and leaned his back against the countertop of the sink. His hand brushed against one of the piles of plaques that were stacked there.

Santino approached Mike and said, "Let's get this done. You know we came for our money and I know you can get it for us. We heard the message you left for your old lady, so there ain't no point in you telling me that you don't know what I'm talking about." He pointed at Anne Marie and continued, "Just tell me where it is and maybe you and her will get out of this alive!"

Ramone picked up the plaque that was on the top of the first stack. It was a "Top Cop" award given to Mike Sullivan for closing the most cases in the previous year. He tossed it over the kitchen table and it landed on the living room rug. He picked up the next plaque that thanked Mike for being a "Boy's Club" mentor in Macon. He flung it over and it skidded off the first plaque on the floor.

He looked at Mike and said, "I'll bet you think you're hot shit, don't you?" and he continued to pick up the plaques and throw them closer and closer to Mike. Santino became aggravated and told Ramone to stop screwing around.

Santino took his hand and smacked Mike on the back of the head. Mike saw stars again. "Just tell me where the money is or I'm gonna have my boy start working on your wife." Santino nodded toward the kitchen and Mike turned his head and watched as Ramone reached into an ankle sheath and pulled out a switch-blade knife. He pressed the button and an ugly blade appeared.

Remembering the description of Sandy's fate at the used-car lot, Mike decided it was time to move. "Ok, I've got the money in the trunk of my car. I'll take you to it, but, how do I know your friend isn't going to hurt my wife while we're getting the money?" Santino thought about this for a second. He knew that once he got the money, this cop and his wife were going to be "dead meat", so he decided to humor Mike for the moment.

Santino looked at Ramone and said, "I want you to be nice to the lady. Just come in here on the sofa and keep your head in the window so he can see you ain't messing with his pretty little wife. He's gonna give us the money and that's all we want, right?"

Ramone walked back into the living room with the shotgun in one hand and the switchblade in the other. He said, "Sure, sure, I ain't gonna hurt her as long as she don't do anything stupid."

He laid the shotgun on the sofa, well away from Mike, but kept the switchblade in his right hand.

Anne Marie got up from her chair and opened the drawer under the sink. She reached in, pulled out the First-Aid kit and opened the lid.

Santino said, "Whoa, what are you doing?" Anne Marie was crying and she responded, "He's bleeding, I need to put a bandage on his head before he goes." "Just put the box on the counter. You do something for me and I'll do something for you. When we get the money, I promise you I'll let you fix his head."

Anne Marie set the large First-Aid kit on the counter next to the one stack of plaques that Ramone had not thrown. Santino pulled Mike onto his feet and said, "Let's go!" As he led him to the front door, Ramone sat back down on the sofa sideways and pulled the venetian blind up so that he could be seen from the outside while still keeping an eye on Anne Marie.

Chapter 132

Charlie Wilson, one of the members of the S.W.A.T. team, saw the window blind going up through the green night scope on his rifle. He immediately spoke into his walkie-talkie. "There's movement in the front window!" Sergeant Rowan replied, "What do you see?" Wilson responded, "I'm looking right at the head of a man and it isn't Mike Sullivan. I've got him covered boss."

"All right, keep me posted."

A few seconds later, the front door opened and two men stepped out onto the porch. Bill Rowan had taken up a position, behind a parked car, on the far side of the street. He recognized the first man out as Mike Sullivan. The man behind Mike had a gun pressed into Mike's back and Mike appeared to be stumbling with one hand held to the back of his head.

Bill looked through his night-vision binoculars and he could see blood covering the back of Mike's shirt. He whispered into his walkie-talkie, telling another member of the team to get a bead on the second man out of the door. Then he contacted the team who was guarding the back of the house and asked them to attempt to get a look inside from the kitchen door.

Santino pushed Mike ahead with the barrel of his gun. He asked Mike where his car was and Mike pointed to the right and said, "Two houses up, on this side." When they got to Mike's car, Santino told him to unlock the trunk, lift it up and then walk over on the lawn.

Mike did what he was told and retreated to the lawn about twenty feet away from his car. Santino said, "Sit down on the grass with your legs folded in front of you and don't try to get up."

Bill Rowan had watched all of this as it happened and he told two of his team to move from the back of Mike's house up two houses and lock onto the man standing up behind the open trunk. "If I say GO, you take him out!"

The man who stayed behind Mike's house reported that he could see someone sitting on the sofa in the living room, but, he was not able to see Mike's wife. Rowan told him to get ready to go through the back door on his call.

Chapter 133

Anne Marie watched as the man pushed Mike through the front door. She never thought that anything like this would ever happen. Mike, on the other hand, had insisted that they at least discuss possible courses of action should they ever find themselves in a life threatening situation.

She didn't have to read Mike's mind to know that these men would never let them go. After all, Mike was a cop and both she and Mike could and would identify them. Well, it wasn't like they hadn't discussed the pros and cons and agreed never to go out without a fight.

Ramone was looking out the front window. Every few seconds he would look into the kitchen to make sure the woman hadn't moved.

Anne Marie decided it was now or never. She watched Ramone as he looked at her and then turned his head back to the window. She reached into the First-Aid kit with her right hand. With her left hand she picked up the bottom plaque from the remaining stack and smiled.

As Ramone turned to check her out again, she threw the plaque at him and said, "Here's one you missed!"

Instinctively, Ramone raised his hands to protect himself from the flying plaque.

Before the plaque had hit the ground, Annie had placed four shots into his chest. They were just to the left of the pocket on his short-sleeved summer shirt and just to the right of the fourth button down from the top.

The four bullets were grouped within a circle that

could be drawn by tracing around the top of a standard sized soup can.

The plaque never came close to hitting Ramone. It landed right-side up about two feet short of where he was sitting. On the plaque, which of course Ramone would never read, was written:

Georgia Rifle & Pistol Association
1977
First Place

Anne Marie Sullivan

299 out of 300
25 meter rapid fire

While the four .22 long rifle bullets would not necessarily have done much damage to Ramone, the fact that two of them pierced his heart did the job.

Chapter 134

Santino kept one eye on Mike Sullivan as he reached into the trunk and unlatched one of the two briefcases lying there. He smiled when he saw the stacks of bills neatly wrapped inside. He turned his head toward Mike and lifted a packet of fifty dollar bills and shook it at Mike. "Two hundred fifty thousand bucks, that's a lot of dough. This, my friend, is what it's all about!"

Mike didn't reply. He just shook his head. Then as he looked beyond Santino, he saw something moving behind a car parked on the other side of the street. "It has to be the S.W.A.T. team", he thought. "They need to get Anne Marie out before they start anything here!"

Suddenly, four sharp cracks rang out. Mike, Bill Rowan and Santino all recognized the sounds as gunfire. Santino hesitated for a second and then he raised his gun and turned toward Mike.

Bill Rowan hadn't hesitated at all. As soon as he heard the gunfire he screamed, "GO" into his walkie-talkie. His voice "boomed" so loudly that his men would have heard it without the walkie-talkie.

The super high velocity round from the sniper rifle took off the top of Santino's head, before he ever had a chance to pull the trigger on his own weapon.

Charlie Wilson came through the front door of the Sullivan house only seconds after his partner had broken in through the kitchen door. What they saw amazed them both. A man was sitting on the sofa in front of the living room window.

Charlie was sure that this was the man he had been watching through his sniper scope for the last fifteen minutes. The look on the man's face showed surprise, if not total disbelief.

Anne Marie was standing with her back to the kitchen counter. She was pointing a Ruger .22 target pistol down at the floor. She was still gripping it with both hands. Charlie asked her if she was all right and she nodded yes. He walked over to the man on the sofa and felt for a pulse. There wasn't one. He spoke into his walkie-talkie, "Mike's wife is ok, I repeat ok, but, there's some guy in here that isn't so ok."

Bill Rowan ran over to Mike. "Anne Marie's ok," he said. Once more he raised the walkie-talkie to his mouth. "Send the EMT's up quick; we've got an officer down."

Charlie Wilson removed the gun from Anne Marie's hand and set it down on the kitchen table. He put his arm around her shoulder and guided her toward the front door. "Let's get you and your husband back together." When they got close to Mike, they saw him already on a stretcher, being slid into the back of an ambulance.

Anne Marie pulled away from Charlie and ran to Mike. She made them stop while she wrapped her arms around Mike. Tears were streaming down her face. Mike looked up at her and said, "Don't worry, honey, I'm gonna be fine. This old Irishman's head is pretty hard. They just want to take some x-rays to be sure."

The EMT said, "Let us get your husband in the ambulance. You can ride along next to him to the hospital."

Chapter 135

Johnny walked over to where Snake had fallen. He had never shot anyone before and he was feeling a little queasy, but he thought about what his family had gone through and whispered to himself, "If anyone ever deserved to get shot, it was this punk."

"Beverly, Linda, you can come out now. It's all over!" Beverly looked at Linda and said, "That's Johnny, let's go." Johnny could hear the rustling of the underbrush as the two girls slowly worked their way out of the trees and toward him.

When they got to Johnny, Linda looked down at Snake's dead body and started to cry. Johnny said, "You aren't crying for this bastard, are you?" Linda shook her head vehemently. "No, no, I don't give a shit about him! I'm just so sorry I got you involved in all of this!"

Johnny said, "What's done is done; now we need to figure out what to do next. Here we are in the middle of nowhere and we can't just stand here waiting for someone to show up."

Beverly interjected, "Why don't we go back to the truck stop. You can call Detective Mike from there. He must be home by now and he can tell us what to do."

They all agreed and got into the station wagon. Johnny turned it around and carefully drove past the convertible. It only took about five minutes to get back to the 76 Truck Stop. Johnny parked next to the phone booth and pulled Mike Sullivan's home phone number out of his shirt pocket.

Linda told Beverly that she had a terrible headache and was going inside the truck stop to get some aspirin and a soda to wash it down. She asked Beverly if she wanted anything. Beverly told her she was going to the rest room and would see her in the store.

The phone was picked up almost immediately. The voice on the other end just said, "Hello." Johnny had spoken to Mike Sullivan enough times to know that this voice didn't belong to Mike.

"Can I speak to Detective Sullivan?"

"He's not available right now, who's calling?"

"My name is Johnny McCord and I was supposed to meet him at his home, but I got detained. Do you know when he will be back?"

Bill Rowan answered the Sullivan's phone and he knew who Johnny McCord was, from his recent conversation with Mike. He said, "Johnny, this is Sergeant Rowan, Atlanta PD. There was some trouble here and Mike was injured. He's on his way to Northside Hospital for some x-rays."

"Is he ok?"

"I think so, but I don't really know. Is there something I can help you with?"

Johnny hesitated. He knew he couldn't just walk away from the scene of a shooting in which he was involved. "Yes Sergeant, I really think I need your help!"

Johnny only told Rowan that there had been a shooting and he was pretty sure that the other person was dead. He told him where he was. Sergeant Rowan told Johnny to wait in his car.

When Johnny described the station wagon to him, Rowan immediately made the connection to the killings at ABC Auto in Rome. "Stay there!" he said. "I'll be there in twenty minutes." Johnny agreed to stay put and they both hung up.

While Johnny was talking to Rowan, he had noticed the girls walking toward the rest room. After his conversation was over, he decided he could use a pit stop himself. As he walked toward the side of the building where the men's rest room was located, he glanced through the large plate-glass window in front. He could see Linda standing in line at one of the check-out lanes. She seemed to be having a conversation with an older man. The guy was sporting a really big, white beard. Johnny probably wouldn't have even noticed if the guy hadn't looked so much like Santa Claus. "Santa Claus in July, what else could happen?"

Linda smiled at the man with the white beard and nodded toward the front of the building. He nodded back at her and pointed toward a navy blue, eighteen-wheeler parked near the entrance.

She paid for the items she had purchased and began walking toward the front of the store. Out of the corner of her eye, she noticed a counter against the wall. Next to the counter were two rotating, carousels that held large selections of picture postcards.

She smiled to herself and walked over to the counter. She selected one of the postcards and, using the pen that was attached by a faux gold chain to the desktop, wrote a note on it. She returned to the cashier and paid for the postcard and left the store.

After taking care of business, Johnny went into the truck stop and ran into Beverly at the check-out counter. They had both gotten a cup of coffee and one of Mrs. Smith's pies. Johnny told Beverly about Detective Mike and what Sergeant Rowan had told him to do.

Neither one of them noticed the trucker, who's resemblance to Santa Claus really was amazing, if they had, they might have recognized the girl riding shotgun. That seat had been empty when the big rig pulled into the truck stop.

Linda had mixed emotions about what she was doing. On the trip down here, from the scene of the original mayhem at McCord's "Farm Fresh" store, she had convinced herself that she should go along with Johnny and Detective Mike and try to get free from all her troubles.

After the recent episode with Snake, she was totally shaken and decided on an alternative. No one actually knew anything about her except that her first name was Linda. She never used her last name and never discussed where she was from. Since she had never been arrested, there wouldn't be a record of her fingerprints anywhere.

She had done her best to help the McCord girls and she could only hope that, with all the rest of her crew dead, Detective Sullivan would let the case be closed.

This truck driver agreed to take her with him to the end of the line, which in his case was San Antonio,

Texas. He was glad to have the company of a pretty young girl and she told him that she would pay for their meals, along the way.

All in all, it was a pretty sweet deal for both of them.

Chapter 136

Johnny and Beverly left the truck stop together. As they approached the station wagon, Beverly looked at Johnny and said, "Where's Linda?" Johnny peeked into the wagon and saw that it was totally empty. They both did a slow 360^0 as they looked across the well-lit parking lot. When they were once again facing each other they both shook their heads.

Johnny said, "I saw her in the check-out line in the mart." Johnny grabbed the door handle and found that the door was locked. He knew that he had left it open when he went to the telephone booth. "Linda must have locked the doors, I wonder why?"

He pulled the key from his pocket and opened the driver's side door. He got in the wagon and started to reach over to open the passenger's side door for Beverly. There, in the middle of the front seat, was a white bag. It had the truck stop's logo on it and there was a word written in large letters with a black marker across the front. It simply said, "SORRY".

As Johnny looked at the bag, Beverly tapped on the window to get his attention. Johnny reached over and pulled up the button that locked the door. Beverly opened the door and got into the station wagon. Johnny lifted up the bag and turned it toward Beverly so she could read the black lettering.

He said, "What do you suppose this is all about?"

"Your guess is as good as mine."

Johnny handed the bag to Beverly and said, "Go for

it." She took the bag from his hand, opened it up and peeked down to view its contents. In the bag, Beverly found a postcard with a note written on it.

The note simply said, "Snake was the last of them and I just want this all to go away. I hope I didn't put you in a bad spot with Detective Mike, but, I just couldn't take the chance. I am really sorry for all that happened to you and your family, maybe you'll hear from me once I get situated."

The note was signed with an *L*.

As Beverly handed the key to Johnny she said, "I guess this means she won't be joining us. It just occurred to me, we really don't know anything about her. I wonder if her name really is Linda."

Johnny replied, "I'm betting that it is or she probably wouldn't have signed the note with an *L*. In any event, I'm happy for her. We could never begin to repay her for what she did for Carol and Gloria. I hope things turn out ok for her."

They agreed not to mention Linda's name to anyone. Once they got a chance to talk to Detective Mike, they would sort out this latest complication.

Chapter 137

Bill Rowan called the Medical Examiner and asked him to meet them at the truck stop. He put one of the S.W.A.T. team in charge of wrapping up at Mike Sullivan's house and asked Officer Phil Burton, another member of the team to come with him to the shooting scene.

On their way to the truck stop, he brought Phil Burton up to speed on what was happening. Bill was a good cop and he made sure to stay on top of all the news that might impact his area of responsibility.

As he mulled over, in his head, the information that Johnny had provided during their conversation, he remembered reading a teletype about a Caprice Classic convertible. The same kind of car that Johnny said this guy Snake had been driving.

Apparently, some poor bastard had been pistol-whipped and his car had been stolen earlier this afternoon. As he recalled, this happened in Tennessee, just across the Georgia border. Rowan didn't believe in coincidences and he calculated that there had been plenty of time for the car to be driven from there to here.

He was sharing his thoughts with Officer Burton as they pulled onto the parking lot. They found the station wagon parked near the phone booth just as Johnny said it would be. They pulled in front of the wagon and stopped.

Johnny and Beverly got out of the wagon and

walked toward them. Bill Rowan and Officer Burton approached Johnny and Beverly.

Sergeant Rowan identified himself by showing them his shield.

Johnny immediately told him that his gun was in the glove box of the wagon. Bill nodded to Officer Burton who pulled a plastic evidence bag from his pocket and retrieved Johnny's Colt 45 and placed it in the bag.

Just then the Medical Examiner pulled up next to them in a rather large pick-up truck with "Medical Examiner" stenciled on the door. He was carrying several gasoline powered generators to power the lights he brought to illuminate the shooting scene.

Johnny watched as Bill Rowan went over to speak with the new arrival. He saw him lean over to the driver's side window and chat with the M.E. Johnny was too far away to hear the conversation, but, he saw the Medical Examiner nod his head and then Sergeant Rowan returned to where they were all standing.

Just to be sure he followed protocol; Sergeant Rowan decided that Officer Burton and Johnny would ride together and Beverly would ride with him back to the scene of the shooting.

They waited for a break in the traffic and then all three vehicles followed each other out of the truck stop with Johnny and Officer Burton leading in the station wagon. Officer Burton was driving and Johnny was giving him directions.

Chapter 138

Once they were on the scene, it didn't take the M.E. long to set up the lighting. Over the hum of the gasoline generators, Johnny and Beverly pointed out where Snake had fallen and where all of the action had occurred. Neither one of them mentioned Linda.

In pretty quick time, the M.E. and Sergeant Rowan concluded that all the evidence supported the story that Johnny and Beverly were telling. Sergeant Rowan called in for an identification of the Chevy convertible and was advised that it was, in fact, the car that had been stolen earlier that day.

Bill Rowan thanked the operator for that information and requested to be connected with Northside Hospital. Bill identified himself and asked to speak to Detective Mike Sullivan, in the Emergency Room.

The duty nurse in the ER, who answered the phone, explained that Detective Sullivan had been treated and was about to be released, but, if he would hold, she would send someone to tell him that he had a phone call waiting.

After a few moments of silence, he heard, "Hello, this is Detective Sullivan speaking."

Bill was relieved to hear Mike's voice and responded, "How are you doing you old son-of-a-gun?" Mike Sullivan recognized the voice right away and said, "Pretty good Bill what's up?"

Bill explained what had happened from the time

he answered Johnny's call at Mike's house right up until now.

He included the fact that the dead man had a piece of paper in his pocket with Mike's name and phone numbers on it.

Mike recognized that Linda's name was conspicuous by its absence in Bill's story. Leaving Linda's name out, he asked, "How are Johnny and Beverly?"

Bill assured him that they were all right, but he didn't mention Linda. The whole Linda thing was very touchy and Mike decided to let it slide until he had the chance to find out what the deal was, from Johnny and Beverly.

"As long as you don't need them for anything else, ask Johnny and Beverly to meet me in the cafeteria at Northside Hospital. Tell them I'll wait for them. It shouldn't take them more than thirty minutes to get here."

"Hold on, Mike, I've got them both right here." Mike could hear Bill talking to them in the background. They agreed to meet Mike at the hospital and Bill told them the shortest and simplest way to get there. Bill got back on the phone and assured Mike that they were on their way.

Mike said, "Anne Marie and I are gonna spend some time with Johnny and Beverly and then we're headed to a hotel. Hopefully, the crime scene folks can wrap up at our house so we can get a cleaning service to get rid of the mess. I'll stop by the precinct after breakfast to fill out a report. Anne Marie will be with me so you can get her whole story, but don't expect to see us before noon."

"No problem, call me from your hotel and I'll have a couple of officers pick up your squad car and bring it to the hotel. Check the front desk for the keys. We'll expect to see you when we see you."

Chapter 139

Mike Sullivan hung up the phone and thanked the receptionist. Behind her desk there was a large wall clock and Mike saw that it was after midnight. Anne Marie had been waiting for him to finish the phone call and now she joined him and held his hand as they walked to the cafeteria.

This was the first chance they had to be alone since all of the mayhem at their home. He squeezed her hand and said, "I can't say that I'm sorry this day is over. I'm sorry that I put you in so much danger. If anything had happened to you...!"

Anne Marie interjected, "Don't even go there. I knew what you did for a living before we were married and you can't say I wasn't prepared, can you?"

"No, I can't. You were fantastic. That bastard who you left on our sofa is the one who wasn't prepared! Now that it's all over, I'll fill you in on some of the details. Let's get a cup of coffee and wait for Johnny & Beverly to show up. I'm sure they've got quite a story to tell and I am dying to wrap this whole thing up and hopefully put it all behind us."

Chapter 140

Mike was on his second refill when he spotted Johnny and Beverly walking in the entrance to the cafeteria. He stood up with his hand on Anne Marie's shoulder and said, "These are two of the kids I've been telling you about." Anne Marie stood up just as Johnny and Beverly got to their table. Mike made the introductions all around and invited everyone to sit down.

Johnny said, "I'm going to get us both a cup of coffee and a sandwich. Can we get you guys anything?"

Mike responded, "I'll walk you up to the counter. It has been a long day and now that you mention it, I think we could eat something as well."

The four of them sat there for almost two hours. There was a lot to talk about and Mike, being the detective that he was, wanted to go over every detail from Johnny, Beverly and Anne Marie.

He came to the conclusion that, just as he had suspected all along, there was no such thing as coincidence and all of the events of the past three days were definitely connected.

At about two-thirty in the morning, they all left together. Johnny dropped Mike and Anne Marie off at a Hilton hotel, which was close by. Then he and Beverly drove back to the McCord home in Marietta.

Epilogue

(One week later)

The money recovered from the two suitcases was counted; it came to exactly two hundred thousand dollars. When Mike Sullivan heard this number, he just smiled and thought to himself, "That's a lot of dough."

Now that things had calmed down and Johnny's Porsche had been repaired, he had decided to return to Virginia. He was going to leave on Monday and had agreed to drive Beverly back to her home in Dublin.

It was a nice, quiet, uneventful Saturday and they were all hanging around the McCord house, taking it easy. The "everyone" didn't include Mr. McCord who was where he always was on Saturdays, at the "Farm Fresh" store.

When the mail arrived at the store, there was a package. It was addressed to "The McCord Family & Beverly". Mr. McCord shrugged his shoulders and decided to take the package home so that everyone could open it together.

Inside the package, there were five individual envelopes. Each envelope had a name or names written on the front. The names were;

BEVERLY
JOHNNY
MR. & MRS. MCCORD
PETE & GLORIA

CAROL

Mr. McCord handed them each the envelope that had their name written on it. They all looked at each other hesitantly and then Johnny opened his envelope. He withdrew a stack of bills wrapped inside a note. The note said, "Sorry for the trouble, maybe this will help some." The note was simply signed:

"L"

Johnny counted the fifty dollar bills. There were one hundred of them. All four of the other envelopes had the exact same contents with the same note.

They all looked at each other and just smiled.

Printed in the United States
By Bookmasters